W9-DAF-578

CLAIMING
MARIAH

★ CLAIMING ★
MARIAH

PAM HILLMAN

Tyndale House Publishers, Inc.
Carol Stream, Illinois

Visit Tyndale online at www.tyndale.com.

Visit Pam Hillman's website at www.pamhillman.com.

TYNDALE and Tyndale's quill logo are registered trademarks of Tyndale House Publishers, Inc.

Claiming Mariah

Copyright © 2013 by Pam Hillman. All rights reserved.

Cover photograph of mountains copyright © 1999 by Photodisc/Getty Images. All rights reserved.

Cover photograph of vintage texture © 2008 by lostandtaken.com. All rights reserved.

Cover photograph of silhouette copyright © by Keith Szafranski/iStockphoto. All rights reserved.

Cover photograph of portrait copyright © by Jasmina/iStockphoto. All rights reserved.

Illustration of calligraphic design copyright © by kandserg/iStockphoto. All rights reserved.

Cover photograph of wood copyright © by AlexAvich/Shutterstock. All rights reserved.

Cover photograph of rope copyright © by blackpixel/Shutterstock. All rights reserved.

Cover and title page designed by Jennifer Ghionzoli

Interior designed by Nicole Grimes

Edited by Erin E. Smith

Published in association with the literary agency of The Steve Laube Agency.

Scripture quotations are taken from the *Holy Bible*, King James Version.

Claiming Mariah is a work of fiction. Where real people, events, establishments, organizations, or locales appear, they are used fictitiously. All other elements of the novel are drawn from the author's imagination.

Library of Congress Cataloging-in-Publication Data
Hillman, Pam.
  Claiming Mariah / Pam Hillman.
    pages cm
    ISBN 978-1-4143-8975-2 (sc)
1. Inheritance and succession—Fiction. 2. Ranch life—Fiction. 3. Murder—Investigation—Fiction. I. Title.
  PS3608.I448C53 2014
  813'.6—dc23   2013023598

Printed in the United States of America

20	19	18	17	16	15	14
7	6	5	4	3	2	1

I'd like to dedicate Claiming Mariah *to my husband, Iran.*

I originally wrote Slade *to be larger than life,*

but first readers scoffed at his amazingly broad shoulders,

six-foot-four frame, gorgeous green eyes,

and large hands that can soothe a small child,

manhandle an ornery cow,

or bring a newborn calf into the world.

But I know the truth. That man does exist.

I married him.

CHAPTER ONE

Wisdom, Wyoming Territory
Late spring, 1882

DUST SWIRLED as the two riders approached the house.

They stopped a few feet shy of the steps, and Mariah Malone eyed the men from the shadowy recesses of the porch. Both were sun-bronzed and looked weary but tough, as if they made their living punching cows and riding fences.

One man hung back; the other rode closer and touched his thumb and forefinger to the brim of his hat. "Afternoon, ma'am."

"Afternoon." Wavy brown hair brushed the frayed collar of his work shirt. A film of dust covered his faded jeans, and the stubble on his jaw hinted at a long, hard trip. "May I help you?"

"I'm here to see Seth Malone." His voice sounded husky, as if he needed a drink of water to clear the trail dust from his throat.

At the mention of her father, a pang of sorrow mixed with longing swept over her. "I'm sorry; he passed away in January. I'm his daughter. Mariah Malone."

The cowboy swung down from his horse and sauntered toward the porch. He rested one worn boot on the bottom step before tilting his hat back, revealing fathomless dark-blue eyes.

"I'm Slade Donovan. And that's my brother, Buck." He jerked his head in the direction of the other man. His intense gaze bored into hers. "Jack Donovan was our father."

Oh no, Jack Donovan's sons.

A shaft of apprehension shot through her, and Mariah grasped the railing for support. Unable to look Mr. Donovan in the eye, she focused on his shadowed jaw. A muscle jumped in his cheek, keeping time with her thudding heart.

When her father died, she hadn't given another thought to the letter she'd sent Jack Donovan. She'd been too worried about her grandmother, her sister, and the ranch to think about the consequences of the past.

"Where is . . . your father?" Mariah asked.

"He died from broken dreams and whiskey."

"I'm sorry for your loss," she murmured, knowing her own father's sins had contributed to Jack Donovan's troubles, maybe even to his death. How much sorrow had her father's greed caused? How much heartache? And how much did his son know of their fathers' shared past?

The accusation on Slade Donovan's face told her, and the heat of fresh shame flooded her cheeks.

"My pa wanted what was rightfully his," he ground out. "I promised him I would find the man who took that gold and make him pay."

Tension filled the air, and she found it difficult to breathe.

"Take it easy, Slade." His brother's soft voice wafted between them.

Mariah caught a glimpse of Cookie hovering at the edge of the bunkhouse. "Miss Mariah, you need any help?"

Her attention swung between Cookie and the Donovan brothers, the taste of fear mounting in the back of her throat. An old man past his prime, Cookie would be no match for them. "No," she said, swallowing her apprehension. "No thank you, Cookie. Mr. Donovan is here to talk business."

She turned back to the man before her. Hard eyes searched her face, and she looked away, praying for guidance. "Mr. Donovan, I think we need to continue this discussion in my father's office."

She moistened her lips, her gaze drawn to the clenched tightness of his jaw. After a tense moment, he nodded.

Malone was dead?

Leaving Buck to care for the horses, Slade followed the daughter into the house. She'd swept her golden-brown hair to the top of her head and twisted it into a serene coil. A few curls escaped the loose bun and flirted with the stand-up lace of her white shirtwaist. She sure looked dressed up out here in the middle of nowhere.

Then he remembered the empty streets and the handful of wagons still gathered around the church when they'd passed through Wisdom at noon. He snorted under his breath. Under other circumstances, a woman like Mariah Malone wouldn't even deem him worthy to wipe her dainty boots on, let alone agree to talk to him in private. He couldn't count the times the girls from the "right" side of town had snubbed their noses at him, their starched pinafores in sharp contrast to his torn, patched clothes. At least his younger brother and sisters hadn't been treated like outcasts. He'd made sure of that.

He trailed the Malone woman down the hall, catching a glimpse of a sitting room with worn but polished furniture on his right, a tidy kitchen on his left. A water stain from a leaky roof marred the faded wallpaper at the end of the wide hallway. While neat and clean, the house and outbuildings looked run-down. He scowled. Surely Seth Malone could have kept the place in better repair with his ill-gotten gain.

Miss Malone led the way into a small office that smelled of leather, ink, and turpentine. She turned, and he caught a glimpse of eyes the color of deep-brown leather polished to a shine. The state of affairs around the house slid into the dark recesses of his mind as he regarded the slender young woman before him.

4

"Mr. Donovan," she began, "I take it you received my letter."

He nodded but kept silent. Uneasiness wormed its way into his gut. Did Miss Malone have brothers or other family to turn to? Who was in charge of the ranch?

"I'm sorry for what my father did. I wish it had never happened." She toyed with a granite paperweight, the distress on her face tugging at his conscience.

He wished it had never happened too. Would his father have given up if Seth Malone hadn't taken off with all the gold? Would they have had a better life—a ranch of their own maybe, instead of a dilapidated shack on the edge of Galveston—if his father hadn't needed to fight the demons from the bullet lodged in his head?

He wanted to ask all the questions that had plagued him over the years, questions his father had shouted during his drunken rages. Instead, he asked another question, one he'd asked himself many times over the last several months. "Why did you send that letter?"

Pain turned her eyes to ebony. "My father wanted to ask forgiveness for what he had done, but by that time he was unable to write the letter himself. I didn't know Mr. Donovan had a family or that he'd died." She shrugged, the pity on her face unmistakable.

Slade clenched his jaw. He didn't want her pity. He'd had enough of that to last a lifetime.

She strolled to the window, arms hugging her waist. She looked too slight to have ever done a day's work. She'd probably been pampered all her life, while his own mother and sisters struggled for survival.

"I hoped Mr. Donovan might write while my father was still alive, and they could resolve their differences." Her soft voice wafted on the still air. "I prayed he might forgive Papa. And that Papa could forgive himself."

"Forgiveness is too little, too late," Slade gritted out, satisfaction welling within him when her back stiffened and her shoulders squared.

She turned, regarding him with caution. "I'm willing to make restitution for what my father did."

"Restitution?"

"A few hundred head of cattle should be sufficient."

"A few hundred?" Surely she didn't think a handful of cattle would make up for what her father had done.

"What more do you want? I've already apologized. What good will it do to keep the bitterness alive?"

"It's not bitterness I want, Miss Malone. It's the land."

"The land?" Her eyes widened.

He nodded, a stiff, curt jerk of his head. "All of it."

"Only a portion of the land should go to your family, if any. Half of that gold belonged to my father." Two spots of angry color bloomed in her cheeks, and her eyes sparked like sun off brown bottle glass. "And besides, he worked the land all these years and made this ranch into something."

Slade frowned. What did she mean, half of the gold belonged to her father? Disgust filled him. Either the woman was a good actress, or Malone had lied to his family even on his deathbed.

"All of it."

She blinked, and for a moment, he thought she might give in. Then she lifted her chin. "And if I refuse?"

"One trip to the sheriff with your letter and the wanted poster from twenty-five years ago would convince any law-abiding judge that this ranch belongs to me and my family." He paused. "As well as the deed to the gold mine in California that has my father's name on it—not your father's."

"What deed?" She glared at him, suspicion glinting in her eyes. "And what wanted poster?"

Did she really not know the truth? Slade pulled out the papers and handed them to her, watching as she read the proof that gave him the right to the land they stood on.

All color left her face as she read, and Slade braced himself in case she fainted clean away. If he'd had any doubt that she didn't know the full story, her reaction to the wanted poster proved otherwise.

"It says . . ." Her voice wavered. "It says Papa shot your father. Left him for dead. I don't believe it. It . . . it's a mistake." She sank into the nearest chair, the starch wilted out of her. The condemning poster fluttered to the floor.

A sudden desire to give in swept over him. He could accept her offer of a few hundred head, walk out the door, and ride away, leaving her on the land that legally, morally, belonged to him. To his mother.

No! He wanted Seth Malone to pay for turning his father into a drunk and making his mother old before her time. But

Seth Malone was dead, and this woman wouldn't cheat him of his revenge.

No matter how innocent she looked, no matter how her eyes filled with tears as she begged for forgiveness, he wouldn't give it to her. Forgiveness wouldn't put food on the table or clothes on his mother's and sisters' backs.

"No mistake." He hunkered down so he could see her face. "You have a right to defend your father's memory, I reckon. But I'll stick by what I said. The deed is legal. And that letter will stand up in court as well. You've got a decision to make, ma'am. Either you sign this ranch over to me, or I'll go to the sheriff."

Silence hung heavy between them until a faint noise drew Slade's attention to the doorway.

An old woman stood there, a walking stick clasped in her right hand. Her piercing dark gaze swung from Mariah to him. He stood to his full height.

"Grandma." Mariah launched herself from the chair and hurried to the woman's side.

The frail-looking woman's penetrating stare never left Slade's face.

He held out his hand for the deed. Silence reigned as Mariah handed it over.

"I'll give you an hour to decide." He gave them a curt nod and strode from the room.

CHAPTER TWO

"Who's that?" Mariah's grandmother stood by her side at the window.

"Jack Donovan's son. The other man—the one by the corral—is his brother."

Her grandmother stiffened. "And Jack Donovan?"

"He's dead."

Mariah watched Donovan's long, steady strides as he marched toward the corral, where his brother waited with the horses. She didn't see Cookie, but she suspected he stood ready with his shotgun. He'd been around long enough to know something wasn't right.

Panic threatened to overwhelm her. The ranch hands

had Sunday off and weren't expected back until late. Did she want to get them involved in something that might lead to bloodshed? She'd never forgive herself if someone got killed.

"After all this time, I'd decided Jack Donovan wasn't going to contact us. I thought maybe he didn't get the letter, or the gold didn't matter that much."

Her grandmother folded her in her arms, and Mariah breathed in the sweet scent of powder and baking bread. Mariah clung to her, wishing her grandmother could fix this problem as easily as she'd kissed away her hurts as a youngster.

"I've wondered if I did the right thing, Grandma. I've even wished I'd never written to him. I thought if I did my Christian duty, God would take care of everything else."

"Hush, child. You did what you thought was right." Her grandmother nodded at the two men leaning against the corral. "That one out there, Donovan's son. What does he want?"

"The land." The knot of anxiety in Mariah's stomach swelled. "He wants the ranch. The whole ranch. And if I refuse, he'll tell the sheriff what Papa did. What am I going to do?"

"Everything?" A frown creased her grandmother's forehead. "Seth said half the gold belonged to him."

"He showed me the deed to the mine. Papa's name wasn't on it. Just Jack Donovan's."

"Well, I'll be."

"I don't know what to do," Mariah whispered. "We might have to leave Wisdom, unless . . . unless I marry Frederick."

"I won't have you sacrifice yourself to save the ranch."

"If I have to marry to provide for you and Amanda, I will."

"If the time comes when you can marry a man because you love him, or even respect him, well and good. But until then, I'll have no talk of marrying for any other reason. Is that clear?"

"Yes, ma'am."

"Now, about this other problem. Seth, bless his heart, did a terrible thing. In the end, he confessed and asked forgiveness. It isn't up to you or me to judge him. The fact remains he stole another man's gold and bought this ranch with it. If his name isn't on that deed, then the ranch—the *whole* ranch—should belong to the Donovans."

"But what about Amanda? Even if I can find work, I won't have enough money to pay for her schooling."

"We'll manage. And besides, the gentleman in charge of that school in Philadelphia is a godly man. He'll understand."

"But what if he doesn't?"

"God will provide." Her grandmother took her by the hand. "Come on, child. Let's go ask our heavenly Father what you should do."

As her grandmother led her from the room, Mariah spied the wanted poster halfway under the desk.

Her father had shot a man?

A whimper of anguish clawed its way up her throat, and she pressed a hand to her lips to stifle the sound. She couldn't bear to tell her grandmother the whole truth.

Not yet. Maybe not ever.

✯ ✯ ✯

Slade leaned against the corral and stared at the house, wondering if the Malone woman had made up her mind. Not that it made any difference. She didn't have much choice. If she stayed, she'd just prolong the agony of leaving as well as letting the whole country know what her father had done. At least she and the old woman could keep their dignity if they left now.

"What happened in there?" Buck stood next to him, his arms resting on a weathered board.

Slade glanced at his brother, wincing at the jagged crescent-shaped scar on his face. A twist of pain pulled at his gut. The wild mustang that stomped his brother had left more than physical scars. Buck had endured the ridicule and gawking of heartless folks until he'd finally taken refuge in working with his beloved horses, avoiding the cruelty of humans most of the time.

"I gave her an hour to make up her mind."

"She alone?"

"No, there's an older woman too. Her grandmother."

Neither spoke for several minutes, their focus on the house standing quiet and still a stone's throw from the corral. Nothing stirred save the swish of the horses' tails as they swatted horseflies. Buck blew out a whistling breath.

Slade clenched his jaw, knowing his brother had something on his mind. "Just spit it out."

"It doesn't seem right to turn them out of their home."

"It's our home. Ma's home." Slade glared at his brother. "What do you want me to do? Just walk away?"

"It's your decision, but I'd at least consider letting them stay until Ma gets here." Buck smothered a cough. "There's no harm in that, is there?"

Slade stalked away. He wouldn't let himself think about where the Malone women would go, what they'd do, or who would take them in.

Their problems were not his concern.

✶   ✶   ✶

Mariah left the storeroom, her decision made. The deed identified Slade Donovan's father as the sole owner of the gold mine, and she wouldn't fight him. It wasn't worth disgracing what was left of her family and her father's memory. Turning the ranch over to the Donovans would set everything to rights, wouldn't it?

She'd be homeless and penniless, but at least she'd have her pride.

Her decision weighed heavy as she looked around the house she'd lived in all her life. Just days ago, she'd complained about the shabbiness of everything. The furniture could use new covers, the house needed a fresh coat of paint, and the roof leaked every time it rained. Even the outbuildings begged for more attention than Red and the hands could spare.

But today, when it seemed as if she'd be leaving forever, everything took on a beloved glow. Her eyes, still stinging from her bout with tears, misted over.

She tamped down a rise of panic. How would she take care of her grandmother and her sister without the security of the ranch? She hadn't thought past the here and now. Hadn't thought what she'd tell Amanda. But she'd deal with that later.

Stepping onto the porch, she came face-to-face with Slade Donovan. A jolt coursed through her when his gaze met hers. What if they'd met under different circumstances? What if he'd been a neighboring rancher or a cowboy looking for work? Somebody to come alongside her and turn the Lazy M around. But he wasn't just another cowboy. He was the son of the man her father had ruined.

A son intent on revenge.

"I'll do it," she blurted out. "I'll sign the ranch over to you. But I want your promise you won't tell our neighbors what my father did. He was highly respected in this community, and his memory and our good name are all we have left."

She searched his face, hoping to find a hint of compassion. He stared at her, his expression hard and unreadable. Would he refuse? Had he decided to contact the sheriff anyway, whether she agreed to leave or not? Would he drag the past into the open, airing it like a musty old blanket? She didn't know if she could bear her friends whispering behind her back, casting pitying glances at her and her grandmother. Her heart thudded against her rib cage.

Please, Lord, let him say yes.

"All right." He nodded. "I'll take you and your grandmother into town in the morning. Just tell me where you want to go."

Mariah turned away. He'd agreed to let them leave without telling the sheriff and the community of Wisdom. She should be relieved that her family's reputation would remain intact.

But knowing her father tried to kill a man over a handful of gold left her feeling as if Slade Donovan had just hung a millstone around her neck and tossed her into the creek to drown.

The breaking of dawn brought rain.

Mariah dropped the curtain into place and stepped away from the window. What did rain on the Lazy M matter anymore? She'd be leaving today. Leaving for good. Let Slade Donovan worry about the rain, the grass, the cattle.

She wouldn't have to worry about the money to pay the hands, the fences that needed mending, or the leaky roof over the bunkhouse. She wouldn't have to worry about why the ranch had steadily declined after her father took sick. Her only worry would be survival: for Amanda, her grandmother, and for herself.

Survival. A place to stay. Food to eat. How would they manage with nothing?

The urge to talk to Reverend Winston grew as she gathered her belongings. But she wouldn't. The shame of what she would have to reveal stopped her. As much as leaving hurt, confessing her father's sins hurt more.

With a heavy heart, she finished packing two trunks

before easing out of her room, careful not to disturb her grandmother. She wrapped a warm shawl around her shoulders and stepped onto the front porch. Hugging the wrap close, she watched the water form small rivulets on the ground, then run together to make larger and larger puddles until little oceans dotted the open space between the house and the outbuildings.

The barn door creaked open, and a tall, broad-shouldered man strode toward the house. Mariah recognized Slade Donovan's confident swagger. He splashed through the widening puddles as if they weren't there, his chin tucked, shielding his face against the onslaught of rain. Just like he'd plowed into her life and laid bare all her family secrets.

He barged right onto the porch, and she stepped back just in time to avoid a collision. He jerked his head up, his gaze locking with hers. Neither spoke, the sound of rain filling the silence between them.

The scent of fresh rainwater clung to his clothes, and widening splotches dampened his brown duster. The dust and stubble from yesterday were gone, leaving a clean-shaven face—a strong, determined face that made her wonder if any part of him could show compassion or gentleness. Somehow she doubted it, and regret clutched at her heart.

If he were kind or gentle, he might offer a compromise, maybe agree to take half the land or only a portion of it. But no, *kind* and *compassionate* didn't describe Slade Donovan.

At least not as far as she was concerned.

Was he married? She rejected the fleeting thought as

suddenly as it occurred to her. What woman would put up with such an overbearing, high-handed man? The poor woman would have to be a saint.

He removed his hat and thrust a hand through his brown hair. This morning, beneath the cloudy skies, his tanned face seemed darker, his eyes bluer. Mariah looked away, annoyed she'd even noticed the color of his eyes or anything else about Slade Donovan.

"Morning, ma'am," he drawled. "Sorry I startled you."

She nodded, accepting his apology.

An uneasy silence settled around them as she waited for him to speak. Would he insist they leave today? She hated to feel as if he governed her life, but he did. She also hated the thought of moving her grandmother out on a morning like this. She started to ask if he'd wait until the rain eased up, but then she pressed her lips together. She wouldn't ask for favors, not even for her grandmother.

Mariah blinked, the grainy feeling behind her lids reminding her of a sleepless night. Even if he offered to delay their departure, she didn't know if she could stand to wait.

Better to get the whole thing over with and get on with her life.

Miss Malone barely acknowledged him. Instead, she stared at the expanse of yard in front of the house, seemingly mesmerized by the puddles. Was she waiting for him to tell her it was time to go? Did she think he'd make her and the old woman get out on a morning like this? He grimaced. He supposed she did. She didn't have any reason to think otherwise.

He gritted his teeth, angry with himself. It didn't matter what she thought. He still wanted them to leave. But he needed answers first.

Answers to ease his nagging conscience.

"Where will you and your grandmother go? Do you have family someplace?"

She took a deep breath but didn't spare him a glance. "We'll manage. After . . . after we drop by the bank to sign over the deed, I'd like to go on to the train station, if you don't mind."

Slade winced at her emotionless words. She appeared tired, as if she hadn't slept much, but her white shirtwaist and dove-gray skirt looked pressed and crisp. She'd combed every strand of her thick golden-brown hair into place, but he suspected before the end of the day her tresses would curl softly around her heart-shaped face just as they had yesterday when he'd first seen her.

He scowled, frustrated with his own indecision. It was a simple matter of telling her they'd wait until the rain slacked up, then be on their way, but he couldn't force the words out. Visions of her willowy form and her elderly grandmother kept him from accomplishing what he'd come here to do. He worked hard, expecting other men to handle their share, to make their own way, and he'd make his. But not women. He remembered the kindness shown to his mother by a precious few.

Hard times from as far back as he could remember had

created a softness in him for women and children, a desire to protect them. Even with the daughter of the man he hated, that soft spot sucker punched him in the gut.

"Miss Malone, I realize it isn't any of my business, but I'd like to know where the two of you are heading."

"You're right." Temper flared in her brown eyes. "It isn't any of your business."

He bit back a rueful smile. He supposed she had a right to be angry and hurting. "I'd still like an answer," he insisted.

She moved away without a word. But Slade could read signs as well as the next man. She wanted to go to the train station, to leave Wisdom, where everyone would whisper behind her back. If she stayed, it wouldn't take long for people to figure out she didn't have the kind of money she should have from the sale of the Lazy M.

And she hadn't so much as said so, but he suspected she didn't have any extended family who could help out. Just her and the old woman. A circumstance that made his demands harsher in the light of a new day.

Why hadn't Malone had a son instead of a daughter? Slade wouldn't think twice about kicking a man off land legally belonging to him. But a man wouldn't have given in so easily. A man would've fought for the land, right or wrong.

He cleared his throat. He'd mulled over Buck's suggestion most of the night. He didn't know if he agreed. But if he turned two women out without a place to go, he would never forgive himself, and neither would his mother. She'd seen enough hard times to feel for others in dire straits.

"It doesn't sit right with me, sending you and your grandmother away knowing the two of you don't have a place to go." He paused. "I take it you don't have much money either."

She stiffened, her lips pressed tight. He'd hit a nerve. Stifling a groan, he tried to come up with a good excuse to let them stay. He shook his head at the irony of wanting to kick them out and provide for them at the same time. He curled the brim of his hat in his fist. Might as well spit it out and be done with it.

"If you and your grandmother could stay on and mind the house until my mother gets here, I'd be obliged." The words stuck in his throat like dust churned up by a thousand head of stampeding cattle.

"Of all the gall!" She faced him then, an incredulous look on her face, color staining her pale cheeks. "Clean my own house and weed and water my own garden, knowing I'm going to walk off and let someone else take over? Mr. Donovan, you've got an inflated sense of who you and your family are if you think for one minute—"

"Miss Malone," he snapped, "I'm trying to be as accommodating as I can. Your father wouldn't have had the money to buy this ranch if he hadn't stolen it from my father in the first place."

They glared at each other for a tense moment before she whirled and stomped to the other end of the porch, presenting him her back, rigid and uncompromising.

*   *   *

Her world crumbled around her. Mariah stared at the mountains shrouded in mist, willing her pounding heart to slow and her careening emotions to subside so she could think.

She gripped the porch railing, feeling the slick dampness of the wood beneath her palms. One image floated to the surface of the jumbled thoughts inside her head. He'd said they could stay. But she didn't want to, not under the circumstances. It would be pure torture to walk through the rooms where she and Amanda had laughed and played. To view the majestic mountains and the rolling pastures, knowing any day might be her last.

But to be able to take care of her grandmother and Amanda for a few more weeks . . .

A weak ray of hope pierced through the cloudy haze. Would it be so bad to agree? It would give her time to plan, to make decisions. She didn't have much choice unless she threw herself on the mercy of Frederick and her other neighbors. A sick feeling assaulted her. Neither option appealed to her, but leaving wasn't exactly an option either. She doubted the small amount of money she had would buy tickets to Philadelphia, let alone see her and her grandmother through until she found a way of making a living.

She wished she could fling Slade Donovan's offer in his face and demand the wagon be brought round so they could leave, rain or no rain. But Amanda and her grandmother deserved better than that. She bowed her head.

Lord, guide me. Show me what to do.

Her stomach churned, uncertainty pulling at her. Should she go? Or stay?

Please, God.

Finally she turned and looked at the man who'd turned her life upside down. He leaned against a post, still and sure of his place in the world. A man who could come and go as he pleased, a man without responsibilities, a man who could disrupt the lives of others and not think twice about it.

A man who spiked her temper and made her blood boil.

"I'll expect the same wages any other housekeeper would get. But don't expect me or my grandmother to be at your beck and call. I don't think I could stomach that."

He stared, unblinking, considering her demand. Finally he dipped his head in agreement. "All right."

"What about meals?" As soon as the question left her lips, Mariah wanted to snatch it back.

"Buck and I will take supper in the house with you and your grandmother. We'll eat breakfast and the noon meal with the rest of the hands."

Another, more alarming, prospect occurred to her, and heat swooshed across her face. "You and your brother will sleep in the bunkhouse as long as we're here. And . . . and we always attend church on Sundays."

"Agreed. Are you done?" The tic in his jaw had returned. Fine and dandy. Let him be irked. It felt good to have the upper hand for a change.

Mariah bit her lip. She couldn't think of anything else. But at least she'd covered the important things, like where he and his brother would eat and sleep.

"What will you tell the hands?" He jerked his head toward the bunkhouse.

She'd forgotten the hands. "What am I going to tell them? You're the boss. What do you intend to tell them?"

"Nothing about your father, if that's what you mean." He lifted an eyebrow.

She searched his face. Could she trust this man's word? He'd ripped everything from her that she held dear, save her family, but as far as she could tell, he hadn't lied to her. "I can tell them you're the new owner of the Lazy M and that Grandma and I are helping out in the house until your mother gets here."

"It's the truth."

She winced. "But not all of it."

"The rest isn't anybody's business."

Mariah glanced at the cookhouse, where a thin plume of smoke told her Cookie had started breakfast for the hands. "Cookie will sense something's wrong. He's known me all my life."

"It'll be up to you to convince him, Mariah. I won't tell him any different." With a slight nod, he turned and headed toward the bunkhouse.

She glared at his retreating back. He'd called her by her first name as if hiring her as housekeeper gave him the right

to be so familiar. Oh, the man made her so mad, she could
. . . she could just *spit*.

Instead, she gritted her teeth and called out, "Supper will
be ready and waiting—*Slade*."

CHAPTER THREE

"GOT ANY COFFEE, old man?"

The stocky fellow Mariah called Cookie whirled around and squinted at Slade, the spatula in his hand pointed like a gun. He shook the greasy instrument. "If you want coffee, you young whippersnapper, you'll call me Cookie. Ain't no *old men* round here," he said, his reedy voice too decrepit to make the threat menacing.

"I'll remember that." The smell of Cookie's breakfast made a man sit up and take notice, so the last thing he wanted was to offend the old codger.

"Coffee's over there." The cook waved his spatula in the general direction of the stove. "Help yourself."

Slade poured a cup of the steaming brew and took a seat. He sipped the coffee: strong, black—exactly how he liked it.

Cookie peered at him over his shoulder as he deftly turned sizzling eggs and frying ham. "You just hire on?"

"You might say that."

"Funny. Red didn't say nothing about it."

"Red?"

Cookie frowned and gave him another squinty inspection. "Red Harper, foreman on the Lazy M."

"I guess he hasn't gotten around to it yet."

Cookie concentrated on setting the food out while men ambled in, making a beeline for the coffeepots on the stove.

Slade took their measure over the rim of his own cup. It didn't take long to pick Harper out. A barrel-chested, beefy man with wiry red hair sticking out in all directions, Harper looked like he'd gotten up on the wrong side of his bunk this morning.

"Name's Red Harper." He poured a tall glass of buttermilk and pulled out a chair. "Lazy M foreman."

"Slade Donovan." He didn't elaborate. The change in ownership of the ranch would be better coming from Mariah. But if she didn't get here soon, he'd have to do the telling.

"Got in late last night." Harper frowned. "Thought I saw two horses in the corral."

"My brother rode in with me. He's not real sociable."

"What brings you to the Lazy M?" Harper acted friendly enough, but Slade detected an undercurrent of tension in his voice.

Cookie pushed between them and placed a platter of hot biscuits in the center of the table. He made a fuss over the steaming plates of eggs and ham. "Food's getting cold. Y'all can talk business after breakfast."

When they'd swiped the last of the biscuits, and the remains of the ham had turned to cold grease, Slade waited for the onslaught from the foreman. He'd decided over breakfast he'd tell the whole bunch the Lazy M had a new owner whether Mariah put in an appearance or not.

"Well, Donovan, now that you've got your belly full, where you headed next?" Harper asked, leaning back. The split-bottom chair creaked under his weight. His studied nonchalance wasn't lost on Slade. He looked coiled as tightly as a rattler about to strike.

Slade glanced around, taking stock of the men lounging at the table. Most of them sipped the last dregs of their coffee, ignoring the conversation. But a couple smirked, clearly interested in how Slade would respond.

A seasoned cowpoke slapped a fresh-faced kid of about sixteen on the back. "Come on, Rio; let's you and me get out of here."

"Aw, Duncan, I ain't finished my coffee yet."

"Hurry up then," Duncan said, his tone gruff. "We've got work to do."

Cookie bustled about behind them, muttering and banging pots and pans together.

Harper leaned forward. "I asked you a question."

Slade reached for his coffee cup with his left hand. "Don't

reckon I'm headed anywhere in particular. I kind of planned on settling right here for a spell."

The foreman's face turned a mottled red. "I don't know what you're up to, mister, but we don't need no trouble on the Lazy M. And we don't need no hands either. So if I was you, I'd just mosey on down the road."

Slade regarded Harper from across the table. "I don't think so."

Harper stood, the sudden movement tipping his chair back to whack against the floor. "If I say you're moving on, you're moving on."

"Red!" Mariah's voice cut across the tension. She stood in the open doorway for a moment before Cookie rushed to her side.

"Miss Mariah, what are you doing? Don't you think you ought to be in the house, out of this rain?"

"It's not raining right now."

"Well, I know that, ma'am, but it might start before you get back to the house. And it's awful muddy out there. You're liable to ruin that purty dress you got on."

Slade felt sorry for the cook. He looked like a banty rooster trying to protect one of his hens.

"It's all right, Cookie." She took a deep breath. "I need to tell you all something. Something important."

She moved to the table, her troubled gaze resting on Slade before shifting to the others. He couldn't help but admire her determination.

"I know this may come as a surprise," she said, "but I

don't know how else to tell you. I've decided to sell the ranch to Mr. Donovan. There are some debts to pay, and . . ." She paused, and a tinge of red crept into her cheeks. "The ranch hasn't been doing as well under my guidance as it did when my father was alive."

Harper moved forward. "But, ma'am, it ain't your fault things haven't gone well for the Lazy M the last few years, what with all the medical bills and the price of cattle being down. . . . We'll do better next year."

Mariah shook her head. "I've already agreed to Mr. Donovan's offer. My grandmother and I will help out in the house until Mr. Donovan's mother gets here. And then we'll be leaving."

Nobody said anything, not even Cookie.

She took another deep breath. "I've let you make all the decisions for a long time, Red, because I felt you knew what to do better than I did. If Frederick hadn't recommended you when my father took sick, I don't know how I would've managed. But from now on, you'll take orders from Mr. Donovan."

Harper glowered at Slade with bulldog intensity, his chin jutted. The moment was fleeting, though, before he reined in his expression and looked at Mariah. "I guess I don't have much choice, ma'am. But I wish you'd change your mind."

"I won't." She turned and left.

Red Harper jammed his hat on his head and stalked from the room.

★　★　★

Slade ambled into the coolness of the barn, stopping to let his eyes adjust to the dim interior. His brother, Buck, whistled as he brushed the coat of a bay mare heavy with foal.

Slade leaned on the stall, watching his brother's face. "I didn't see you at breakfast this morning."

"Not hungry."

"Here. Saved these for you." Slade held out a bundle wrapped in cheesecloth. "Cookie's a fair-to-middling cook."

Buck hesitated, then dropped the brush, took the biscuits and ham, and settled on a bench against the wall. The tantalizing smell of fried ham filled the barn as he unwrapped the offering.

Slade made himself comfortable against the stall and stared at the mountains behind the house as his brother ate his breakfast. Slade's jaw tightened. Buck had always been a quiet sort, even as a child. But then, they both were.

They'd grown up hard and fast and hadn't had time for a lot of fun and games. No time to go swimming with the other boys or to fish for the sheer fun of it. All their fishing had been serious business.

Since Buck's accident, he'd retreated into a world of horses, avoiding people even more than usual. He'd insisted on making the trip from Texas to Wyoming, even though Slade was dead set against it. Buck hadn't completely gotten over a bout with pneumonia this past winter, and Slade could just see the two of them getting caught in a storm and Buck taking sick again. But they'd arrived safely at their destination no worse for wear. Buck's coughing spells seemed to come on less and less, so maybe he truly was on the mend.

The soft whisper of Buck brushing the crumbs from his clothes broke the silence. "What happened this morning? I saw that redheaded barrel of a man come out of the cook-house mad as a hornet."

"That's Harper, the foreman here. Miss Malone told the men I'm the new owner of the ranch."

Buck whistled. "She told them the truth?"

"Not exactly. She said there were some debts to be paid, and she'd sold the ranch."

"Well, I reckon that's true, isn't it?" Buck asked, scratching his jawline.

Slade shrugged. "I reckon so."

The steady pounding gave Mariah great satisfaction. She punched the dough with her fist, visualizing Slade Donovan's face in the doughy blob. She folded the dough before slapping it again.

She should've turned down his offer to let them stay.

If she had enough money, she'd go to Philadelphia lickety-split. Surely she could make twice as much in the city cooking and cleaning as she'd make here. She flipped the dough on the wooden work surface, and puffs of flour flew in her face, fueling her anger.

The Lazy M hadn't turned a profit in two years, and they'd

barely squeezed by the year before that. Slade might have enough to pay the other hands and purchase some much-needed supplies, but where would that leave her?

Without, more than likely!

She slapped the dough again. Hard.

"If you beat that dough any longer, child, it's going to be tougher than an old boot."

Mariah glanced at the mound of dough she'd pulverized. "Sorry, Grandma."

She formed a smooth oval and choked off a section, expertly rolling it into a biscuit with both hands. "I should've stood up to him. I should've told him to take us to court. The people of Wisdom would stand by us." She glanced at her grandmother, expecting to see agreement on her weathered face.

Faded brown eyes, once as bright as her own, gazed back at her. Disillusionment filled their depths. "You think so?"

"Don't you?" Mariah asked, dismay coursing through her.

"Stealing is a hard thing, Mariah. It isn't easily forgiven. I reckon folks have to work so hard for what they get, they don't want someone else taking it away from them."

"But Papa was a good man," Mariah argued, tamping down thoughts of the wanted poster Slade had shown her. She'd hidden it in the bottom drawer in her father's office, tucked inside an old ledger. She never wanted to see the thing again. And she certainly didn't want her grandmother to see it. "The people in Wisdom respected him."

"I know. When Seth wrote your grandpa and me and told us to come to Wyoming Territory, that he'd bought all this land, it surprised me. I didn't expect anybody to go to California and strike it rich—well, he might not have been rich, but it was more money than the likes of us had ever seen. But others did it, so I just figured the Lord blessed him. I never dreamed he'd stolen it." Her grandmother's thin shoulders slumped.

Mariah wiped her hands on her apron and hurried over to her grandmother. "Oh, Grandma, I'm sorry. I hadn't thought how much all of this has hurt you, too. It'll all work out." She gave her a tight hug.

Her grandmother patted her shoulder. "Don't worry about me, child. You did the right thing. There's nothing we can do about the past. It's the future we have to think about. We've got to do right in God's sight, and the rest will fall into place."

"Such an easy thing to say, but much harder to believe."

"All we can do is pray and have faith. You never know what might happen to change things before we have to leave here." Her grandmother smothered a yawn. "I do believe it's time for a short nap. Do you need help with anything else?"

"No, you go ahead. I'll call you when supper's ready."

Mariah watched her grandmother totter from the room. How could the old woman survive this upheaval? Her grandmother had often said that she was done moving. She wanted to be buried by her husband in the cemetery in Wisdom. Mariah turned back to the mound of dough and formed another biscuit.

"Lord, what am I going to do?" she whispered.

*　　*　　*

What was he going to do?

Slade regarded the ranch house. Mariah had gone on and on with her demands, getting more worked up by the minute. When she'd blurted out the question about meals, he'd told her he would eat supper in the house just to raise her ire.

He hadn't counted on having to face her at the supper table night after night. He slapped his hat on his head and marched across the muddy expanse between the barn and the house. Nothing for it now. He wouldn't back down from his impulsive attempt to needle her. He stepped onto the porch and scrubbed the mud from his boots. He stopped when he heard humming.

The tune brought back memories.

His mother used to hum that very song as she worked around the house.

The kitchen door stood ajar, so he could see Mariah's shadow as she moved about putting the finishing touches on supper. She hummed as she flitted from the stove to the table, the heat from the stove casting a becoming blush across her cheekbones. Her neat bun from earlier in the day was mussed, just as he'd suspected it would be. He smiled. The slightly messy appearance wilted a little of the starch out of her.

Her humming turned to words as she absentmindedly sang a few lines of the hymn.

He rapped on the open door, capturing her attention.

If possible, the color on her flushed cheeks ratcheted up

another notch. She tucked an errant strand of hair behind her ear and motioned to the table. "Supper'll be ready any minute now."

He raked a hand through his hair, pushing the damp strands into place, before hanging his hat on a wooden peg by the door.

"I set a place for your brother." She cleared her throat. "Is he joining us?"

"Buck ate with the men."

"I see." She smoothed both palms down her apron before abruptly turning toward the stove. "Would you like some coffee?"

"Yes, ma'am. Black."

Mariah poured a cup and set it on the table, pushing it toward him. The scrape of the cup across the scarred oak table sounded loud in the silence of the kitchen. He took a sip and nodded. "Good."

"I'm glad it meets your approval." Her chin tipped up a notch.

His gaze snapped to hers and saw the challenge there. "All I meant—"

He broke off as the elderly woman eased into the room, her arthritic, blue-veined hands gripping a walking stick.

"Grandma, I thought you were resting." Mariah helped her to a chair and turned back to the stove.

"I heard voices." She speared Slade with a look. "Sarah Malone."

"Ma'am."

Mariah carried the stew to the table, skirting the chair where he sat. As she leaned toward the center with the heavy pot, she gasped. The pot tilted, and Slade grabbed for the handles, his hands closing over hers.

"You all right? Are you burned?"

"No, my hand slipped." Roses bloomed in her cheeks again, and she tugged against his grip. "I've got it now."

Conscious of the warmth of her fingers beneath his, Slade let go.

His mouth watered as she grabbed a pan of biscuits with golden-brown tops and carried them to the table. Then she sat down next to her grandmother and folded her hands in her lap, not sparing him a glance. "Grandma, would you say grace, please?"

Slade lowered his head along with the women. When was the last time he'd bowed his head in reverence while someone blessed a meal? As a child, his mother insisted that they pray over the food, at least as long as his father wasn't around. And when she thought she could get away with it without a beating, she'd scrubbed them up good and taken them to meetings anytime a preacher bravely ventured into the lower part of town. The memories of those long-ago days had grown hazy.

He hadn't attended a brush arbor meeting since he'd found his father dead in an alley behind the Golden Chance Saloon in Galveston. Even his mother's gentle admonitions to forgive and forget couldn't penetrate the cold, hard knot festering down deep inside.

"Dear heavenly Father, thank You for the food we're about to eat, and bless the hands that prepared it. We give You praise for our health and happiness. Your will be done. Amen."

He looked up to find Mariah staring at him with a bemused expression. His gaze flickered over the smooth planes of her face, across her full lips, to her hair, and back again. She dropped her head as a becoming shade of crimson flooded her cheeks.

Warmth exploded in Slade's chest, shocking in its intensity.

He'd come seeking revenge, but a longing for something more swept over him. Something he'd glimpsed in the shimmering depths of Mariah Malone's brown eyes.

CHAPTER FOUR

"I TOLD YOU not to ever come here."

Emmit's flat black eyes bored into Red. He hated it when his half brother looked at him like that. Like he was too stupid to live. It had always been that way. Red was big and rawboned and a little clumsy. Mostly he liked being big. Being stocky came in handy working cattle. But Emmit always made him feel like a big, dumb ox.

As soon as Emmit had shown a talent for cards, Red's stepfather had started grooming his son to follow in his footsteps. Red stayed with his mother, but he longed to be included in their excursions. They'd be gone for days, sometimes weeks, coming back with fancy duds, their pockets flush, full of tales of the places they'd been and what they'd seen. The more worldly and sophisticated Emmit became, the more backward and uncouth Red felt.

When Emmit had gotten in trouble with the law six years ago, their ma had scraped up enough money to pay the fine and begged Red to keep him out of trouble. He'd been bailing him out ever since.

"Something's happened." Red paced back and forth. "Something you should know about."

"What is it?"

"Miss Malone sold the ranch."

"What?" Emmit straightened. "Who bought it?"

"He's not from around here. Name's Slade Donovan."

"Does he know anything about ranching? About cattle?"

"I think so." The knot in Red's stomach mushroomed and threatened to consume him. "He could cause trouble. A lot of trouble."

One time, and one time only, Emmit had promised. But one time led to two, then three, and now the whole thing had been going on for way too long.

He scowled. Some big brother he'd turned out to be. Emmit had managed to dig himself into a pit deeper than ever before.

And this time, he'd pulled Red in with him.

A rolling flush swept up Mariah's neck. Now would be a good time for the kitchen floor to open up and swallow her.

Slade Donovan had caught her staring at him. And to make matters worse, he'd stared right back. Why had she been watching him when she should have had her head bowed in reverence for the blessing? She had no excuse, other than the fact that his presence dominated the kitchen, making the space feel small and intimate.

Had the harshness she'd seen in the line of his jaw softened to something akin to regret and longing? She focused on her plate. Surely she was mistaken. What regrets could he possibly have?

Heart pounding, she stole another glance at him, noticing the sweep of thick lashes across his sun-darkened cheekbones and the tiny lines feathering out from the corners of his eyes.

She studied his hands. Strong and capable, as she'd known they would be. He gripped his spoon before lifting a bite of the thick stew. He kept his attention focused on his plate, and Mariah jerked her gaze back to her own meal, heat suffusing her face.

Would every night seated across from him be as torturous as this one? They had nothing to talk about, no common interests, other than ranching. And talking about the Lazy M didn't seem to be the best topic to settle on under the circumstances. The soft clink of spoons against bowls and the rustle of their movements filled the room, but the lack of conversation started to grate on her nerves.

Please, Lord, just let this meal be over.

Her grandmother broke the silence. "Where did you say you were from, Mr. Donovan?"

"I'd prefer Slade, ma'am."

Mariah glanced at her grandmother and caught a speculative gleam in her eyes. After a moment, her grandmother nodded. "All right. Slade it is."

"I grew up around Galveston, ma'am, but I've traveled here and there over the years. Working cattle mostly."

"So you know a good deal about cattle, then?" A definite edge laced her grandmother's voice. Sarah Malone might be feeble, but her mind remained as feisty as ever.

"I reckon."

"Hmph. You think you can turn a profit here?"

"Grandma . . ." Mariah bit back her response. The very topic she wanted to avoid. If she didn't watch out, her grandmother would have both of them thrown out on their ear, money or no money.

Slade shifted in his chair. "I don't see why not. Good grazing land around these parts. And the cows seem to have fared all right through the winter."

"Our cows are the finest in this part of the country, mark my words," her grandmother replied with a proud tilt to her chin.

Slade lifted his coffee cup to his mouth, but not before Mariah caught a glimpse of a slight smile. The upward quirk of his lips created deeply slashed lines beside his mouth.

He was laughing. She glared at him, but he ignored her.

"I'm sure they are, ma'am."

"More coffee, Grandma?" Mariah stood and lifted the coffeepot from the stove.

Her grandmother held up a hand, halting her at half a cup. "No more. I don't want to stay awake all night."

Mariah turned to Slade, frowning at the hint of amusement lingering on his face. She topped off his cup and moved away. She didn't know whether to be glad or angry he found her grandmother amusing.

"What about the hands? What do you intend to do about them?" Her grandmother continued her verbal sparring regardless of Mariah's subtle hints that they'd finished supper.

One by one, the old hands had drifted away, until Mariah didn't know any of the ranch workers anymore. Cookie was the only one who'd been around for any length of time. And he really couldn't be counted as a hand. Cookie just sort of came with the bunkhouse.

The uneasy silence following her grandmother's question magnified Mariah's worries.

"What do you think I should do?" Slade sat forward, his attention trained on her grandmother. He didn't look angry, but curious and slightly wary.

Her grandmother paused, taking her time before she answered. "You'll know—if you know men and if you want this ranch to succeed." She sat back in her chair, a pleased expression on her face.

Mariah watched as her grandmother and Slade sized each other up. He drained his coffee cup and stood. "I'll keep that in mind. Thanks for supper, Mariah." He nodded at her grandmother. "Good night, ma'am. Pleasure talking to you."

"Good night."

He stepped out into the night and left them alone.

Mariah stared at her grandmother. "What was that all about?"

"I just wanted to see if he had any smarts about him." Her grandmother gave her an innocent look. "I've never had any use for some of the men Red has hired."

"Everybody makes mistakes." But Red seemed to make more than most when it came to hiring dependable hands.

"You know, Mariah, I think that young man just might be what the Lazy M needs. Too bad we won't be here to see him make a go of it." She pursed her lips. "I wish . . ."

"What?" Mariah prompted.

"Nothing." Her grandmother stood, groaning with the effort of getting to her feet. "Here, child, help me to bed. It's time for my prayers. Me and the Lord have some serious business to attend to."

Mariah laughed as she took her grandmother's arm. "You and the Lord always have serious business."

"And who better to talk to when things get serious?"

"I can't think of anyone better, Grandma."

Once she settled her grandmother in for the night, she returned to the kitchen, pondering the conversation over dinner. Her grandmother had taken a liking to Slade Donovan, of all people.

And by his reaction to her questions, the feeling seemed mutual. Too bad he didn't care one whit for Mariah. Still, she supposed it might be a good thing her grandmother intrigued him. Maybe he'd think twice about forcing them to leave before she saved enough money to get them to Philadelphia.

She made quick work of washing the dishes, then gathered the leftover scraps in a bowl and stepped outside. Daylight gave way to a pink-and-yellow sunset as the sun sank toward the horizon. A slight wintry nip remained in the air, but the heat of summer would be here soon enough. The cats twined themselves around her skirts as she picked her way to the woodpile at the edge of the yard, careful to avoid puddles left by the rain.

"Hello there, Prissy." Bending down, she scratched a calico cat behind the ears. Prissy arched her back into the gesture. A rotund black-and-white cat waddled toward them.

Mariah laughed as she ran her hand down the expectant feline's back, the feel of her soft, silky fur soothing. "So you want a little petting too, do you?"

The cat purred with pleasure.

Mariah poured out the scraps, saving a small portion in the bottom of the bowl. She squinted into the fading light, trying to get a glimpse of the half-wild tomcat that shared the others' meals. A movement past the smokehouse caught her attention.

"Hey, Yellow," she crooned, easing toward him.

She stopped within a few feet of the tomcat, scraped out the remains of the stew, and backed away. He sidled toward the offering and started eating, his yellow eyes darting in her direction every few bites, keeping a careful watch on her movements.

Taking care not to startle him, she whispered, "Hey, boy, what you been doing today, hmm?"

She inched closer. They played this game night after night. She moved another inch and waited. He'd grown more used to her, letting her draw nearer over the last several weeks, and she knew she'd eventually tame him.

Suddenly his ears perked, his head jerked toward the porch, and he darted into the shadows. Mariah turned and caught a glimpse of Slade beside the porch.

"Sorry." His voice drifted to her on the evening breeze. "Didn't mean to scare him away."

"It's all right. He wouldn't have let me touch him anyway."

"You think he'll let you pet him someday?"

She wished she could hightail it back to the house. He probably thought her childish, wasting her time trying to tame a half-wild tomcat. Being a man, he wouldn't have time for such silliness. But what did his opinion matter? She didn't have to explain her actions to him.

"I hope so." Lifting her chin, she headed toward the house.

"You're a lot like my brother." A deep chuckle rumbled out of him, the sound catching her off guard. "You'd better be careful, or he's liable to give you a run for your money and try to tame that tomcat himself. He's got the patience of Job when it comes to animals and such."

"And you don't?" She couldn't see Slade Donovan being patient about much of anything.

"I'm not as patient as Buck, but I have my moments." A faint smile lifted one corner of his mouth.

"Not many, I would imagine," she quipped, desperately trying to break the spell woven by the encroaching darkness and his amused drawl.

"You'd be surprised at the level of patience I can muster when the need arises."

Shadows cast by the evening sun danced across his features, and the tiny smile on his face faded away. She forced her attention from his mouth to his eyes, squinted against the light of the lantern on the porch. What was it about the evening breeze and lengthening shadows that made him seem more approachable, more relaxed, concerned even?

An owl hooted, and she jumped. What was she thinking? "I'm sorry; did you want something?"

"I'm heading into town in the morning now that the rain's let up. I'd like you to ride along, and we'll sign over the deed." The words came out in a hushed tone, flat and emotionless. His gaze bored into her, serious, unblinking.

But his demand, couched as a polite request, wasn't lost on Mariah. They'd come to an uneasy truce this morning, and she could agree quietly or let loose her temper and start another argument. But what good would that do?

An argument wouldn't change the inevitable.

The next morning dawned bright and clear. Mariah hurried out to gather the eggs while her grandmother stoked the fire in the old woodstove. She didn't know what time Slade wanted to leave, but she'd be ready. She didn't want to keep him waiting.

Halfway across the barnyard, she decided to check on the mare due to foal in a couple of weeks. She entered the barn, blinking in the dim interior. The scent of fresh hay, leather, and horses swirled around her. Someone had been hard at work organizing the tack along the wall to her left. Slade? She doubted it. Maybe his brother had a penchant for organization.

Across the open area in the middle of the barn stood Slade's brother. His rail-thin body made his height more pronounced. His shirt hung loosely from his shoulders, and the threadbare pair of breeches belted at his waist looked a couple of sizes too big. Had he been sick?

She watched as he brushed the pregnant mare, his attention focused on the animal, murmuring as he worked. Dusty's ears twitched toward the sound, showing her pleasure at the attention.

Mariah smiled. Yes, she and Buck were much alike. She stepped closer and he glanced up, his face shadowed by the brim of a floppy hat pulled low over his brow.

"Good morning. I'm Mariah. You must be Buck."

He nodded but didn't face her. "Yes, ma'am."

His voice sounded like a faint imitation of Slade's deep baritone. A little less worn and trail-weary, but the determination she'd heard in Slade's voice resided in Buck's as well.

"Her name's Dusty." She motioned toward the mare. "It's her first foal, so we thought we'd better keep a close watch on her."

He nodded again.

"I don't know if Slade mentioned it, but he'll be eating supper in the house every night." She moved closer, surprised and pleased Buck wasn't as gruff as his brother. His bashful nature made her want to befriend him as she'd befriended the yellow cat. "You're welcome to join us."

He glanced sideways in her direction and then jerked his head down in another nod and brushed Dusty with quick, sure strokes. "Thank you, ma'am, but I'll eat with the others, if it's all the same to you."

Mariah shifted her feet, moving some hay back and forth, and looked over at the next stall. What should she say? She'd never met anyone as shy as Buck. He wouldn't even look at her here in the dim interior of the barn. No wonder he didn't want to come to the house and sit with strangers at the supper table. Now she wished she hadn't embarrassed him by asking.

"Well," she said with forced cheerfulness, "if you change your mind, you're always welcome."

She beat a hasty retreat to the henhouse and gathered the eggs, her mind straying to the Donovan brothers. For siblings, they acted nothing alike. Slade plowed in and got what he wanted by being downright overbearing, while Buck's shy and unassuming personality made her wonder if he had any backbone at all. She frowned. What if Slade ran roughshod over his brother like he'd done over her?

Mariah reached for another egg and pondered the situation. The sound of raised voices from the other side of the barn wafted toward her as she placed the last egg in her basket.

"What's the matter, Bucky-boy; don't you like us?" The mocking voice belonged to Giff Kerchen.

She heard the taunt clearly, and her heart lurched. Red had definitely made a mistake when he hired Giff a few months ago. The man made her uneasy. At first, he'd come to the house offering to fill the wood box, start the fire in the kitchen, even volunteered to drive her and her grandmother into town on occasion. And she'd done nothing to encourage him.

Come to think of it, he hadn't bothered her since the day Frederick had stopped by and Mariah had told him how uncomfortable the man made her feel. Maybe Frederick had said something to Red. Regardless, Mariah was glad of the reprieve from Giff's unwanted attentions.

". . . where I please." Buck's answer was broken up by a muffled cough.

"Now, that ain't friendly, is it, boys?"

She gritted her teeth. Giff's tone was anything but friendly. It was downright hostile.

"Not a bit, Giff," someone else answered. A low rumble of laughter followed.

"Big brother ain't here to take care of you now, Bucky-boy, so I'll just have to do it myself. What say we just mosey on over to the cook shack and all have a nice little breakfast together?"

"No thanks."

Mariah had heard enough. Maybe if the men saw her coming out of the chicken coop, they'd leave Buck alone. She hurried to the hinged gate, latching it on her way out.

The sight that greeted her as she rounded the corner of the barn put a knot of fear in her stomach. But the wave of anger and protectiveness swelling up inside overrode her anxiety.

Giff and another burly cowboy grabbed Buck, each holding an arm while dragging him toward the cookhouse. Buck's reed-thin frame bowed as he dug in his heels and resisted the men. He jerked away, the buttons on his shirt ripped free, and he lurched back toward the barn.

In that instant, Mariah saw the scar racing down one side of his pale face and the misshapen jaw that pulled his mouth down on one side. She caught a glimpse of puckered flesh on his rib cage and torso just before he sprawled into the dirt, his stricken gaze caught in hers. But the raw pain she saw in his face had nothing to do with the scars he carried on the outside.

Giff bent over, clutching his stomach, laughing.

White-hot rage overtook her, and before she realized what she was doing, she stomped behind him and dumped the entire contents of the basket over his head. Fresh eggs cracked and dripped in thick rivulets onto his shoulders and arms.

He whirled to face her. "What the—?"

"You should be ashamed. Can't you see he's been hurt enough?" She swung the basket at him, uncaring how ineffective the weapon was. He backpedaled, the sudden attack catching him by surprise. But he recovered quickly. Anger flashed across his face, and he ripped the basket out of her hand and tossed it away. The basket bounced on the ground and tumbled to rest against the watering trough a few feet away.

"Why, you—" He took a step toward her, the slimy yellow egg yolks oozing down his shirt.

Dread snaked up her spine. But she stood her ground. If she backed down, he'd do as he pleased.

Buck, pale as death, stepped in front of her. She bit her lip. What had she done? Giff probably wouldn't actually hit her, but he wouldn't think twice about taking his anger out on Buck, even if it was obvious he'd been hurt bad and recently.

"Giff! That's enough," Red called from the bunkhouse. "Get yourself cleaned up and get on over to the north pasture. That water hole needs cleaning out."

The ranch hand's angry glare shifted between Mariah and Buck. He turned and stalked away, the others following.

A wave of relief rolled over Mariah.

"You shouldn't have done that, ma'am." Buck's quiet voice broke across her relief.

"I know." She sighed and squinted at him. He still looked pale and weak, emphasizing the crescent-shaped scar covering the entire left side of his face. "I wasted all my eggs."

Shock registered on his face before an amused little smile lifted one corner of his mouth. If not for the scars and his thin frame, he'd be a handsome young man. His lips twitched as he fought to contain the grin. "What a sight to see. A big man like that stopped dead in his tracks by a basket of raw eggs."

Mariah giggled.

He bent down to pick up her basket, turning the scarred side of his face away from her, the movement so smooth and practiced she knew he'd done it hundreds of times before. A muscle twitched in his jaw, reminding her of Slade.

"I guess I should be mad at you for stepping in. No man likes to think he can't take care of himself."

"It's no shame to have been hurt, Buck." What had happened to him? She wouldn't humiliate him more by asking.

"Yes, ma'am."

His defeated tone told her he didn't believe the words he'd uttered. "Well, you just come on over to the house with Slade tonight. A few good meals will help you build your strength up."

He threw a glance in her direction, and a grin crossed his uneven features. "Thank you, ma'am. I might do that."

Mariah smiled back at him as he handed her the empty basket.

Soon after breakfast, the lumbering sound of the wagon drew Mariah to the front porch. Slade sat atop the buckboard, the reins clasped loosely in both hands. He set the brake, jumped down, and faced her, hands on his hips.

"Do we have to take the buckboard?" Mariah finished pinning on her hat, studying the narrow seat. "I wouldn't mind riding."

"Got to pick up a few things."

She started to pull herself up, but he held out a large,

work-roughened hand. She stared at it for a moment. How could the man be so considerate and so coldhearted at the same time?

Reluctantly she placed her hand in his, her fingertips registering the calluses on his palm—calluses that told of countless hours working with cows, horses, and the land. She couldn't ignore their warmth or their strength as his fingers wrapped around hers and steadied her as she stepped up into the wagon.

All too soon, he settled beside her. She inched to the edge of the seat, uncomfortably aware of his wide shoulders taking up more than his share of the room. She stared straight ahead, gripped the edge of the seat, and resigned herself to an uncomfortably close ride into Wisdom.

As they lurched down the rutted lane toward the dirt road leading to town, every jolt threw her shoulder against his immovable solidness. He shifted his weight, but the movement did little to give her more room. It just served to remind her of his nearness.

The creak of the wagon and the jingling harness were about as unnerving as the intermittent jostling against her companion. Finally she blurted out, "I met your brother this morning."

"Well?"

She frowned in his direction. "Well, what?"

"What did you think of my little brother?" Mariah didn't miss the underlying wariness in his question.

Should she tell him about the incident with Giff? Would Buck want her to? She hesitated. "He's been hurt real bad."

"That's obvious." He gave a slight snort as if any idiot could see that.

"That's not what I meant." Mariah grabbed the metal railing and held on as the buckboard inched over a washed-out place in the road so deep it rattled her teeth.

"What *did* you mean?"

"By people. He's been hurt by people who make fun of him."

"Some people act like they've never seen anyone with a scar before," he muttered.

She nodded. She knew all too well how the jeers of people could twist like a knife in a person's soul. She'd lived with people making fun of her sister nearly all her life.

When they topped a rise, the small town of Wisdom came into view. There wasn't much to see. A smattering of weathered buildings faced each other across a wide main street. A couple of side streets branched off, meandering in various directions into the countryside. Slaughter's Sawmill and the railroad were about the only things holding the town together. A schoolhouse that doubled as a church nestled in a grove of trees off to their right.

"What happened to him?" The buckboard bounced across the railroad tracks, then started the slow descent into town.

"A wild mustang. Buck got thrown, and the horse stomped on him before I could get to him. He almost died. Took months before he could even walk across a room. He had another setback this past winter when he took sick with pneumonia."

"It's a miracle he's alive. He's got a lot to be thankful for."

"Thankful?" He gestured at the town laid out before them. "He couldn't even walk down those streets without every mother in sight shielding her children from him. And what about a wife and family? What woman will want to marry him?"

The bitterness in his voice masked his pain for his brother. She knew exactly how he felt: his guilt for not protecting his brother, the worry over how different Buck's life could have been, what the future might hold.

Oh yes, she knew all about that.

Her thoughts turned to her sister. Amanda wouldn't care about Buck's scars. She'd care for the man inside. "Someday, a woman will love him for himself," she spoke with conviction. "No matter what he looks like."

Slade didn't believe her, but now was not the time to argue as he guided the wagon into town. Wisdom resembled hundreds of other small towns he'd been through. And he figured the people were the same: close-knit, taking care of their own, suspicious of others.

He'd been an outsider all his life. He supposed he could thank his father for that. He couldn't count the times he'd dragged his father out of some seedy saloon in Galveston, or the times he'd begged some cowboy to help him lift his drunken pa up onto an old swayback mare so he could take him home.

He'd known their pity and hated it, but his mother needed his help, needed him to take care of her and the rest of the family. So he'd swallowed his pride and did what had to be done.

After a while, it didn't bother him that people didn't trust him, didn't think he belonged in their circle of friends, in their churches, or in their town meetings. He'd learned to live with rejection a long time ago. He didn't need their approval.

But he wanted Buck and his mother and sisters to be accepted. He wanted a better home for them than some shack down by the tracks in Galveston. His mother deserved that after what his pa had put her through.

With the deed to the Lazy M, they'd have a chance at a new start. Making friends might take a while, but acceptance would come. He'd make sure of it.

He glanced at Mariah. A worried frown marred her smooth forehead, and her drawn lips thinned into a tight line. She pointed toward the far end of the street.

"The bank's over there."

They didn't speak again until he drew up in front of the squat, whitewashed building with bars on the windows. He helped her down and saw the hopelessness written on her face. Then she replaced it with stoic acceptance.

His jaw clenched, and he turned away. He couldn't let her plight sway him from his goal. Her thieving father had sent his father to an early grave and forced his mother to toil day and night to support her children.

Mariah was the interloper, not him.

He'd do well to remember that.

Inside the bank, Mariah fidgeted as they waited for Mr. Tisdale. She'd promised herself she wouldn't look at Slade again, but almost against her will, her gaze slid across his blue visage, hardened with purpose and determination. Her heart skipped a beat. Did he hate her father that much? The look in his eyes and the threats he'd flung at her on Sunday told her he did.

The banker hurried out of his small office, and Mariah pasted on an artificial smile. He greeted her warmly. "Mariah. What a pleasure to see you." He glanced at Slade, questions surfacing in his expression.

Mariah introduced the two men. "Mr. Tisdale, do you have a moment? I need . . . That is, Mr. Donovan and I have some business to discuss with you."

He lifted an eyebrow but, without questions, simply nodded. "Of course." He stepped aside, allowing her to precede him into his office.

Thankful for Mr. Tisdale's discretion, she sank into one of the plush leather chairs facing his desk. The men sat down and the banker folded his hands together.

"How's your grandmother?"

"Fine. Thank you for asking."

"Now, what can I help you with, my dear?"

Where should she begin? She glanced at Slade but received

a hardened stare for her effort. *Lord, help me,* she prayed silently.

She cleared her throat and plunged in. "Mr. Tisdale, I've decided to go to Philadelphia to be with Amanda. Mr. Donovan is going to be the new owner of the Lazy M."

There. She'd told him. Had she said too much? Too little? She didn't want to lie about the circumstances leading up to the transfer of the deed, but what else could she do?

Surprise crossed the banker's face, but he masked it quickly. "I think that's an admirable decision, Mariah. I know how hard it's been for you since your father died. Maybe life in the city close to Amanda will be better for all concerned."

"I hope you're right." She let out a slow breath and produced a small smile, thankful he didn't ask for details. Her hands fluttered. "About the deed."

"Of course." He pushed away from the desk. "I'll be right back."

A heavy silence descended on the room. Mariah clasped her hands tightly in her lap to keep them from shaking. She wouldn't look at Slade. She couldn't.

Mr. Tisdale returned shortly, deed in hand. Before she lost her nerve, she signed the document where he indicated and passed it to Slade.

Slade pulled a leather wallet out of his breast pocket. "I'd like to open an account."

The banker smiled.

Mariah rose from the chair. "I'll wait outside if you don't mind."

Both men stood. She hurried outside, head held high, then steadied herself against the buckboard. She'd done it. She'd signed away the Lazy M. Almost penniless and at the mercy of Slade Donovan, she felt a terrifying sense of panic. What would she do if he threw her and her grandmother out now? How would they get to Philadelphia? Would she be able to find a job there? How would she take care of Amanda? The questions jumbled up in her head like the jar of mismatched buttons at the bottom of her sewing basket.

"Oh, Lord, did I do the right thing?" she whispered.

CHAPTER FIVE

THE SIGHT OF MARIAH slumped against the buckboard reminded Slade of his mother. Too many times he'd seen her with that look of defeat on her face, wondering where she'd get enough money to put one more meal on the table or to bail his father out of jail. But Mariah didn't have to worry about food or a place to stay. At least not for now. And he'd see to it that she made it to Philadelphia when the time came.

As much as she refused to believe him, he wasn't that heartless.

Slowly he walked toward her. She stood with her head down. He drew closer, noticing her lips moving. He stopped abruptly, not wanting to be privy to her prayers.

Her eyes, awash in tears, flew open and focused on him. He didn't see accusation or anger, but a haunted look of vulnerability—a look he knew all too well. She turned away, fumbled in her drawstring bag for a lace handkerchief, and dabbed at her tears.

"Who's Amanda?" Resting his forearms on the side of the buckboard, he stared across the street at the mercantile.

She sniffed and threw him a glance. "My sister."

"You didn't tell me you had a sister."

"You didn't ask." She tilted her chin. "She's been going to school in Philadelphia for about a year now."

He sighed. Another complication. Not only did Mariah have an elderly grandmother to take care of; she had a sister intent on a fancy education. "Mariah, I'm sorry it has to be this way. Just remember, you and your grandmother are welcome to stay at the Lazy M as long as you need to."

"I'll stay until I have enough money to get us to Philadelphia. I don't know how I'll manage when I get there." Bitterness tinged her voice, and she shrugged. "But you wouldn't know anything about that. Being a man, you can come and go as you please, without any responsibilities."

"You're wrong, you know."

The look she gave him dared him to explain himself. He had a sudden urge to prove to her that life hadn't been a smooth ride for him either.

"My father drank himself to death by the time I turned nine. The bullet that almost took his life lodged in his skull, and he lived with the pain until the day he died."

Mariah's face turned white, and Slade could have kicked himself for reminding her that it was her father who'd fired the shot that almost killed his. But the truth couldn't be sugarcoated. "I don't ever remember him working a steady job. And when he did make a little money, he spent it all on whiskey. My mother worked day and night to keep a roof over our heads and food on the table."

Her face softened, but he continued doggedly.

"I got my first real job at eight, but I'd been doing odd jobs and errands around town from age five or six."

He felt her hand on his arm and looked down into her chocolate-colored eyes, now filled with compassion.

"I'm sorry, Slade. Sorry for the little boy you never got to be, and sorry that my father was the cause of it."

He tried to ignore the warmth of her hand. "I don't need your pity, Mariah. All that's over and done with. But I want you to understand that I'll do whatever I can for my family. They deserve better than they've got." Abruptly he straightened, already regretting blurting out part of his past. "I need to go to the lumber mill," he muttered. "You got any errands in town?"

"I've got a list from Cookie for the mercantile. Do you want to see it?"

"No. Just put it on the Lazy M account."

"All right."

He watched her walk across the street, thinking of the way her face had softened when he'd told her about his childhood.

His gut twisted. She'd had the same look when she'd tried

to get the stray cat to eat: tender, caring, loving. Like she cared about his childhood and his family. Like she could *fix* what happened, make it all better.

But it couldn't be fixed. Nothing and nobody could undo the past.

He jammed his hat on his head, climbed into the wagon, and released the brake. He made his way through town, noticing the well-kept stores with boardwalks running between them for those days when the mud could bog a wagon up to the hubs. A handful of flowers graced the entrance to the boardinghouse nestled close to the train depot. A weathered sign invited visitors to try the daily special at the café next door. The train station itself looked fairly new, and the wagons gathered at the lumber mill indicated a thriving business.

Slade halted the team in front of Slaughter's Sawmill. The whine of the saw filled the morning air, one man running the saw and another removing the boards. A cluster of men stood outside under a huge shade tree, and Slade nodded as he hopped down from the wagon.

The men welcomed him into their circle. One older man with a shock of white hair sticking out from under his hat held out his hand. "Good morning, stranger. John Riker."

Slade shook hands. "Morning. Slade Donovan."

"Nice to meet you, Donovan. Those look like Lazy M horses. You working for the Malones?"

"No, sir." Slade rubbed his hand over his neck and glanced toward the mercantile. "I'm taking over the Lazy M."

"You don't say? Mariah finally decided to up and sell the

place, huh?" Riker grinned. "We'll be neighbors then. My place is out that way."

A stocky man spoke up. "That girl's had it kind of rough the last couple of years, what with her pa getting sick and her sister in Philadelphia and all."

"And don't forget Mrs. Malone," Riker added. "She ain't no spring chicken either. She's about the same age as Ma, and Ma's nigh onto ninety."

The men nodded.

"You got family, Donovan?"

"A mother and two sisters who'll be along shortly. My brother came with me." He headed off their next inevitable question. "We're from down Galveston way."

One of the men poked a younger man in the arm. "Girls, Charlie. You hear that?"

The young man called Charlie turned beet red when the group laughed at his expense.

The saw blade ground to a halt, and a man Slade assumed was the owner walked over, removing his gloves. Sawdust clung to his sweaty forearms, but he didn't seem to notice. He scooped up a dipperful of water from a bucket and gulped it down, then motioned down the hill toward a shed filled with lumber. A couple of youngsters were tying down some of the lumber on a wagon. "John, the boys have got you loaded."

"Thanks. This is Slade Donovan. He bought the Malone place." Riker headed down the hill. "Nice meeting you, Donovan. Don't be a stranger now. The turnoff to my place is not far from yours. Only three or four miles. You can't miss it."

"Thanks."

The man stuck out his hand. "Thomas Slaughter, owner. What can I do for you?"

"I need some lumber to fix up the corral."

"Got good seasoned boards down in the pole barn. Come on and I'll show you."

Slade followed the man down the hill and picked out the lumber. He paid with cash, and Slaughter's two boys helped him load the wagon.

Slaughter grinned. "Enjoyed doing business with you, mister."

"I'm hoping to snake some logs out this winter." Slade squinted at the man. "Would you take part of the lumber as payment? On halves, maybe?"

"Sounds good." Slaughter glanced at the cluster of men standing under the shade tree. "Better get back to work. Just let me know when you're ready and we'll work out the terms."

Slade turned the wagon around and headed toward the post office, the letter to his mother burning a hole in his pocket. A feeling of satisfaction gripped him as he posted the letter. He'd instructed Mr. Tisdale to wire enough money to Galveston for her expenses.

A wagon rattled past, loaded with lumber. The man on the seat dipped his head in a subtle sign of recognition. Slade nodded in return. The life he dreamed of for his family moved closer to his grasp.

The specter of his drunken father's name wouldn't overshadow any of them here.

* * *

Mariah riffled through the small selection of cloth in the mercantile while Mr. Thompkins filled Cookie's order. But her mind wasn't on the blue-checked gingham or the flowered calico.

Her thoughts centered on a small brown-haired boy desperately trying to provide for his family. She squeezed her eyes shut and prayed.

Lord, help me to be grateful. I've had a good home for twenty-three years. I've never worried about where the next meal would come from, if I would have a roof over my head at night or clothes on my back. I don't know what tomorrow will bring, but You've supplied my needs all these years, and I know You'll provide for me for the rest of my life.

She took a deep breath.

And, Lord, reveal Your love and mercy to Slade and Buck. They're both hurting, Slade more than Buck, I think. Help him to learn to trust You and do Your will—

"Mariah."

Startled, she looked up and found herself face-to-face with Frederick Cooper. One hand went to her throat and pressed against the collar of her high-necked shirtwaist. "Frederick, you scared me."

"Sorry about that." He offered her an apologetic smile. "What are you doing?"

"I was praying. For a . . . an acquaintance." She smiled. "How are you?"

"I'm fine. Headed to Laramie for a few days." He propped an arm on the stack of cloth, his stance blocking any hope of a graceful exit. The barest hint of a smile still played about his lips, never touching pitch-colored eyes that gauged her every move. "I stopped by the Lazy M on my way into town to tell you good-bye, and your grandmother said you were here. We had a nice long chat."

"Oh?" She fingered a piece of red calico, her gaze drawn to his manicured fingers. An image of Slade's work-scarred hands handling the reins of the team on the way into town tumbled into her thoughts, and she wondered if that was what bothered her about Frederick. He just seemed too perfect. Perfectly groomed, perfectly dressed. Perfectly boring, down to his perfectly styled mustache.

He leaned in, demanding her attention. "Mariah, darling, I heard a disturbing rumor yesterday."

She wasn't his darling, but she let the familiarity go unchallenged. Frederick had a habit of calling her "darling" and "dear." She'd given up convincing him to stop. He also had a habit of asking her to marry him, but she'd managed to avoid giving him a direct answer up to now.

"A rumor? Frederick, you shouldn't be spreading rumors." She laughed off his somber mood, moved away, and pretended to be engrossed in a bolt of green-sprigged gingham. If he was in a hurry to make it to the train station, he wouldn't take the time to ask her to marry him right in the middle of the mercantile.

"I heard you sold the Lazy M."

Her gaze jerked to meet his. "Where did you hear that?"

"Is it true?"

"It's true." No need denying what the whole town would know before long.

"This Donovan." His lips curled. "What do you know of him? Where'd he come from?"

"I don't really know anything about him." Mariah bit her lip. She wasn't obligated to answer Frederick's questions. "You'll have to ask him yourself."

Something flickered in his eyes but was quickly masked. "You should have asked my opinion. I'm sure I could have gotten a better price for the land."

"I got the best price I could." She lifted her chin.

"I think I've hurt your feelings. I'm sorry." He flashed a disarming smile. "Actually, you've probably done both of us a favor by selling now. You'll have the money, and we won't have to worry about finding a buyer once we're married."

Mariah turned away. "Frederick, I have never said I'd marry you—"

"But it's just a matter of time."

"I don't—"

He took her fingers and kissed the back of her hand. "Think it over while I'm gone, Mariah. Like I said—it's only a matter of time before you say yes."

She stood rooted to the spot as he left the store, calling out a cheerful good-bye to Mr. Thompkins. She sighed.

Other suitors had come to call after her father had died, but none had been as persistent as Frederick. Maybe he truly did care for her. She moved to the window and watched him stride away from the mercantile toward the train station. Could he be the answer to her prayers?

The Lazy M wagon, groaning under a load of lumber, rattled to a stop in front of the store. Slade set the brake and jumped down from the wagon, settled his hat more firmly on his head, and strode toward the door, full of purposeful intent. Mariah's attention swung from the man who wanted her to stay to the man who wanted her to go.

Lord, it would be much easier if I just cared enough for Frederick to marry him. Then he would take care of everything.

Soon they were on their way back to the ranch. Mariah twisted the corded drawstring on her handbag. How should she broach the subject of money? Or rather, the lack of it. She peeked at Slade. "Uh . . ."

"Something on your mind?"

"Yes, actually there is. I couldn't help but notice the lumber. I don't think buying lumber on credit is a good idea. It takes every dime to pay the hands and keep Amanda in school." Hastily she added, "I'm not trying to tell you how to run things. I just thought you needed to know. About the money, that is."

He studied her for a moment before replying, "I've got a little savings. I can afford a few pieces of lumber."

She nodded, relieved.

He lightly slapped the reins against the horses' rumps, and they picked up the pace. "Do you mind if I ask a question?"

"No, of course not."

"Why is your sister in Philadelphia at some fancy finishing school if the ranch has been doing so poorly lately? Seems a mite selfish to me."

Finishing school? Was that what he thought? "Amanda doesn't have a selfish bone in her body. She's—"

"Just seems like the money could be better spent on the ranch."

Mariah pressed her lips together. He hadn't given her a chance to explain. He didn't care about Amanda; he'd only asked because of the money. "Maybe I want her to have a better chance in life, just as you want for your family."

Turning away, she stared at the familiar countryside, blinking back hot, frustrated tears. Slade didn't know Amanda was the sweetest, most giving person in the world. It wasn't her sister's fault she couldn't enjoy what most people took for granted or that she would probably never marry and have a family of her own.

And it wasn't Amanda's fault she would never see the light of day again. The fault lay entirely with Mariah—and she would never let herself forget it.

CHAPTER SIX

THE CREAK OF METAL SPRINGS and leather harness drifted over the still afternoon. Mariah wiped her hands and stepped to the edge of the porch, shading her eyes to get a better look at the rig headed down the lane toward the house.

A smile tugged at her lips. The buggy and gelding belonged to her best friend, Sally Winston. Mariah waved, and Sally slapped the reins against the gelding's hindquarters. The horse trotted faster.

When Sally stepped down from the buggy, Mariah hugged her. "It's so good to see you. What are you doing out here in the middle of the week?"

"I needed some fresh air." A smile graced Sally's round

face. "George is working on his sermon for Sunday. He's pacing back and forth and driving me crazy. He says he can't think of anything *profound* to say."

Mariah laughed. Sally could always be relied on to find humor in every situation. She linked arms with her friend and led her inside. "Won't you stay for supper?"

"Thank you, but no. I can't stay long."

Sally took off her bonnet and smoothed her hair as they entered the kitchen. "How's your grandmother?"

"She's fine. Napping right now." Mariah busied herself at the stove, making a fresh pot of coffee. "Her joints have been acting up lately, but today she's doing much better. I'll wake her. She'll be so glad to see you."

"No, don't. Let her rest. I'll step in and say hello before I leave."

As soon as the coffee boiled, Mariah poured two cups and offered Sally a tea cake from the batch she'd made yesterday. Then she sat down and chose a cookie for herself.

Sally crumbled her cookie on the plate and fidgeted with her cup. "Mariah, I heard a rumor this morning in the mercantile and just had to come see for myself."

Mariah's heart skipped a beat. Had Mr. Thompkins overheard Frederick's latest proposal? So far, she'd managed to keep his interest in her from becoming the talk of the town. "You did? About Frederick?" Sally was one of the few who knew he'd asked her to marry him, not once, but several times.

"No. It's all over town that you've sold the Lazy M."

Mariah lifted her coffee cup and took a sip of the steaming liquid, debating how much to reveal. "It's true. When the new owner's mother arrives, Grandma and I will go to Philadelphia to be with Amanda."

"You're leaving?" Sally reached across the table and clasped Mariah's hand. Tears shimmered in her eyes. "What will I do without you?"

"We can't stay. Amanda needs us. She needs *me*." Mariah blinked back her own tears and looked away. Leaving the friends she'd known her entire life would be harder than she'd ever dreamed. "If there was any other way, we would stay. But I can't run the ranch and see to Grandma and Amanda as well. The last few months have proven that."

"I know. It's just that I'll miss you so."

"I'll miss you too. But I don't have much choice." Mariah hated keeping things from Sally, the one friend she could count on to keep her confidence. Sally had never been one to gossip or carry tales. Now that she thought of it, Sally made the perfect preacher's wife. Compassionate, concerned, loving, and discreet, she would never spread anyone's private agonies around town.

But the very thought of telling her best friend what her father had done turned her stomach.

Sally wiped away her tears and smiled, her plump cheeks dimpling. "Well, look on the bright side. You'll be able to take care of Amanda and live comfortably with the money from the sale of the ranch. And when she's through with school, you can move back home. Home to Wisdom."

And risk the community finding out about her father's past? Mariah's heart squeezed as the truth dawned.

She could never return to Wisdom.

✯   ✯   ✯

Dust mites danced on the sunlight streaming through the wide opening into the cool interior of the barn. Slade dismounted and led his horse inside. Cookie sat on a milking stool, a scowl on his face, one gnarled hand rubbing the back of his neck. Buck worked at the far end of the barn shoveling out a stall.

"Afternoon, Cookie. What's the matter?"

Cookie rubbed harder. "Got a crick in my neck."

"I've got some liniment that would help," Buck volunteered from the recesses of the stall, the laughter in his voice evident.

Cookie snorted. "Don't want no horse liniment, you young whippersnapper. That stuff stinks worse than a polecat."

Slade grinned. "But does it make you feel better?"

"Don't know. And I ain't aiming to find out neither."

"Who's that over at the house?"

"The preacher's wife. She's a nice little thing, good friends with Miss Mariah. She was raised right down the road. Riker was her maiden name."

"Her pa is John Riker? I met him in town the other day." Slade unsaddled his horse and started rubbing the animal down. "Seemed friendly enough."

"Yeah, that's him. Funny, but I never pictured Miss Sally as a preacher's wife. But I guess there's somebody for everybody."

"What about you, Cookie? You ever been married?"

"Nah."

"But you just said there was someone for everybody."

Cookie scowled.

They all turned at the sound of horses coming into the barnyard. Duncan and Rio rode double on Rio's horse, trailing Duncan's bay mare on a lead rope.

The mare limped up to the barn, her right front leg wrapped in bloody strips of cloth.

"What happened?" Slade reached for the lead rope.

"Easy, girl." Buck soothed the trembling mare, his voice gentle.

Duncan slid off the back of Rio's mount. "We were over in the south pasture checking fence like you told us. My horse got tangled up in some barbed wire. She spooked, and before I could cut her loose, she'd managed to get all cut up."

Slade squinted at Duncan. "You hurt?"

Duncan shook his head. "Nah, I'm fine. About scared the daylights out of me, though. I thought for sure we were both gonna get wrapped up in that stuff."

Slade turned his attention back to the mare. "We'll need to clean up that wire tomorrow. I don't want anybody else to get hurt."

Buck moved his hands down the horse's cannon, gently unwinding the makeshift bandages.

Slade winced at the deep lacerations on the mare's mangled leg. "How bad is it?"

"I don't know yet. Let's get her in the barn, and I'll clean her up."

Cookie heaved himself to his feet. "Well, iffen you're gonna drag out that awful-smelling salve of yours, I'm gonna go check on my stew."

Slade put his hands on his hips. "Are you sure you don't want some, Cookie? It'll make you feel better."

"Not me," the old man muttered as he left the barn. "I can't abide the smell of that stuff."

Cookie shuffled out of the barn as the men focused on the injured mare.

"What do you think, Buck? Is she gonna be all right?" Duncan asked, a worried frown on his face.

Buck pointed to a ragged gash about three inches above the hoof. "I think she needs stitches here. If not, it might not heal right. And we'll have to doctor her morning and night and keep a close watch." He shrugged. "We'll just have to wait and see."

"We might have to put her down." Slade glanced at Duncan, gauging the older man's reaction. Like most men he knew, Duncan put a lot of store in his string of horses.

Duncan pushed his hat back. "Not if Buck can fix her up. She's a good ol' gal, the best cutting horse I've got."

"All right. We'll see how it goes."

Buck stitched the gash, then cleaned the rest of the mare's cuts before applying the salve. The pungent smell of the liniment filled the barn, but Buck didn't seem to notice. He just kept talking to the horse, ignoring the rest of them. Gradually, the mare stopped trembling. Slade nodded in satisfaction. If anybody could get that horse well, Buck could.

"Rio, go see if Cookie's got some clean rags we can use."

Rio hurried off and returned shortly with a ragged sheet. Slade tore it into strips and handed the pieces to Buck.

When they had finished bandaging the mare, Slade went to wash up for supper. He threw his hat on a peg, rolled up his sleeves, and grabbed a bar of soap. Giff rode into the yard just as Buck exited the barn and headed toward the house. The ranch hand rode so close, Buck had to alter his steps to keep from being run down. Giff laughed and continued on to the barn. Slade leaned against a post, fist clenched. His brother wouldn't appreciate him stepping in.

Buck stepped onto the porch, his gaze not quite meeting Slade's.

Slade grabbed his hat and slapped it against his leg a couple of times, knocking the dust off. He squinted at his brother. "What was that all about?"

He'd heard the men talking about the incident with the eggs, but Buck hadn't mentioned it at all.

"Nothing." Buck shrugged. "Giff's just feeling his oats. Give me a minute, will you?"

"Sure." Slade threw him a surprised glance. He waited while his brother washed up, wondering what made him change his mind. Slade hadn't pressured him, let him take one day at a time joining the living again, but he'd go along with anything that helped Buck come out of his shell.

He pondered the situation with Duncan's horse. They'd only been here a few days and Buck had already started a good-natured banter with Cookie, and now he seemed to be more comfortable around Duncan and Rio. Already Duncan recognized Buck's healing touch with animals. The seasoned cowpoke wouldn't let just anybody doctor his horse. Maybe Buck would feel like he'd found a home here when the others recognized his skill and learned to focus on his uncanny way with animals instead of looking at his scars.

"You ready?" Buck asked.

"Yeah." He straightened.

They entered the kitchen together. Mariah bustled about putting food on the table. Slade hung his hat on a hat-rack peg and inhaled the tantalizing aroma drifting through the kitchen. A big pot of chicken and brown gravy graced the center of the table, and his mouth watered in anticipation when Mariah pulled a skillet of steaming biscuits from the oven.

Mrs. Malone sat at her customary place at the table. "Evening, boys."

"Evening, ma'am." Slade nodded, then turned toward Mariah, his attention caught by the light glinting off her hair. "Mariah."

She threw him a quick glance. "Evening."

Her cool tone reminded him of their conversation in the buckboard. He frowned. If her sister couldn't see the ranch needed money more than she needed a fancy education, then she *was* selfish. There just wasn't two ways about it. Mariah was too stubborn to admit it.

Maybe she loved her sister so much she ignored her faults, but when it came to letting the ranch run down, he would have put a stop to such nonsense long before now.

She turned her back on him and spoke to Buck. "I'm glad you decided to join us, Buck. Have you met my grandmother?"

"No, ma'am." Buck hovered near the door, hat in his hand.

"Nice to meet you," Mrs. Malone said. "Cookie's been telling me how good you are with horses."

"Yes, ma'am."

"You're not scared of them, not after what happened to you?"

Slade glanced at Buck. His brother didn't like to talk about the accident.

"No, ma'am. It was my own fault for thinking I could handle that wild bronco. Broke horses are real gentle once they get used to you." He dipped his head and smothered a cough. "It's people that I have a hard time with."

Mrs. Malone smiled at him, looking him square in the face without flinching. She didn't appear shocked or horrified by his misshapen jaw or the scars. And for some reason, Buck didn't seem to feel the need to shield his face from the wizened old woman.

"Just be yourself," she said. "Eventually people will accept you for who you are, not what you look like. And if they don't, they're not worth the trouble anyway."

"Yes, ma'am." Buck nodded, a short, quick jerk of his head.

Mrs. Malone chose to see the man, not the scars. Buck must have sensed that, because he took to her right off. But, of course, the old woman's stark honesty had earned Slade's respect from the beginning, so he wasn't surprised she'd won Buck over as well.

Mariah smiled. "Buck, would you like some coffee?"

"Yes, ma'am."

She handed him a cup, then turned toward Slade, her smile dimming. She quirked a brow. "Coffee?"

Slade snagged a cup from one of the hooks on the wall and held it out. Mariah steadied the mug as she poured, and the tips of her fingers brushed against his. He froze. Her nearness, the touch of her fingers, the scent of her hair, the shape of her lips, all hit him at once, and the only thing he could do was stare.

A hint of a blush stole over her cheeks; then her gaze lifted and collided with his before she turned away. Perhaps it was the heat from the stove, or maybe she'd felt the same jolt he had when they'd touched. Whatever the reason, he liked the way her cheeks bloomed with color and her brown eyes sparkled in the light cast by the lanterns.

He sipped his coffee, aware of every movement she made. Soft tendrils of brown-sugar hair resisted the neat bun gathered at her neck, softly framing her face. His fingers itched to tuck the wayward curls behind her ears. He turned and found Buck watching him with a curious look on his face. Slade scowled, moved to the table, and sat down.

Just like Buck to see something where nothing existed. Nothing at all.

Nothing except a scalding-hot cup of coffee and an over-heated kitchen.

Dawn gave way to a cool, clear day. Mariah rose with the sun, stoked the fire in the woodstove, and headed to the chicken coop to gather eggs. She wrapped a shawl around her shoulders to ward off the chill as she made her way across the barnyard.

It wouldn't be long before the sun would chase the coolness away and she'd be comfortable without her shawl, but for now early morning still carried a wintry bite. She filled her basket with eggs, then stopped in the barn to milk the cow and check on Dusty.

Alone except for the animals, she took her time milking. She liked the early morning quietness, hearing the ping of the milk as it hit the bottom of her pail, the *squirt-thunk* as the bucket filled.

She rested her forehead against the cow's flank, closed her eyes, and let the barn sounds wash over her in waves. The cow munching on hay, the swish of her tail. The snort of a horse in the next stall. She lifted her head and took in every nook and cranny of the barn she'd explored from the time she could walk. She'd miss the barn, the house, and the animals.

The cow switched her tail, slapping Mariah in the face.

She swatted the coarse strands of hair away. And yes, she'd even miss the cow.

Dusty nickered from the next stall over. Mariah set the pail of milk to the side and rubbed the mare's velvety nose, scratching one hand along the horse's long, hard jawline. Dusty whinnied and nudged her arm.

Mariah laughed. "Hey, Dusty girl. When are you going to drop that foal?"

She rubbed a hand along the mare's distended belly. The maiden mare's dam was notorious for foaling early, but who knew if Dusty would follow suit? Other than carrying low and heavy, she hadn't bagged up, but they'd started keeping her in the stall at night, just in case. Mariah determined to ask Buck what he thought when she saw him. She gave the horse another pat before turning to go. The black-and-white mama cat met her on the way out: slim and trim and obviously not expecting kittens anymore.

"Well, what have we here?"

The cat ignored her and headed to the far corner of the barn. Mariah waited a moment and followed.

She eased around a stack of hay toward the corner stall, a catchall for anything and everything no one wanted or needed anymore. A faint mewling sound caught her attention.

Pausing, she squinted into the dim corner and listened for the kittens again. She heard a faint snuffling sound and a whimper. She bent down and peered beneath a jumble of old harness and rope. There, out of reach, in the corner on a bed of old sacks, a litter of newborn kittens nursed. The mama cat reclined on the sacks, eyes half-closed, a contented purr emanating from her.

Mariah was trying to figure out how to reach the kittens when a movement in the open doorway caught her attention. She grinned at Slade, unable to contain her excitement. "We've got kittens."

He came closer and squatted down to see the mama cat and her offspring. "Looks like she's got a good-size litter."

Mariah leaned over and peered into the cozy nursery. "How many are there? Can you reach them?"

He pushed the harness to one side and reached toward the kittens, managing to grab one around its belly and haul it out. He held out the tiny animal for her inspection.

Gently she scooped up the black-and-white ball of fur and cradled it, marveling at the soft tufts that were ears and the pink nose not even as big as the tip of her little finger. "Isn't it the cutest thing you've ever seen?"

He reached for another kitten and held it up in front of him, giving it a once-over. "I reckon they're cute enough. At least they're good for something. When they get bigger, they can catch mice."

The yellow kitten squirmed and mewled its displeasure at being dangled in the air away from the warmth and safety of its mother. The mama cat's ears perked up and she meowed in protest.

"Slade, it's scared." Mariah's own kitten lay snuggled against her, emitting a quiet snuffle every once in a while. "Here. Give it to me." She reached for the kitten and placed it next to its sibling. The yellow kitten mewled and snubbed around for a moment before settling into the warmth of Mariah's arms. "Poor baby. The big, bad man scared you to death, didn't he?"

She glanced at Slade. He was crouched down, back braced against the barn wall, watching her, an amused smile on his face.

Her face grew warm at his scrutiny, and she ducked her head and studied the kittens again. "What's so funny?"

"You." A crooked grin creased his face. "Cuddling and talking to those kittens as if they were babies."

Mariah concentrated on the kittens, idly rubbing one finger over their backs. The black-and-white kitten took a deep, shuddering breath. "They're not babies, but they're still sweet." She hoped her voice didn't carry the wistfulness she felt in her heart.

"Why haven't you married, Mariah?"

Her heart skipped a crazy beat, and she kept her attention firmly on the kittens. "Because the right man hasn't come along."

Until now.

Her hand froze in midstroke along the kitten's back. Where had such an outrageous thought come from? She hoped Slade couldn't see the blush that stole over her face. "And . . . and I've been busy taking care of the ranch and my family. Then Papa got sick. I really haven't had time to get married. And I haven't found a man I wanted to marry either."

She clamped her mouth shut to stop herself from babbling like an idiot. What would he think of her?

"Here," she said, needing to get away from him before she embarrassed herself further. "Put the kittens back. Grandma will be wondering what's happened to me."

As Slade tucked the kittens in beside the others, Mariah's heart turned over. For all his gruff talk about the kittens, he showed a gentleness with them he'd never shown with her. She wondered what he acted like with his mother and sisters, and a sudden, deep longing to know the kinder, gentler side of this man swept over her—a longing that shocked and surprised her.

She hefted the pail of milk and the basket of eggs and hurried toward the house, her heart aching with a need she couldn't—or wouldn't—identify.

Slade watched her go, then stood and dusted off his jeans. One minute she'd been talking, and the next she'd almost thrown the kittens at him and rushed out of the barn.

He frowned as he went to saddle his horse. When he asked her why she wasn't married, she'd run like a scared rabbit. Maybe she'd been jilted, or maybe she felt the same way he used to feel about marriage. He'd never intended to get married and force a wife and children to live the way he'd lived as a kid.

Marriage was for men who could provide a home for a wife and kids, take care of them, and make sure they had a normal life like everybody else. He placed a blanket on the gelding's back and reached for his saddle.

Now that he had a home, land, and a future, there was nothing to stop him from finding someone to spend the rest of his life with.

As he pulled the cinch tight around his horse's belly, he pictured a family—his family—riding into Wisdom in a wagon. They'd ride down the street, friends and neighbors calling out greetings to them. The Donovan name would be respected here in Wisdom, if he had anything to say about it.

Slade let the elusive dream play itself out. He imagined pulling up in front of the mercantile and jumping down to help a small girl with sparkling brown eyes out of the back of the wagon, while a boy with dark, curly hair tumbled out on his own, skinned knees and all.

He imagined walking around the wagon and reaching up to help his wife down. He lifted his gaze, coming face-to-face with a hazy vision of Mariah Malone smiling down at him from the wagon seat.

Slade's daydream disappeared faster than Mariah's biscuits, and he shook his head. Mariah as his wife? Even if she did have a soft spot for kittens and babies and could cook better than any woman alive, she'd never consider marrying him, not with the bad blood between their fathers.

He swung into the saddle, his daydreams left to die on the sawdust floor of the barn.

CHAPTER SEVEN

THE HOE SWUNG in a downward arc, the blade turned at the perfect angle to slice through the dirt. One jerk, and Mariah plucked a clump of weeds out by the roots. She dreaded the chore, but someone had to do it if they were going to eat. She glanced toward the end of the row. Another ten minutes and she'd be finished for the day.

Long minutes later, she breathed a sigh of relief and wiped her brow. Three more rows to go. She trudged back to the house, deciding she'd work on those tomorrow. When she reached the porch, she scooped a dipperful of water and sat down on the steps, cooling off in the shade of the porch before she went inside to start dinner.

Buck exited the barn. She gave him a wave, and he headed

across the way. "I thought I'd come out to check on you. I figured it might be way too hot out there in that garden."

"You figured right." Mariah fanned herself with her apron.

"Is it usually so hot this time of year?"

"No. We need more rain." She took another sip of water. "What about down in Galveston? What's it like there?"

"Galveston's not so bad. The breezes from the ocean keep it pretty cool this time of the year."

"It sounds like a nice enough place."

"It is, I reckon."

"You don't miss it? Or miss your friends?"

Buck stood hipshot, watching her. "I didn't make many friends back home. I preferred being with horses to people."

"You mean after your accident?"

"No, even before. A lot of young fellers wanted to sneak off to the saloons, but I wasn't interested in that."

"Because of your father?"

He gave her a questioning glance.

"Slade mentioned that he used to . . . drink a lot. . . ." She trailed off. "I shouldn't have said anything."

"It's all right." Buck dropped to the porch steps beside her, draped his arms over his knees, and stared into the distance. "They called our pa Black Jack Donovan down in Galveston. Everybody knew him as the town drunk."

"It must have been hard growing up like that."

"Harder for Slade than for the rest of us, him being the eldest. He always had to go find our pa and drag him home when he got drunk, listening to his drunken rages for hours on end. Our sisters were small when Pa died, so they don't remember him at all, and I remember very little."

"I'm sorry."

"Don't be." Buck shrugged. "It wasn't your fault."

Mariah pleated her apron between her fingers. "That's not the way Slade sees it. He blames my father for what happened to your family."

"It's my turn to say I'm sorry. I guess hauling Pa home night after night from the saloons in Galveston and listening to him rant and rave about the misfortune that befell him because of your father did something to Slade down deep inside." He squinted at her, a sad look on his thin, misshapen features. "I didn't read that letter you sent, but I knew Slade might do something he'd regret if I didn't stop him. I finally convinced him I could travel and had a hankering to see Wyoming."

"And did you have a hankering to see Wyoming?"

One side of Buck's mouth tilted in a lopsided smile. "Not as much as I wanted to keep my brother out of trouble."

It made her feel better to know that Buck didn't share Slade's bitterness. Did Buck know the whole truth, or had Slade kept part of it from him, too? She bit her lip. "Do you blame my father for what happened to your family?"

"I don't know what happened between our fathers, but I do know that one person shouldn't let another have that much power over them. No matter what your father did, it shouldn't have caused Pa to turn into a sot drunkard for the rest of his life."

Mariah's eyes misted with tears. "Thank you, Buck."

Buck gave her his uneven smile. "Now what did I say to make you cry? I tried to make you feel better."

"You did." She sniffed. "It's just that I wish Slade had the same attitude as you do about what happened all those years ago."

"Yeah. Things might have turned out differently if he did. But there's no arguing with him when he gets his mind made up. And Pa's name is on that deed. No question about that."

Mariah tried to smile.

Buck turned to walk away, and Mariah reached up to wipe the tears from her eyes.

"Mariah?" Buck faced her again.

She looked up. "Yes?"

He scratched his head, looking unsure of himself. "There's something else I think you should know. It might help you understand why Slade is so bitter at your father."

"All right."

"Slade was nine years old when he found Pa dead outside a saloon in Galveston. He's never forgotten it."

Buck turned away and trudged toward the barn, his shoulders slumped. Mariah stared at his retreating back, wondering if laying claim to the land would be enough to erase the bitterness rooted deep in Slade's soul.

For his sake, she prayed it would.

The mingled smells of warm bread, ham, and peas filled the air, but Slade barely noticed. Instead, his thoughts and his gaze lingered on Mariah. All day, he'd tried to concentrate on something—*anything*—else, but then he'd find himself thinking about her and the way she'd looked cuddling those kittens. Next thing he knew, he'd be wondering what she was doing: weeding the garden, bustling around the kitchen, or helping her grandmother. Then he'd get mad at himself all over again for letting his mind wander into forbidden territory when he should be working.

Mrs. Malone looked up from her place at the table. "Evening, boys. Did you have a good day?"

Mariah turned from the stove, and Slade glanced away, not wanting to be caught staring. He focused on her grandmother. "Yes, ma'am. Good but busy."

"The work on this ranch never ends. But then I suppose it doesn't anywhere else either."

Mariah placed a pan of piping-hot corn bread on the table. "How's Duncan's horse?"

"She's mending." Buck pulled his chair up to the table. "There's still a lot of swelling, but she's eating and her leg looks good. We'll just have to wait and see."

"That's good. Duncan sets a lot of store by that horse. I'd hate to see her put down." Mariah took a seat. "Grandma, would you say grace, please?"

Slade bowed his head and listened to Mrs. Malone's prayer. Sometimes she blessed everybody in and around Wisdom. He'd learned a lot about the community listening to her prayers.

"Lord, thank You for this day, and bless this food and the

hands that prepared it. We ask that You ease the widow Ames. She fell and broke her hip, and she's in a lot of pain. And bless old Mr. Dickinson. He's been feeling poorly lately. Take care of us all, and help us all to have a good night's sleep. Amen."

Mrs. Malone passed Slade a bowl of peas. "Tomorrow's wash day, in case Cookie hasn't mentioned it. You boys leave your dirty clothes on the porch, and Mariah and I will see that they're washed and mended."

Slade shook his head. "That's too much trouble, ma'am. We can just wash our stuff down at the creek."

"It's not a lot of trouble. Most of the hands only have one or two changes of clothes. We've got to heat the water anyway, and it costs too much to take them to town. No, we'll do it. Another shirt or two won't make much difference." She peered nearsightedly at the rip in Slade's shirtsleeve. "Bring that one. I'll have Mariah mend the tear. If it's not fixed, you're going to ruin a perfectly good shirt."

"Grandma," Mariah protested.

"Thank you for the offer, ma'am." Slade picked up his fork.

But he had no intention of letting Mariah or her grandmother anywhere near his clothes.

★   ★   ★

"You've been mighty quiet tonight. Is something ailing you?"

"I'm fine." Mariah opened a drawer and pulled out her grandmother's nightgown. "Just thinking about leaving Wisdom. Leaving my friends."

94

And thinking about Slade and the feelings he'd stirred in her heart.

"What did Sally say when you told her?"

"She was disappointed, of course." Mariah fingered the tatted lace on the nightgown. "I didn't tell her everything."

"Oh?"

"Slade promised not to tell the community what Papa did." She shrugged and slipped the nightgown over her grandmother's head. "I just don't think it's anybody else's business."

"Perhaps you're right. People can twist things out of proportion, given enough fodder to gossip about." Her grandmother gave her a long, searching look. "Mariah, I hope you don't let this situation with the Donovans make you bitter."

"I'm not bitter. Angry, yes, but I'll get over it . . . eventually."

"Angry at Slade or at your father?"

She turned back the covers, considering the question. She sighed. "Both."

"Slade did what was right by law."

"He took everything we owned."

"The deed told the tale. We didn't really own anything. We never did. Slade's father, and now Slade and Buck, are the rightful owners. You can't blame him."

"I know."

"And besides, just as I suspected, that boy's whipping this ranch into shape. Have you noticed he's got the hands hopping to and fro repairing the corral and the cook shack and anything else he can find for idle hands to do? He's no slacker, that one."

"I noticed."

"You did, did you?" Her grandmother smiled as Mariah helped her into bed. "Did you also notice he's got a right nice smile and beautiful dark-blue eyes?"

"Grandma!" Heat rose to Mariah's cheeks.

"I see." Her grandmother chuckled. "So you noticed that as well." Suddenly she grew serious. "You could do a lot worse than Slade Donovan."

"Don't be getting any ideas." Mariah pulled a quilt over her grandmother. "I can't imagine Slade looking twice at me, let alone getting the urge to court me, not with the history between our families."

"Well, it was just a thought." Her grandmother pouted. "But if it's the Lord's will, it can be done."

"True. But I don't think bringing Slade Donovan and myself together could possibly be in the Lord's will."

Her grandmother pulled the covers up to her chin, a tiny smile on her face. "You'd be surprised, Mariah. You'd be surprised."

Exasperated, Mariah turned down the wick on the lantern, puffed the flame out, and plunged the room into darkness. "Good night, Grandma."

★　　★　　★

Slade rolled out of his bunk at the crack of dawn and reached for the shirt he'd thrown over the back of a chair. It was gone. He couldn't find his pants either. He hunkered down and looked underneath his bunk.

Nothing.

Buck had taken Mrs. Malone up on her offer to wash their clothes.

He found a faded denim shirt that should have been tossed in the rag bin years ago. The material was so thin it would split right down the middle if he muscled up and bowed his back to a hard task. But it would have to do for now.

A pair of pants hung on a nail beside Duncan's bunk. He grabbed them. They were too short, but that couldn't be helped. Maybe if he hurried, he could get his clothes back before Mrs. Malone and Mariah started on the wash.

At least he still had his socks. He stomped into his boots and stumbled toward the door.

The sun peeked over the horizon as he hurried across the barnyard to the porch. Sure enough, a mound of sweat-stained laundry lay in a heap near the door. His clothes were in that pile somewhere. He'd be hanged if he let Mariah Malone see his holey underwear. He squinted through the early light, trying to find the clothes Buck had taken hostage. He spotted one of his shirts.

Just as he started pawing through the laundry, the door flew open and banged against the side of his head. Caught off-balance, he fell backward, landing solidly on his rear with his and Buck's dirty clothes spread all around him.

"Oh, I'm sorry! I didn't realize you were there."

He jumped at the sound of Mariah's voice.

She bent over, plucking jeans and shirts off him. When

she picked up his long johns, he cringed. So much for trying to get his clothes back before she saw them.

"Are you all right?"

"I'm fine." He forced the words through gritted teeth and stood, wanting to slink off like a polecat caught raiding the chicken coop.

"Let me see." She frowned at him. "The door hit the side of your head pretty hard."

"It's all right, Mariah. I'm not hurt." Hands on his hips, he glared into her brown eyes, filled with concern and riveted on his cheek.

She reached up and touched the side of his face. Her fingers felt like velvet fire on his cheekbone. Her startled gaze met his in the misty haze of early dawn. Then she focused on the tiny grazed spot on his cheek. "It's okay. Not even bleeding."

"Told you," he grunted, his skin burning more from her touch than the whack from the door. Her lips parted, soft and dewy as rose petals in the half-light. Slade fought the urge to see if her lips tasted as soft as he imagined. He edged closer. Her fingers slid ever so gently down his cheek until they rasped across his unshaven jaw.

At the sound, she jerked her hand away, blinking like a doe caught in the open, poised to take flight at the slightest noise. "Well, I . . . I guess I'd better get started. Looks like we're going to have a busy day."

"Yes, ma'am." He reached up to tip his hat, and his fingers met air.

What in the world had happened to his hat?

CHAPTER EIGHT

"Here." Mariah handed her grandmother one of Rio's shirts. "See if you can find a button for this one."

"Land sakes, that boy must've tangled with a mountain lion." Her grandmother inspected the shirt, clicking her tongue. "I'll have to darn a good two inches before I can even sew on a button."

They worked in silence, her grandmother sewing, Mariah scrubbing. She swiped her damp forehead, then pushed wayward strands of hair behind her ears. No use trying. She couldn't escape the sweltering, grueling work of wash day. But the heat didn't stop her thoughts from returning to her encounter with Slade on the porch. Whatever had made her reach up and touch his face like that?

His cheekbone had felt strong and solid beneath her fingertips. She'd resisted the temptation to let her fingers linger on his sun-darkened jawline and trace his lips. The very idea that she'd had such a wanton thought shocked her all the way to her toes.

She turned away, shielding her flushed face from her grandmother, hoping she'd think the blush on her cheeks had to do with the heat and the boiling water instead of the thoughts tumbling around in her head. It wouldn't do for her to find out about this morning. Not after what she'd said last night. Surely there wasn't anything to her grandmother's daydreaming? She'd just been teasing.

Hadn't she?

Surely the Lord couldn't work that kind of miracle in Slade's heart. And did she want Him to? Her hands trembled. Even though she hadn't admitted it to her grandmother, she hadn't completely forgiven Slade for laying claim to the ranch even if he did have the right. Granted, he'd seen to their well-being when he hadn't been obliged to. She would give him credit for that consideration.

But complete forgiveness? No, that would be a long time coming.

Her grandmother's blather from last night and this morning's encounter were pure coincidence. The early morning shadows, his proximity, and the fact that she'd almost knocked him unconscious made her lose her head and think things that were better off forgotten.

She dropped another soiled shirt into the boiling water.

Then she reached for a cake of lye soap and shaved several pieces into the pot. She beat the shirt with a heavy stick, hoping the tedious chore would take her mind off Slade.

"Let me help you with that," her grandmother chided from her rocking chair in the shade. "I'm almost done with this shirt."

"It's all right. I can do it."

Buck came back from the creek with two more buckets of water. When he reached the shade of the large oak tree where she'd set up her wash pot, she straightened, the pain in her back from being hunched over easing a bit with the movement. "Thank you, Buck."

"It's no trouble."

"I appreciate it anyway. It sure has saved me a lot of walking back and forth."

The sound of a horse drew her gaze to the road. She waved when she recognized Sally's pa, John Riker. "Mr. Riker," she called out. "How are you?"

"Howdy, Mariah. Mrs. Malone." His friendly nod included Buck.

"Howdy." Buck tipped his hat and sauntered in the direction of the barn.

Mariah watched him go, wishing he would have stayed. John Riker was one of the kindest men she'd ever met. He wouldn't shun Buck, no matter what he looked like.

"Why don't you sit a spell, John?" her grandmother offered, motioning to a bench under the tree.

The leather on his saddle creaked as he dismounted.

"Don't mind if I do. But I can't stay long. Got a pile of work to do."

"How's your mother?"

"She don't get out like she used to, ma'am. She frets about not being able to go to church or visiting. She mentioned you the other day. About how she wished she could see you."

"I wish I could see her too." A wistful smile crossed her face. "I remember how we used to visit regularly. When Mariah and Amanda were small, we'd have quilting bees and barn raisings and share recipes. We're all too busy, or too old, to visit like we used to."

"We'll make plans to visit her soon." A feeling of guilt swept over Mariah. Her grandmother hadn't seen her dear friend in ages, and once they left Wisdom, she'd never see her again. Her grandmother glanced at her, and Mariah knew she was thinking the same thing.

Mr. Riker nodded. "She'd like that. Is that young man around? The one who's so good with horses. My bull is down sick, and I was hoping he'd know what to do."

"Oh no, the one you got from King Ranch in Texas?"

"The very one. I'd sure hate to lose that animal." Mr. Riker slapped his hat against his thigh, and Mariah noticed for the first time the worry that lined his face. The entire community knew he'd paid a handsome price for that bull.

"That was Buck you saw a few minutes ago." Mariah dried her hands on her apron. "I'll see if he can head on over to your place right away."

"I'd be obliged. Mrs. Malone, you should ride over with the young feller and visit with Ma while he's there."

Her grandmother nodded. "I just might do that."

"I'd better be getting back then. Just tell him to come on out to the barn when he gets there. I sure appreciate this, Mariah." Mr. Riker jammed his hat on his head, mounted, and urged his horse into a trot back toward home.

Mariah found Buck in the barn. "Mr. Riker's bull is sick, and he wants you to come take a look at him."

"I don't know . . ."

"Riker's a good, decent sort. And he's mighty worried about his bull. He's liable to die if you don't go see about him."

Indecision warred across Buck's face.

Mariah put her hand on his arm, forcing him to acknowledge her. His troubled blue gaze bored into hers, looking so much like his brother's that it hurt. "I know you don't want to go because of your face, but if you don't go, and that bull dies, you'll regret it. I know you will."

After a long moment, he nodded. "I'll get my stuff."

"Wonderful. Could you hitch up the wagon? Grandma wants to visit with Mrs. Riker, so she'll ride along and show you the way."

He turned back, a sheepish grin tugging at one corner of his mouth. "You knew all along I'd go, didn't you?"

Mariah smiled. "I knew you couldn't refuse to help a sick animal. It's just not in you."

★　★　★

Red settled in for a long night of cards. He didn't really care for the game himself, but Emmit did, so Red played.

His brother ignored him most of the time, which stuck in Red's craw. But since nobody around these parts knew they were brothers—or even called Emmit by his real name—he'd have to live with it. But what he wouldn't give to be able to walk away and leave Emmit to his own devices.

He cashed out early and watched, listening to the talk around the table. His brother fancied himself a card shark, in control of the game, but nobody was ever in charge of cards, unless they cheated. And Red could tell Emmit wasn't cheating tonight.

Emmit would laugh and say that playing cards with the ranch hands around Wisdom honed his skills for bigger and better things, and since they were playing for a few dollars, it didn't matter if he won or lost. His day would come, and when there was a big stake, he'd turn up the heat and win the whole pot.

None of it made sense, but that was Emmit.

The spitting image of his old man.

All these years later, Red couldn't figure out what his mother had seen in Emmit's pa. The man had been a gambler, a drifter, and a womanizer until the day he died, but she'd married the smooth talker anyway.

He eyed Emmit's fancy getup.

Yep. Just like his pa.

Except Emmit's pa had never skirted on the wrong side of the law as far as Red could tell.

After supper, Slade shut himself in the office and tried to make sense of the Lazy M ledgers for the second night in a row. A lamp sputtered on the table, and a cup of Mariah's coffee sat within easy reach.

Slade jotted numbers on a smudged piece of paper. He didn't have much schooling, but he knew enough about ranching to keep books, and numbers had always come easy for him. But trying to decipher the Lazy M ledgers made him wonder if he knew as much as he thought he did.

Seth Malone's chicken scratch, what little there was of it, made no sense at all. There were very few notations to explain the numbers, and half the time there weren't even any dates. One page with *1878* scrawled at the top showed a total of two entries for the entire year. At roundup, Malone had tallied the number of cows counted with calves by their sides. He'd entered the number of cattle they'd driven to market. No other notations for the year. No details about income and expenses or profit. Under the circumstances, Slade was glad to have that much to go on. He turned the page, the paper crackling loud in the silence of the office.

The next two years Malone had kept better records, but it was still like tallying toothpicks. He ran his finger down a column of numbers, spotting a notation where Mariah's father had bought some lumber at the sawmill and supplies at the mercantile on the same day. Weeks passed with nothing; then he made some more notations during roundup. Slade jotted the figures on his piece of paper, making note of the year. He was pleased at the number of head the ranch ran. More than he'd thought, considering the run-down state of the house, outbuildings, and fences.

He grunted when he saw a notation for a large sum to a doctor in Philadelphia. With Malone sick, they'd probably used every resource available to see if something could be done for him. That would account for where the money had gone for the last few years.

He ran his finger down the columns, lingering on the larger sums. One jumped out at him, and he squinted at the scrawled notation on the left. All he could make out was *Philadelphia* and *school*. He shook his head in disgust.

Finishing school cost a lot more than he'd even imagined. The handwriting on the next page changed to a neatly flowing script. Mariah's handwriting, he guessed, since she'd been running the ranch since her father took sick. Her fancy writing was even harder for him to decipher than her father's printed scrawl, but the numbers she'd written down were the important thing.

One after the other, day after day, neatly penned transactions marched down the page. She'd methodically put the expenses in one column and the income in another, making it easier to follow. A few small entries showed where she'd sold eggs, butter, and cream at the mercantile. But as was the case for most ranches, there was no cash money to speak of until roundup.

He flipped several pages and zeroed in on the income for last year's roundup, anxious to see how the ranch had fared. The dollar amount staring up at him was disappointing.

Granted, the price of beef had been down the last couple of years, but a niggling in the back of his brain told him the figure was less than it should have been considering the number of head the ranch ran.

He jotted down the number of cattle tallied during roundup and compared it to the sparse accounts he'd found in her father's handwriting from the previous years. He frowned, checking his totals again. Had he penciled in the wrong figures? The number of head brought in during roundup had dropped a lot in the last two years.

No wonder the Lazy M was in such disrepair.

A light rap broke his concentration, and he scowled. "Yes?"

Mariah pushed the door open. "There's a little coffee left. I'd hate for it to go to waste."

Slade held out his cup, and she filled it with the steaming brew. The flickering light from the lantern cast shadows over her face.

"Your father wasn't much on record keeping, was he?"

"No. He always said he kept the numbers in his head." She gave him a sympathetic look. "The books are a mess, aren't they? I've just about pulled my hair out trying to understand it all."

"There's not much to go on until you started keeping up with things. The last couple of years make a lot more sense."

Slade sat back in the leather chair and took a sip of coffee. "Except for a couple of things."

"Like what?"

"It looks like the ranch has been losing money from just a few months after your father took sick."

Indignation washed over Mariah.

She'd worked hard to keep good records from the moment her father's health began to fail, documenting every penny that had passed through the Lazy M accounts for the last two years. She plopped the coffeepot on the edge of the desk and crossed her arms.

"Are you saying I'm incompetent?"

"No, I'm not saying that. But something has happened." He leaned forward and tapped the books. "From the number of cows your father recorded at branding time a couple of years ago to the number recorded last year, the ranch lost several hundred head."

Mariah leaned closer and peered at the numbers. "That isn't unheard of."

"That's a big loss without somebody being able to explain it." He pinned her with a direct look. "Did you ask Harper about it?"

"Of course. He gave the usual reasons. Drought, poisoned water holes, sickness, snakebites, bogs." Mariah squirmed, wishing she'd paid more attention to Red's reasons for the lost cattle, but she'd been at her father's bedside night and day for months—and had her grandmother and sister to worry about as well. She'd blocked out much of that time and didn't want to remember.

"Rustlers?"

"He didn't mention it, but it's always at the back of any rancher's mind, and then there's the occasional poacher who kills a cow here and there."

"Does your sister know what kind of strain her tuition to that fancy school has put on the ranch?"

"Excuse me?" Mariah jerked her head up.

"The cost of your sister's schooling in Philadelphia would pay three men's wages for a year and then some." He thumbed through the ledger.

She took a deep breath. The last time they'd had this conversation, Slade hadn't given her a chance to explain. Maybe now was the time to clear the air about Amanda. Surely he'd be more understanding if he knew the truth. "Slade, Amanda's—"

"If you want to send your sister to a finishing school so she can find a rich husband, I guess that's your business, but to let the ranch go under is beyond me."

Mariah's jaw dropped as she stared at him. He really didn't care to learn the reason she'd sacrificed everything to send Amanda to Philadelphia. She crossed her arms. Well, if he didn't want to know, she wouldn't go out of her way to tell him. It wasn't any of his business.

"Amanda doesn't know anything about the trouble the ranch has had, and if I have my way, she won't ever know.

I'm glad I sent her to Philadelphia, and if I had it to do over again, I would."

She grabbed the coffeepot and stomped out of the office.

Why did Slade have to keep bringing up her sister? For once, just once, she wished he might ask *why* Amanda was in Philadelphia.

It all boiled down to money or the lack of it. Her brow creased as a Bible verse entered her thoughts. *"The love of money is the root of all evil."*

Did Slade's preoccupation with the cost of Amanda's schooling stem from his impoverished childhood and the desire to regain everything he'd lost?

It seemed that with every step she and Slade took toward reconciliation, their pasts hammered a thicker wedge between them.

CHAPTER NINE

BAM! BAM! BAM!

Mariah winced with every slam of Slade's hammer out at the corral. He'd been at it all day, and the incessant hammering had frayed her nerves to no end. It didn't help that she'd tossed and turned all night after their altercation over the Lazy M accounts.

She started to turn away from the window when a movement down the road caught her attention. She stood on tiptoes and peered past the windowsill, trying to make out the visitor coming up the lane. The smart black two-seater with a fringed canopy could only belong to Frederick.

An uncomfortable knot of unease formed in her stomach.

She turned from the window and faced the sweltering kitchen. Slade and Buck could arrive for supper at any time. But there was no way she could avoid this visit, even though she wanted to. She hurried to the stove, stirred the pot of stew, and closed the damper to a tiny crack.

A twinge of guilt shot through her. She hadn't even thought about Frederick's proposal. She'd been too distracted by Slade and Buck's arrival, the shock of losing the ranch, and what the future held for her and her grandmother.

An unwanted proposal had been the least of her worries the last few days. What would she tell him? How could she convince him she wasn't interested? She resolved to be polite and treat him with kindness. And she would tell him no for the last time. Since she'd be leaving for Philadelphia in the next month or so, he'd forget about her and find someone else to marry.

As Mariah made her way to the front door, she smoothed back her flyaway hair and feathered her fingers over her face and shirtwaist, brushing away dustings of flour. In the hall, she paused, closed her eyes, and whispered a quick prayer.

"Lord, help Frederick accept once and for all that I can't marry him. Please help him move on and find someone else to share his life with."

At his knock, she swung the door open and offered him a wide smile. "Frederick. What a surprise."

"Afternoon, Mariah." Frederick tipped his hat and stepped over the threshold. Mariah stepped back but wasn't quick enough. He snagged her elbow and leaned down. She turned her head just in time. His lips, cool and dry, brushed her cheek.

"How was your trip to Laramie?"

"Better than expected." He smiled. "A couple of deals were very lucrative."

"That's good news."

"Yes, very good news." He laughed.

She led him into the parlor, noticing the shabbiness of the room. A musty odor permeated the area, even though she'd aired the room last week. She lifted her chin. She wasn't ashamed of her dwelling.

Then she remembered. It wasn't her home anymore. It belonged to Slade. With a heavy heart, she motioned to one of the chairs. "Please, have a seat."

He eased down on the horsehair settee. At least his clothes were black, so the horsehair wouldn't show up too much. His gaze traveled around the room to the faded curtains and the battered furniture that had seen better days. He turned toward her again, a considering look on his face. "You know, Mariah, it's probably a good thing you didn't pour money into this old house now that you've sold the place."

There hadn't been any money to spend on the house in years. The doctors in Laramie and Philadelphia had seen to that. But Frederick didn't need to know how desperately she'd hoarded every penny.

"I suppose you're right."

He crossed his legs, flicking an imaginary speck of lint off one pressed trouser leg. An unexpected visual of Slade dressed in dusty boots and a sweaty shirt, pounding nails to mend the corral, flitted through her mind. Somehow she couldn't help but compare the two men, and in many ways Frederick came up lacking.

"Mariah, I want to apologize for what I said the other day in town. It sounded like I didn't trust your judgment about selling the ranch. I know you did the right thing. I hope you're keeping the money at the bank and not out here." He lifted a brow in silent question.

"Um . . . it's not here; I'll grant you that." She pleated her skirt with her fingers, dreading the moment when he asked her once again to marry him.

"I knew I could count on you to be sensible." He leaned forward. "As a matter of fact, this turn of events has made me consider selling out and moving back east."

Mariah gasped, stunned by his sudden announcement. "You'd do that? Just up and sell your land? But you've only been here a few years."

"I've decided I'm not cut out to be a rancher. I'm much more suited to the city." He waved a hand. "We can be married within the week and on our way to Philadelphia. You wouldn't have to worry about a thing."

Mariah stood, trying to make sense of this new development. While the thought of turning all her worries over to Frederick had its appeal, she couldn't marry him. She didn't love him, and she couldn't see herself spending the rest of her life by his side. It wouldn't be fair to mislead him into thinking otherwise.

"Frederick, I'm sorry; I can't accept your proposal."

* * *

A fancy rig with a well-appointed mare sat in front of the house. Slade admired the horse. Whoever had come to call knew good horseflesh. He walked around to the back porch, washed up, and followed the smell of beef stew and baking bread into the kitchen, sniffing appreciatively.

Mrs. Malone looked up from her seat at the table, a frown of concentration knitting her brow. The sound of muted voices floated in from the parlor.

"Evening, ma'am."

"Slade." She shifted in her seat and waved a hand at the stove. "Stir that pot of stew, young man. I thought Mariah would be back by now, but it sounds like Frederick intends to stay awhile."

Slade dipped a ladle into the pot and stirred. "Who's Frederick?" The name sounded vaguely familiar, but he couldn't place where he'd heard it.

"Frederick Cooper. Owns land north of the Lazy M. Kind of a newcomer. He seems nice enough, but a bit of a dandy if you ask me. I have to admit that when Seth took sick, he was a godsend. Made sure we had plenty of help around the place, that we lacked for nothing."

Slade forked up a chunk of meat. His stomach rumbled in anticipation of the tender morsel.

"He's been after Mariah to marry him for a coon's age."

The fork froze in midair. Funny, Mariah hadn't said anything at all about Cooper when she'd insisted on taking the

115

first train out of Wisdom or when he'd asked her why she wasn't married. She hadn't even mentioned the man.

Suddenly he remembered where he'd heard the name. Frederick Cooper had recommended Mariah hire Red Harper. Slade dropped the meat back into the pot, scowling. He'd lost his appetite.

"Frederick, please!" Mariah's distressed voice pierced the air.

The hair on the back of Slade's neck stood on end, and he clenched his fist. He glanced at Mrs. Malone. She sat, her head cocked to one side as if listening for more. The low rumble of Cooper's voice floated to them, but Slade couldn't make out the words.

"See what's going on." Resolve flickered across Mrs. Malone's face. "Make him leave if you have to."

"It's not my place, ma'am . . . especially if Mariah intends to marry him."

"Haven't you heard a word I said? Just because a man asks doesn't mean a woman plans to say yes. Oh, fiddlesticks." She started to heave herself up. "I'll do it myself."

"Never mind. I'll handle it." Slade gently pushed her down.

He strode toward the parlor and rapped on the door. He was turning the knob at the same time Mariah called out a breathless "Come in."

Slade stepped through the door just in time to see Cooper let go of Mariah's arm. She stepped away and wrapped her arms around her slender waist, not meeting Slade's questioning glance. But he didn't miss the way she rubbed the tender flesh above her elbow. A jolt of protectiveness surged through him, and he clenched his fist. Had Cooper hurt her?

He studied the man at her side, taking in the expensive coat, gold watch chain, and polished boots.

"I don't believe we've met." A smile crossed Cooper's face, creasing his thin lips but not reaching his eyes. "Frederick E. Cooper's the name. I own the spread north of here."

"Slade Donovan."

Cooper's brows lifted as he in turn raked Slade from head to toe, taking in his worn shirt and dusty boots. "The new owner of the Lazy M?"

Slade nodded.

"I'm sorry, Mr. Donovan. I didn't realize who you were." The smile grew into a mocking grin. "Been out supervising the hands, have you?"

"You might say that." He turned to Mariah. "Supper's getting cold."

"I take it that's my cue to leave." Cooper focused his attention on Mariah.

"You'll stay for supper, won't you?"

Slade crossed his arms and waited. Was it wishful thinking that made Mariah's offer sound less than enthusiastic?

"Thank you for the kind invitation, but I must be on my way. I'll be back in a few days when you've had time to think about my proposal." Cooper eyed Slade even as he pressed his lips against the back of Mariah's hand. "I'll let myself out. Give your grandmother my regards."

Cooper strode across the room, face devoid of the amusement he'd displayed for Mariah. A cold, calculating mask shuttered his features as he brushed past Slade.

Neither Slade nor Mariah moved until they heard the front door close.

Slade turned to Mariah. "Are you all right?"

"I'm fine." She lifted a hand and smoothed back a wayward strand of hair. "Why shouldn't I be?"

"You don't look fine." His chin jutted. "Did he threaten you?"

"No, of course not." Her laugh sounded strained. "He asked me to marry him."

"Didn't sound like any proposal I've ever heard."

"You were eavesdropping?"

"No. You were just overly loud."

She bit her lip. "I turned him down, and he became, uh, persistent."

"Why?"

"What kind of question is that? He wants to marry me because he loves me."

"Do you believe that?" He scowled.

She looked at him like he'd lost his mind. Maybe he had, but the thought of her marrying the man who'd just left turned his stomach.

"Why else would he want to marry me?"

"Maybe he wants your land. Have you ever thought about that?"

Mariah grabbed her skirts and pushed past him, eyes

flashing. "Well, that's certainly something you'd know all about, isn't it?"

"Do you believe that?"

Slade's question reverberated through Mariah's head as she cleaned up the kitchen after supper. She slapped a pan hard against the stove and winced at the clatter. She'd wake her grandmother if she didn't get her emotions under control.

Why had Slade asked her that?

He didn't have a high opinion of any of the Malones, other than her grandmother. He thought her father a thief, her sister a spendthrift, and that Mariah herself was incapable of running the ranch. But did he think she was unlovable as well?

Hot tears stung her eyes. She wanted to slam another pot against the stove but resisted the urge.

Frederick had been after her to marry him for almost a year. No man would wait that long unless he cared about a woman. Would he? Slade must be addle-brained to think Frederick wanted something other than marriage. He had a fine house and plenty of land of his own. He didn't need hers.

She winced. She no longer had any land.

But Frederick didn't know that.

She let her hands drop into the dishwater and stared out the window, absently focusing on a twinkling star hanging low in the sky.

Could it be possible that Frederick had never loved her

and only wanted the land as Slade suggested? It wasn't so far-fetched. More than one man had come calling after her father had died, making no bones that they wanted to get their hands on the Lazy M. Could Slade be right about Frederick?

There was one way to find out.

The next time he asked her to marry him—if there was a next time—she could tell him there was no money. If he truly cared about her, he wouldn't mind that her family was destitute.

Her heart stuttered against her rib cage. Was proving Slade wrong worth revealing the truth to Frederick?

CHAPTER TEN

"LET'S CUT OUR LOSSES."

A rumble of agreement sounded among the motley group of men gathered in the shack, lantern light barely casting enough of a glow to tell who'd spoken. Red squinted, recognizing the haggard-looking drifter Emmit had met in a saloon over in Laramie.

Emmit lifted his head, eyes narrowed, flat and black like the sky before a freak storm. When he was gambling, Emmit could keep a poker face until the cows came home, but tonight he held all the cards, and there was no need to fool anybody in the room.

"You think so, Slick?"

Red tensed. A storm was brewing for sure.

"Yeah, boss." Slick leaned against the wall by the door, looking like a stiff wind might blow him over. "It was one thing to skim cattle off that girl and her grandma because nobody was the wiser, but since Donovan's bought her out, it's too risky."

"And just what do you plan to do with the cattle we rebranded?" Emmit spared Red a glance. "How long before those brands are healed and we can move them?"

"Another week, maybe two."

"So we just take off, leave two hundred head of cattle with my brand on them for Donovan to find?" Emmit smiled—if you could call it that. More of a snarl, really. Red didn't like the way this conversation was going. Not one bit.

He'd like to get out too, but Emmit had a point.

Slick didn't answer, and Emmit stood, his fancy waistcoat at odds with the dusty, trail-worn clothes the other men wore. "Giff, you and the others move the cattle to the canyon tomorrow night. Donovan won't look for them there. When they heal, we'll get rid of them, and we'll be done here. Red, you stick around the ranch and keep an eye on Donovan."

Red breathed a sigh of relief. At least he wouldn't have to move the stolen cattle this time. The whole business gave him ulcers.

"I'll just mosey on down the road, if it's all right with you fellers." Slick straightened, jammed his hat tighter on his head, and turned for the door. "It's not worth the risk."

"Slick?"

"Yeah?" Slick seemed oblivious to the hard, cold tone, but Red didn't miss the deadly calm in his brother's voice.

"Nobody walks out on this job until I say so."

The room spun in slow motion, and the men eased to the side, leaving a clear path between Emmit and Slick. Red's stomach clenched. Something was different in Emmit's voice. Something deadly, menacing. Something he'd never heard before. He needed to stop his brother.

But he knew he couldn't stop Emmit.

Emmit was a loose cannon packed tight with coiled rattlers when he was mad. He simmered, then exploded, lashing out with lightning speed when the storm hit.

"Emmit—"

The blast of a Colt 45 drowned out Red's protest.

"Cookie's here, Grandma," Mariah called as she grabbed her Bible and checked her hair one last time. "Ready?" she asked as her grandmother tottered out into the hall.

"Ready as I'll ever be. I hope Reverend Winston can keep his mind on the sermon today. Ain't never seen a man unable to keep his eyes off his wife like that. And him a preacher and all."

"Oh, Grandma, Reverend Winston and Sally are still practically newlyweds. I guess he just can't help himself."

"Well, if you ask me, he needs to get his mind on his sermons."

She helped her grandmother down the steps and called out, "Good morning, Cookie."

"Morning."

She jerked her head up. Slade Donovan stood beside the buggy, not Cookie. A sinking sensation curled in the pit of her stomach.

"Cookie's not feeling well, so he asked me to take you ladies to church this morning."

"His neck still bothering him?" her grandmother asked as Slade gave her a hand up into the buggy.

"Yes, ma'am."

"I can manage the buggy," Mariah said. "You don't have to come along."

"Cookie said you'd say that." He gave her a fleeting smile. "He made me promise to take you, no matter what. Said he'd rest easier if he knew you ladies were being taken care of."

"But I—"

"Mariah, quit arguing," her grandmother interrupted, "or we'll be late."

Slade grinned and held out his hand. Mariah allowed him to help her into the backseat of the buggy. He hoisted himself up with ease to the driver's side, and they were on their way.

Her grandmother tapped him on the shoulder. "I hope you're planning to attend church with us."

"Sorry, ma'am. I'm not dressed for church."

"Ah, fiddlesticks. We don't stand on ceremony in Wisdom. A clean shirt and a decent pair of pants will do nicely." She looked him over. "And a haircut, if you don't mind my saying so."

"Yes, ma'am." He glanced back at Mariah, amusement in his eyes.

Mariah listened as her grandmother pointed out landmarks on the way into town. She didn't try to join in the one-sided conversation—much easier to let her grandmother do all the talking. Slade must have realized the futility of interrupting too. He just nodded in agreement every so often.

Her gaze lingered on Slade, noticing how his too-long dark-brown hair brushed his collar beneath the shadow of his hat. Her grandmother was right. He could use a haircut. She'd kept her father's hair trimmed during his last few years, when her grandmother's shaking fingers hadn't been up to the task. What would it feel like to comb Slade's unruly locks into place and snip off the curling ends?

She tried to concentrate on the passing countryside, but the opportunity to study him unobserved was too tempting. She couldn't make out anything above his chiseled cheekbone with his hat shading the upper portion of his face, but a faint shadow of a beard covered his jawline.

Suddenly he turned his head, and his blue gaze, heightened by the midmorning sunlight, caught and held hers. He quirked an eyebrow. Mariah jerked her attention away and tried to look engrossed in the countryside.

She stole glances at him the rest of the way into town, being careful not to get caught staring again.

An hour and a half later, Mariah sat on the hard church

pew and did her best to concentrate on the end of the sermon. As promised, Slade didn't accompany them to church, and she wondered where he'd gotten off to. She'd managed quite well throughout the singing, the prayer for Martha Edwards and her new baby, and the announcement of the upcoming church picnic. But as Reverend Winston wound down his sermon on Abraham and Sarah, her mind wandered.

A faint rumble sounded in the distance, and a sigh went up from several of the children. Mariah smiled. The sound of the train coming—a sign that Reverend Winston had to wrap up his sermon if he didn't want to be drowned out by the whistle and the steam engine. The noon train had always been an effective deterrent to any long-winded sermons on Sunday mornings.

As soon as he said the last prayer and the train passed on by, she put her hand on her grandmother's frail arm. "Why don't you wait here, Grandma, and I'll have Slade bring the buggy around."

"All right, child."

She left her grandmother chatting happily with her friends and made her way outside. She shaded her eyes against the noonday sun and looked around for Slade.

"Mariah."

She turned to find Sally behind her. Mariah embraced her friend. "Sally. How are you?"

"Feeling a little peaked these days." A smile broke over Sally's face. "Especially in the mornings."

Mariah's heart skipped a beat. "Really?"

"Yes, really." Her friend's lips twitched as amusement danced across her expressive face.

"Why didn't you tell me the other day?"

"I just found out myself a couple of days ago. I didn't want to say anything until I knew for sure."

"Oh, Sally! I'm so happy for you." A twinge of disappointment stabbed her. "But I won't be here when the baby's born."

Sally reached out and hugged her. "I'll write and tell you all about him or her when the time comes."

"What does Reverend Winston say?" Mariah couldn't bring herself to call the pastor by his first name, even if Sally had been her best friend forever.

Sally shrugged. "Oh, he acts like it's nothing to get excited about. But did you hear his sermon today? Abraham and Sarah?" She laughed. "I'm sure we'll hear all about Mary, Elizabeth, and Hannah in the next few weeks."

"Sally, you're incorrigible."

"Enough about me. How are you doing? And how's Amanda?"

"Amanda's fine. I got a letter the other day. She passed another major milestone."

"What?" Sally's eyes lit up with interest.

"She had to walk from the school to the farmers' market, purchase a very specific list of fruits and vegetables, and take them back."

"Alone?" The interest in Sally's face turned to surprise.

"Yes." Mariah shook her head. "Amanda assured me the

market is close to the school and it's perfectly safe. She had made the trip several times with an escort and knew the route, but still, it scared the daylights out of me. She seemed to take it in stride."

"Adventurous Amanda—that's what I used to call her. I'll keep praying for her."

"Thank you, Sally. I knew you would."

A broad-shouldered form by the railroad tracks caught her attention, and Mariah's gaze slid past her friend. Slade stood beside the tracks, chewing on a piece of straw and watching the conductor inspect the train. In the distance, two children walked along the tracks, making their way toward town.

Sally turned to see what had caught Mariah's attention. "Those poor children."

"Do you know them?"

"They moved to town a month or so ago. Their father is a drunk. He doesn't have a job, and when he does get a little money, I'm certain he spends it all on whiskey."

"How sad."

Sally shook her head. "I've tried to help all I can by taking the mother vegetables and such. I've invited her to church and told her to come by and see if any of the clothes in the mission basket might fit the children. But she's too proud or maybe too scared. She won't accept any handouts."

Mariah's heart ached as she looked toward the tracks again, her gaze going past Slade to rest on the children. The little boy appeared to be about seven, and his sister was maybe four or five. She chewed her lip. The boy wasn't much younger than Slade had been when he had to take on the responsibilities of an adult.

The children drew nearer to Slade and stopped, both of them staring up at him. He said something to them, but she couldn't hear anything at this distance. The boy dug one toe in the weed-infested dirt beside the tracks and cast a sidelong glance at Slade. Then Slade pulled something out of his pocket. It glinted brightly in the sunlight as he handed it to the little boy. The child's face lit up with a smile, and Mariah heard him say something that could have been "Thanks, mister!"

Then the boy took his sister by the hand and hurried off. Slade turned away, and Mariah let out a breath she hadn't even realized she'd been holding.

"That's the man who brought you and your grandmother to church, isn't it? Is he the new owner of the Lazy M?"

"Yes." Mariah nodded.

Sally leaned close. "He's mighty handsome, don't you think?"

Mariah frowned at her friend. "You're a married woman, Sally. And to a preacher, no less."

"I'm not interested for myself." Sally shrugged, elbowing Mariah. "Maybe you won't have to go to Philadelphia after all."

Mariah shook her head. "I'm afraid it's not that simple. I don't think Slade Donovan would be interested in me."

"Why in the world would you say that?" Sally asked. "He's not married, is he?"

"No." She couldn't tell Sally why Slade wouldn't look twice at her. "But that doesn't change the fact that he would never want to marry me."

✳ ✳ ✳

As the two children headed back down the tracks, Slade wished he could do more. It hadn't taken long to see how poor they were. He'd seen their tattered clothes, the haunted, hungry look on their faces, the hopelessness. He recognized the signs, and his heart squeezed with compassion for them.

But he'd done all he could for now. He'd watch out for the little boy around town and try to help when he could.

A chattering drew his attention toward the church. Several people milled around outside, indicating the end of the service. Time to gather up Mariah and her grandmother and head back to the ranch. He searched the small crowd and found Mariah talking with a young woman about her own age.

He made his way toward them, admiring Mariah's slender form as he drew nearer. Her grandmother had been in such a hurry to get to the church this morning, he hadn't had time to really look at her. She looked even prettier today than the day he'd arrived.

Her soft brown skirt draped in folds from her small waist, a waist he could probably span with his two hands. And her cream-colored shirtwaist gave her skin a soft glow, like a rose-colored sunset. Her gaze met his, her brown eyes reflecting the deep shades of her skirt. He moved forward, and her friend held out one hand, smiling broadly.

Mariah introduced him to the preacher's wife.

"So glad to meet you, Mr. Donovan. Welcome to Wisdom."

Slade tipped his hat. "Pleased to meet you, ma'am."

"The next time you bring Mrs. Malone and Mariah to church, feel free to join us. We'd love to have you. Mariah sings solos, you know." The woman tapped him on the arm with her gloves and smiled. "Come to church next Sunday, and I'll make sure she sings."

"Sally . . ." Mariah swatted the woman's arm.

Slade bit back a smile as Mariah tried to hush the friendly preacher's wife. "Thank you, ma'am. I'll think about it."

But he had no intention of setting one foot inside that church—even if Mariah Malone could sing like a mockingbird.

CHAPTER ELEVEN

THE CREAKING OF SADDLE LEATHER broke the stillness, but for once the men were silent.

Slade slouched in the saddle and let his gelding find his own way back to the ranch. The ranch hands had spent the entire day repairing the section of fence that had injured Duncan's horse. Giff had done his share of complaining, and Red had finally growled at him to shut up.

Which was a good thing. Slade's patience was worn to the breaking point, and he'd come within inches of telling Giff to pack his things and get out. But they were shorthanded, and as long as he did his job, Slade was willing to give him a chance.

Stretching his aching back, he'd like nothing better than to go down to the creek to wash the sweat and dust from his body before sitting down to one of Mariah's home-cooked meals.

He dismounted and saw Mariah coming back from the creek, a sturdy pole with a bucket dangling from each end draped over her shoulders. Water sloshed out of the buckets as she trudged toward her small garden.

Slade unsaddled his horse, ignoring Rio's chatter that started right back up where he'd left off earlier. He caught glimpses of Mariah as she carefully rationed water on each tender plant. When she'd emptied the first bucket, she repeated the process with the second one before lowering it to the ground.

She pushed her bonnet back and wiped her face with her sleeve, then massaged her neck, letting her head roll backward and then to the right and the left.

He knew how she felt. He'd been riding fences all day, forcing nails into fence posts gone hard with age, stretching half-rusted wire, trying to make ends meet. And they'd barely gotten started.

Mariah pulled her bonnet up to shade her face and hooked the buckets to the pole again, then bent down to lift the contraption to her shoulders once more. As she wove her way back toward the creek, he shook his head. She looked much too tired to tote one bucket, let alone two. She disappeared into the line of trees bordering the creek bank.

Absentmindedly, Slade rubbed the gelding down and

turned him into the corral. Then he followed after Mariah. Might as well offer to carry the buckets for her. He strode through the trees and along the briar-lined path. He spotted her at the edge of the water, struggling to fill one of the heavy wooden buckets.

She slipped in the mud and the bucket tipped, drenching her skirt. A groan broke from her throat, and she glared at him. "Do not say a word."

"I won't. I promise." He grinned.

He sidestepped down the steep bank and reached for the still mostly full bucket. Mariah yelped when his fingers closed over hers. He stilled, and she tried to tug her hand from beneath his, but he didn't let go. Slowly he peeled her hand away from the bucket and turned it over.

Her hand felt small and delicate in his, like a fragile bird anxious to take flight. For all its smallness, though, her hand's reddened calluses proved she worked hard around the ranch. Lugging the buckets back and forth had taken a toll, though. He feathered his thumb over her palm before lifting his gaze to hers.

"You should be wearing gloves."

"They're wet."

"I see." His eyes dropped to her lips, looking full and lush as if the sun had ripened them just for him. Awareness crackled between them, and she dipped her head, the edge of her bonnet shielding her face against his scrutiny. He let go of her hand, took both buckets and slid farther down the bank, hunkering down to fill them from the creek.

"Watering the garden is my job."

"It won't hurt me to tote the buckets back this once. Besides, the faster you get through watering the garden, the faster you'll have supper on the table."

"All right, but only because you're already here."

She turned, grabbed a handful of sodden material in each hand, and trudged up the path toward the house. Slade grinned at the mud caked on the back of her faded skirt. She wouldn't be happy when she realized the state of her skirt. Suddenly she stumbled and cried out. Her bonnet flew back, revealing her pain-filled expression.

"What is it?" Slade dropped the buckets and grabbed for her.

"Nothing." She spoke through clenched teeth, tears pooling in her eyes.

"Mariah . . ."

"It's just a thorn. I'll be fine in a minute."

In spite of her protests, she clung to his arm, teetering on one foot. Turning one of the buckets upside down, he pointed. "Sit." When she obeyed, he knelt and reached for her foot. "Let me see."

"No, it's all right." She pulled out of his grasp.

Exasperated, he blew out a breath. "Mariah, let me see your boot."

He grabbed her ankle before she could protest again. She flicked her voluminous skirt over her ankles. He grunted. Women and their propriety.

Wiping the mud off, he inspected the bottom of her boot.

He didn't see any thorns, but he did see the hole in the leather where her stocking foot peeked through, stained crimson by the thorn she'd stepped on. He raised his head to meet the guilty look on her face. "Mariah, the sole of your boot is worn through."

She tugged her foot from his grasp.

He let go and grabbed the other boot, glancing at the bottom of it. "Why in heaven's name are you traipsing around out here with these boots on? You might as well go barefoot."

"These are my work boots. I save my other pair for Sunday." She lifted her chin.

Slade had seen her other pair when he'd helped her into the buggy Sunday. Even though she'd polished them and they were presentable, they were almost as old and worn as the pair she wore today.

"Why don't you buy a new pair for Sunday and wear your other ones for every day?" He rocked back on his heels and glowered at her.

"It takes money to buy boots."

"That's right; you don't have the money. You'd rather send every dime you can get your hands on to your sister. You've let this ranch fall down around your ears, and you're walking around all but barefoot just so she can prance about in high society."

"I'll have you know, Slade Donovan, that I'll do whatever I want with my money. If I want to walk around *barefoot*,

I will. And there's not one thing you can do about it!" Mariah struggled to her feet. He didn't know anything about Amanda, and she'd be hanged before she'd tell him.

She groaned as her tender foot touched the ground. Walking with as much dignity as she could manage, she limped toward the house, watching for more thorns. *Please, Lord, just let me get away from that man.*

Suddenly he grabbed her from behind and swept her up into his arms.

"Ooooh," she gasped. "Put me down!"

"Not on your life," he growled. "Do you think I want to watch you hobble all the way to the house like a wounded buffalo? If you want to be stubborn, you can. But I don't have to watch such foolishness."

A wounded buffalo?

Mariah clamped her mouth shut and remained rigid in his arms as he stomped toward the back porch, thankful no one was around to witness her embarrassing predicament.

As soon as he deposited her on the porch, she limped into the house without a backward glance. She hobbled into her bedroom and cringed at the dirt and mud clinging to her soggy skirt.

Just look at the mess he'd caused. If he'd left her alone, everything would have been fine. She could have finished watering her garden in peace. Now, she'd have to finish the chore in the morning and get all hot and bothered all over again.

She changed clothes, lined her Sunday boots with a

piece of soft cotton, and tested her weight on her sore foot, thankful the quickened pain of the thorn had eased a bit. By tomorrow her foot should be fine.

Not so her relationship with Slade. They took two steps back for every step forward. She'd tried to explain why Amanda lived in Philadelphia. But he hadn't given her a chance. He'd made it plain that as soon as his mother arrived, she would be out of a job and out on her ear.

Did he think so little of her that he couldn't accept the idea that she had a good reason for supporting Amanda? A feeling of hopelessness swamped her. He would never look at her as a woman, respect her talents, and applaud the areas she excelled in.

Instead, he would only see her faults because that's all he wanted to see. He thought so little of her, he didn't even believe Frederick could love her. She stomped toward the kitchen, ignoring the smarting pain in her foot, wishing she could ignore the man who'd caused it.

As she passed by the kitchen window, she spotted movement at the edge of her garden, and a bit of her anger leached out of her. She stood transfixed as Slade carefully watered each and every one of her precious plants.

CHAPTER TWELVE

"I'm heading into town." Slade hefted his saddle onto his horse, glancing at Buck. "You want to go?"

Probably not, but it didn't hurt to ask. Buck's health had improved a lot in the last few months, but he still shied away from people. When he'd insisted on accompanying Slade to the Lazy M, they'd avoided towns along the way as much as possible.

But Buck had come out of his shell since they'd arrived at the Lazy M. He'd taken Mrs. Malone to see the Riker woman the other day, and he'd started eating supper in the house. A trip to town would do him good, wouldn't it?

Buck hesitated for a moment before nodding. "I need

more medicine for Mr. Riker's bull, so I might as well ride along with you."

Slade didn't offer to help Buck saddle his horse. And to his surprise, his brother managed fairly well on his own. Mariah's cooking and the hard work around the barn were paying off. Buck pulled the cinch tight and swung into the saddle. Slade swallowed a grunt of satisfaction and relief as he turned away. Buck was finally on the mend.

Without seeming to, he let Buck set the pace as they rode away from the Lazy M. Once on the open road headed into town, Buck pulled his horse to a slow walk. "You think Ma is going to like it here?"

Slade thumbed his hat back. Buck always cared about others—what they thought, how they felt. And if he couldn't pour out compassion on another person, he'd find some poor, sick animal to nurse back to health. "I figure she will. She's always dreamed of getting out in the country away from town."

"I reckon." Buck didn't sound convinced.

What did that mean? Slade frowned, mulling over Buck's response and coming up empty-handed. Finally he asked, "What's really on your mind?"

"I just can't stop thinking about Mariah and her grandmother." His brother sighed. "You know she's got a sister, don't you?"

"I gathered as much." He didn't tell Buck her sister's schooling was part of the reason the ranch was doing so poorly. The very thought made his jaw clench. If Amanda cared anything at all for Mariah and their grandmother, she would be at home instead of letting Mariah pay her way at that fancy school.

"I just feel sorry for them, that's all. Mariah's treated me pretty nice." He chuckled. "I can't get over the way she lit into Giff Kerchen with that basket of eggs."

"You'd better watch yourself. I don't imagine Giff thought it was funny."

They slowed at the creek that ran across the Lazy M and let the horses take a breather. Buck rested his forearm on the pommel of his saddle. "It's just that I can't help but wonder what they're going to do when they leave."

An uneasy feeling hit him square in the chest, and he threw Buck a hard glance. "You sweet on Mariah?"

"Of course not. She wouldn't think of me like that."

"Don't be too sure."

"I'm sure. But I have seen the way she looks at you." Buck grinned.

"You're loco." Slade scowled at his brother. "There's too much bad blood between our families for Mariah to ever look twice at me."

He urged his horse into a slow trot as Wisdom came into view, hoping to curtail Buck's chatter. But it would take more than that to stop the thoughts of Mariah churning around and around in his head.

Slade stopped by the post office and picked up a letter from his mother. She'd started preparations for the journey, but it would take time to cover the distance between

Galveston and Wisdom. The women would have to travel part of the way by stagecoach and part by train. He passed the letter to Buck and let him read it for himself. Before long, his family would all be together again.

A couple of buckboards sat in front of the mercantile, and three horses stood loose-jointed at the hitching rail. Unease pricked at Slade as he glanced at his brother. He shouldn't have asked Buck to accompany him to town.

Ever since the accident, it had been a recipe for disaster when Buck walked into a crowded store. The folks would all grow quiet and pretend to be busy, casting sideways glances at him. Then, before long, most would gather their purchases, sidle toward the door, and ease out, probably to speculate on his battered face. Slade and Buck dismounted, and Slade took a deep breath and led the way, not expecting today to be any different.

It wasn't.

A sudden quiet filled the store as everyone looked up at the newcomers. Slade counted a couple of farmers, a woman with a small boy, an older well-dressed woman, and the clerk. They all stared at Buck for a shocked moment before turning away and becoming engrossed in the stock on the shelves.

All except the boy.

The kid stared at Buck with the unblinking gaze of someone with a lot of questions.

"Hey, mister, what happened to your face?"

"Matthew!" His mother grabbed his arm, her face turning

bright red. She glanced at Buck, then down at her son. "Apologize. It's not polite to ask personal questions."

"It's all right, ma'am," Buck murmured.

Slade held his peace, letting Buck handle the situation as he saw fit.

Buck hunkered down to the boy's level. The youngster stared at him with childlike wonder. "I was trying to break in a wild mustang and got thrown. I didn't get out of the way in time, and that old horse decided to stomp on me."

The boy's mouth rounded. "Really?"

"Yeah."

An excited glint came into the little boy's eyes. "Wait until I tell Dan about this."

"To tell you the truth, I knew that mean old mustang wanted to get me. I should have stayed away from the corral until my brother or someone else got there. But I was too cocky. I thought I could handle him alone, but I couldn't."

"I want to be a horse wrangler when I grow up."

Buck tapped the boy's shirt with his forefinger. "Don't do anything foolish like I did."

"I won't."

His mother leaned down. "Say good-bye, Matthew. We need to go."

Matthew shook Buck's hand before leaving with his mother.

Slade glanced around. The faces of the men held a grudging respect while the nicely dressed woman dabbed at her cheeks with a handkerchief before turning toward the dry goods and taking an intense interest in a spool of black thread.

A feeling of pride at the way Buck handled the situation coursed through Slade. If Buck could learn to live with people's gawking, then eventually he'd be able to ignore them and get on with his life. Once the people of Wisdom got to know him, they'd see the kind of man he was inside, instead of focusing on the scars.

Slade fished a piece of paper out of his shirt pocket and handed it to the shopkeeper. "Can you fill this order?"

The man scanned the list and nodded. "I think I've got everything. It won't take long."

"Thanks. I'm in no hurry."

The shopkeeper smiled and stuck out his hand. "The name's Thompkins. Jed Thompkins. You must be the new owner of the Lazy M. I saw you in town the other day with Mariah but didn't get a chance to introduce myself."

"Slade Donovan." He shook the shopkeeper's hand and thumbed over his shoulder in Buck's direction. "And that's my brother, Buck."

"Welcome to Wisdom. Heard you bought the Lazy M from Mariah."

"That's right."

"A mighty fine spread. And the Malones are good folks. Couldn't ask for any better." He shook his head. "That Mariah's had it rough, though. Glad to see someone buy that ranch. Too much work for a woman to handle alone."

Slade nodded, not knowing what else to do. He'd promised

Mariah he wouldn't tell the townspeople what her father had done, and he wouldn't go back on his word.

Mr. Thompkins held up the slip of paper. "I'd better get your order filled, or I'll be here jawing all day."

Buck wandered away, studying the bottles of cure-alls and medicines lined up on a shelf behind the counter.

While he waited, Slade looked at the odds and ends, the bolts of brightly colored cloth, and tins of meat. In one corner, Mr. Thompkins had string beans, new potatoes, and fresh eggs for sale. Had Mariah intended to sell the eggs she'd dumped on Giff Kerchen? If she had, her temper had cost her a pretty penny.

He moved on and came to a low shelf with a small selection of sturdy boots on display. He picked up one of the boots, admiring the handiwork. He rubbed his thumb over the leather uppers, feeling its cool suppleness.

The pleasing scent of new leather tickled his nose, and he placed the boot back on the shelf, knowing that such boots would be expensive. They were the kind men wore to church and fancy gatherings or if they were going courting. And since he didn't intend to do any of the above, he didn't have a need for a pair of fancy boots.

A dainty pair of women's boots tucked beside the larger ones caught his eye. Out of curiosity, he picked one up. The brown leather was soft but sturdy, with two rows of hooks marching up the side. He hefted the small boot in the palm of his hand, remembering the holes worn in the bottom of Mariah's.

He frowned and plunked the boot back on the shelf. She had made the choice to live without boots. There wasn't anything he could do about it.

A sudden commotion outside drew everyone's attention to the front window. A man lurched drunkenly down the middle of the street, blocking a farm wagon pulled by two draft horses.

"Git outta the way, you lazy no-account drunk!" the driver shouted.

The man waved offhandedly at the driver before weaving his way toward the mercantile.

"A sad case, that one."

Slade glanced at Mr. Thompkins.

"He lives down on the other side of the tracks. Got a timid little wife and two kids. A boy and a girl. He's done a few odd jobs around town. Does a good job too, but he don't stay sober long enough to work more'n one or two days, and he's at it again."

The shopkeeper shook his head and turned away to finish Slade's order. Slade tried to ignore the man slumped against the porch steps of the mercantile, but his thoughts wouldn't let him. The whole situation reminded him too much of his own father. His father had stayed drunk, hardly knowing—or caring—if the rest of them had anything to eat or clothes to wear or even a roof over their heads.

He thought of the little boy he'd given the money to. Could this man be the boy's father? More than likely. There probably weren't too many drunks in a town the size of Wisdom.

"All right, mister, here's your order," Mr. Thompkins said.

"Put it on the Lazy M tab, will you?"

"Sure thing."

Slade picked up his supplies and headed out the door, Buck right behind him. A little boy stood beside the drunken man.

"Pa?"

The man grunted. "Wha'? Wha'cha want?"

"It's time to come home, Pa."

The man brushed the kid away. "Leave me 'lone. Can't you see I'm sleepin'?" He curled himself up on the porch.

Slade stuffed his saddlebags with his packages, unable to ignore the child as he tried to rouse his pa. As he suspected, it was the same boy he'd met down by the railroad tracks. Somehow he'd known those kids were hungry. They hadn't asked for money or a handout. But he'd known.

"Pa, you've got to come home." The youngster tugged on his pa's sleeve. "Ma's got some rabbit stew cooking. Don't you want some stew?"

"Don' want no stew."

Desperation clouded the boy's expression. "But, Pa—"

The shopkeeper stepped through the door. "Better get him out of here." He sounded apologetic. "Or I'll have to call the sheriff. Can't have him running off all my customers. Especially the women. They won't come in here with him plastered all over my porch."

"Please, Mr. Thompkins, don't call the sheriff." Fear shot

across the boy's face. "Ma don't want Pa to go to jail again. He's almighty mean when he gets out."

"I know, son, but he's got to go." Mr. Thompkins glanced at Slade, clearly in a quandary.

Slade looked at the boy. "How about if I help you get your pa home?"

"Would you, mister? I'd be mighty obliged." A light of hope shone in his eyes.

"What's your name, young man?"

"Jimmy—" He drew himself up tall. "Jim Denton."

"I'm Slade Donovan, and this here's my brother, Buck."

As Slade pulled the man to his feet, Jimmy's pa glanced around wildly. "Where we goin'?"

"Goin' for a little ride." Slade helped him up on his horse. Denton groaned and slumped over the saddle horn.

Buck jerked his head toward his own mount. "You want a ride out to your house, Jim?"

Jim nodded, his too-long bangs flopping into his eyes. "Yes, sir."

Buck helped him up onto the gentle horse, and Jim led the way out of town. They crossed the railroad tracks past the church and headed down a rutted lane. Less than a mile from town, they came to a dilapidated shack.

Jim slid off Buck's horse and ran toward the house. A thin young woman with light-brown hair came to the door. A look of relief eased her tired features when she saw her husband.

"Mr. Slade and Mr. Buck brought Pa home."

"Ma'am." Slade touched his hat.

It didn't take much effort to haul Denton off the back of the horse and propel him toward the porch steps. He disappeared inside.

The woman turned to Slade, her gaze not fully meeting his. "Thank you."

"Welcome, ma'am."

Little Jim studied the ground.

Slade ruffled his thick shock of hair. "Jim, we could use some help out at the Lazy M. Would you be up to doing a little work this summer?"

"Could I, Ma?" The boy's face lit up.

Mrs. Denton glanced toward the open door of the shack and twisted her hands in her faded apron. "You'd have to ask your pa."

The boy's face fell.

"You do that, Jim." Slade gathered up his horse's reins. "I'll be by later in the week and we'll see about it, okay?"

"Yes, sir," Jim mumbled, head lowered as he toed the dirt.

They rode home in silence. Slade knew he and Buck were both thinking about the abject poverty the Dentons lived in. The kind of poverty they both were familiar with. The kind that seeps into your pores and stays with you for a long, long time.

But not anymore. Slade took a deep, cleansing breath. His mother no longer lived in a drafty shack on the edge of town. He fingered the letter in his pocket, anticipating the day she'd arrive. He couldn't wait for her to see the Lazy M ranch house. It might need work, but it was a mansion compared to where she'd lived for as long as he could remember.

Only one thing tempered his bright new future.

Mariah and her grandmother would pack up and leave as soon as his mother arrived, and he only had himself to blame.

CHAPTER THIRTEEN

THE YELLOW TOMCAT sat still as a statue, watching Mariah, unblinking. Slowly he lowered his head and nibbled at the leftover pot roast.

"It's all right, Yellow," she murmured, her voice whisper-soft. "I won't hurt you."

He kept his suspicious gaze on her but continued to eat. Mariah forced herself to relax. Maybe she should forget about trying to tame him. The exercise involved too much effort. Right now, she needed to be in the house finishing supper, not crouched out here trying to lure a half-wild cat to her. What good would it do to keep trying since she'd be gone before long?

She tossed another piece of meat near him when he finished the first one, making sure it landed a little closer to her. He inched his way toward it, still eyeing her. She held her breath. She could reach out and touch him if he'd let her. But she didn't dare. Not yet.

He tore off small pieces of the meat, and she thought about how sad his life had been. Not long after Giff had come to work for the Lazy M, he'd brought a new dog to the ranch. A rangy, mean-looking critter that despised cats. If the dog caught one, he'd kill it.

In self-defense, the barn cats had taken to the woods behind the house. Mariah had tried to feed them, but the dog guarded his territory ruthlessly and the cats had to fend for themselves for months. None of them would come close to the house or any of the barns with the dog around.

Then one day the dog disappeared. Mariah didn't know what happened to him, and she didn't ask any questions. Gradually the cats returned, along with a litter of half-grown kittens. Skittish Yellow, born and raised in the woods, didn't take to farm life like the other cats. He lurked in the shadows, running off if anyone came near.

Mariah's foot went to sleep, and shifting her weight, she stood. Yellow darted away but stopped and watched from a distance. She murmured soothing words, encouraging him to let her get closer. He crouched, eyes narrowed, wary. Wary, tough, and alone.

His guarded stance reminded her of Slade.

Even their hardscrabble lives were similar. Living from

hand to mouth, on the fringes of society at an early age. Dependent on no one. As much as she felt sorry for the cat, shouldn't she feel more compassion for the man?

Confusion wafted through her, and she chewed her lip. Why should she feel sorry for Slade? Because of him, she didn't even have a home anymore.

She sighed. Grandma was right. He'd only done what anybody in the same circumstances would have. What would her father have done if the tables had been turned? Why, he would have produced the deed and demanded justice. He would have fought tooth and nail to provide for her, Amanda, and Grandma.

What had happened years before? Did he have accomplices? Had her father walked up on Donovan's claim and robbed him at gunpoint or snuck up on him at night? A hard knot formed in her middle. She couldn't picture her father robbing anyone—and certainly not holding a gun on them. It didn't seem possible. He hadn't been a particularly religious man, but he'd been a good man and a good father. People had liked and respected him.

All the speculation just tied her stomach in knots and left her more frustrated than before. She'd probably never know what had happened between her father and Slade's, and worrying about it wouldn't accomplish a thing.

The sound of horses drew her gaze to the road. Slade and Buck rode side by side, headed to the barn. Slade sat tall in the saddle, shoulders broad. Confident. He pointed toward something, and Buck nodded. She slipped into the kitchen, knowing it wouldn't be long before they'd be ready for supper.

Mariah set the table, trying to dredge up the anger and resentment she'd felt when Slade first demanded the ranch. But she couldn't. She only wanted—

Confusion flooded up from her midsection and swamped her.

What did she want?

She wanted everything to be all right. She wanted Amanda to finish her schooling and come home. She wanted the ranch back. And . . . and she wanted a chance to get closer to Slade, to bring him into the light and help him see that he'd been living on the fringes too long. Her heart thudded against her rib cage.

Could this yearning be love? Or did she just want to fix the man as much as she wanted to fix the poor lonely cat that lived in the woods behind the house?

Her feelings for Slade had started slowly enough. First with his tales of hardship as a child, then when he'd held the kitten out to her, and again when he'd watered her garden.

Lord, give me strength. Strength to resist whatever flight of fancy made her ache for a life with Slade—the most unlikely man for her to fall in love with.

An urge to run to her room and pack up her grand-mother's and her belongings came on so strong that Mariah shook her head and pushed the thought out of her mind. She hurried to the stove and checked on the biscuits. She'd never been a quitter, and no matter the unfamiliar feelings churning inside her, she wouldn't shirk her duty. She'd cook and clean even if being around him killed her.

Her pulse spiked the minute she heard the sound of Slade and Buck washing up on the back porch. They came in a short while later, hands and faces scrubbed clean. Mariah was painfully aware of every movement Slade made. Would he sense anything different about her?

He slapped his hat on one of the pegs by the door, and his damp hair gleamed in the lamplight. She engrossed herself in preparations for supper. Why, oh, why, did his presence affect her so? He would never forgive her for the past. Obviously there was only one thing to do.

Pray.

Pray that the Lord would deliver her from wanting something she could never have.

If Mariah had taken one bite, Slade hadn't seen it. She'd spent the entire evening pushing peas back and forth on her plate.

And she wouldn't look at him.

The more she ignored him, the more he wanted to get a glimpse of her flashing brown eyes, of the smile that lit up her face. The more he wanted to hear her laughter and her teasing comments to her grandmother.

He frowned into his coffee cup, his senses alert to every nuance of her movements, the flat tone of her voice when she thanked him for passing the butter, the swish of her skirts when she got up to pour more coffee. She'd given brief answers when Buck and her grandmother tried to pull her into the conversation. Something was bothering her, and he couldn't figure out what.

"That was good eating." Buck pushed his plate away. "Thanks, Mariah."

"Glad you enjoyed it." She stood and started clearing the table as if she was in a hurry to shoo them out of the kitchen.

Mrs. Malone shifted on her straight-back chair. "Do either of you play checkers? I've got a hankering for a good match, and Mariah doesn't care for the game at all."

"Buck's a better player than I am, ma'am." Slade glanced at the feisty old woman. He didn't have any doubt she'd beat the socks off his brother.

"Are you?" She pinned Buck with her gaze.

"I guess so." Buck shrugged.

"Well, come on into the parlor." Mrs. Malone stood and began to shuffle out of the room. "We'll see how good you are."

Slade finally caught Mariah's eye.

"She really is very good."

"Buck'll put up a good fight."

"Good." She finished clearing the table. "She beats me in a handful of moves, and I never know what hit me."

Mariah bustled about the kitchen, dumping scraps into a bowl for her cats, covering the leftover pie and storing it in the pie safe. She kept her back to him, her hands busy. "Can I get you something else? Another piece of pie? More coffee?"

"I'm fine." Slade sipped his coffee, wishing she'd stop

flitting about the kitchen like a skittish colt. "You didn't eat anything. Is something wrong?"

She stiffened. "No—nothing's wrong."

"How's your foot?"

"Fine, thank you."

Slade grunted. He'd seen how she favored it when she walked.

She finally glanced his way, all hint of laughter and sunshine absent from her expression. "Thank you for watering the garden. I appreciate it."

"You're welcome." He dipped his head and gave her a tiny smile, but she didn't smile back. She blinked, looked away, and started washing dishes, movements quick and efficient.

While she worked, he took stock of the small, sturdy kitchen. Mariah's kitchen. She knew where every pot went, where to store every plate. Somehow he couldn't picture this kitchen without her. But he'd have to. She'd be leaving soon, and he'd never see her again. Unsure how he really felt about that, he drained his coffee cup and carried it to where she stood at the sink, hands immersed in hot, soapy water.

He held out the cup, his gaze roaming over her face, stoic in the lamplight. She took the cup, glancing at him out of the corner of her eye but not making eye contact. He clenched his jaw. He'd already asked what was wrong, and she'd brushed him off, claiming everything was fine. He wouldn't ask again.

"Thanks for supper, Mariah. It was good, as always."

"It's my job." She shrugged, a tiny movement of her shoulders.

The resignation in her voice brought him up short. How could he have forgotten she wouldn't even be here if she had the money to leave? He strode to the door, picked up his hat, and jammed it on his head.

"Slade?"

He paused, his hand on the latch. "Yes?"

"When do you expect your mother and sisters to arrive?"

"A couple of weeks, maybe a month. She had some things to settle in Galveston."

"Thank you. I was just wondering."

"Good night, Mariah."

"Good night," she whispered, her voice sounding close to tears.

He waited, the silence broken by her vigorous scrubbing of the plate in her hand. Finally he unlatched the door and strode into the night, pondering her reaction. Relief that she could leave so soon? Or disappointment that she might have to stay another month? An ache squeezed his chest. He settled his hat more firmly on his head and stomped across the yard toward the barn.

The idea that she might want to get away from Wisdom as soon as possible, away from *him*, bothered him more than he liked to admit.

CHAPTER FOURTEEN

MARIAH REACHED FOR another stick of firewood, planning her day's work. She had a lot to do to whip the place into shape before Slade's family arrived. The furnishings might be tattered and worn, but everything would be neat and tidy when she packed her trunk and left for the last time.

Pounding hooves interrupted her thoughts, and she shaded her eyes against the morning sunlight. She spotted Slade's horse loping down the lane toward the house, and her heart ricocheted against her rib cage. But she tamped down the joy that bubbled up inside and trudged toward the porch.

No need to dally. He'd feel obligated to speak to her, and her heart had been trampled enough already. She had to get through the next few weeks without making a complete and utter fool of herself, and the least amount of contact they had with each other, the better. How would she survive the daily ache of seeing him, being near him? She'd pour all her energy into spring-cleaning and the garden. Work was her only hope.

He headed straight for the porch instead of the barn, and she spotted a small boy on the back of the horse, his arms wrapped securely around Slade's waist. He swung the child to the ground, and Mariah recognized the little boy she'd seen down by the railroad tracks.

Slade tilted his hat back; his blue eyes flickered over her face before he jerked his head at the boy. "Mariah, I'd like you to meet Jimmy Denton."

"Jimmy." She dumped the wood in the wood box and focused on the boy, trying not to notice how Slade's shoulders filled out his worn shirt, the shadow forming on his unshaven jawline, or how he kept his prancing horse under control with ease.

The boy ducked his head and dug in the dirt with his big toe. "It's Jim, ma'am."

Mariah suppressed a smile. "Oh, I'm sorry. Jim it is."

"Could you rustle up some breakfast for Jim, then send him out to the barn?"

"Of course."

"Soon as you get a bite to eat, Jim, I'll show you around."

"Yes, sir." Jim grinned, showing a gap where he'd lost a front tooth.

"I'm counting on you. Now, go on with Miss Mariah." Slade reined away.

Mariah led the way into the kitchen, where she sliced two biscuits and placed a thick piece of fried ham between each. "Here you go."

Her heart ached when the thin youngster gulped down a huge bite as if he hadn't eaten anything in days.

"Do you like buttermilk?"

"Yes, ma'am." He nodded, floppy bangs waving wildly.

"I had a little left from breakfast. It'll keep me from having to drink it or feed it to the cats." She filled a pint jar and slid it across the table. "I'll tell you a secret. The cats don't like buttermilk much. It sticks to their whiskers."

He took a swallow and grinned at her, his upper lip covered in buttermilk.

She tidied the kitchen while Jim concentrated on his breakfast. Why did Slade need the boy out in the barn? What was going on?

"Jim?"

"Yes'm?" he mumbled around a mouthful of biscuit.

"Did Mr. Donovan offer you a job?"

The boy swallowed a big gulp of buttermilk. "Yes, ma'am. I want to make enough money to buy a horse. I ain't never had one." His brown eyes, older than his years, gazed fearfully at her as if he expected her to send him back home. "I promise to work really hard."

"I'm sure you will." She patted him on the back, feeling

his thin shoulders through his threadbare shirt. "Finish your breakfast. I'll be right back."

She marched toward the barn. Once inside, she blinked against the dimness, searching for Slade. She saw him in the shadowy recesses of one of the stalls.

"Where's Jim?" he asked.

"Still eating." She crossed her arms and glared at him.

He draped his arms over the top of the stall and cocked a brow at her.

"He's just a little boy. He's not big enough to do a man's job."

"Who said anything about a man's job?" He frowned, pushing his hat back. A tangle of dark hair fell over his forehead, and Mariah scrambled to hold on to her displeasure.

"Jim did. He said if he did a good job, you'd pay him. Maybe even give him a horse." She stared hard at him. "What exactly are you going to make him do?"

He jerked his head at the cluttered stall behind him. "For starters, he can learn to muck stalls, gather eggs, take care of the horses, and milk the cows. There are lots of things he can do. Then he can learn to ride. Did he tell you how much he likes horses?"

She nodded but didn't let the question sway her from her purpose. "It's too much. He can't do all that."

Slade gazed steadily at her. "It's the only way. His ma won't let me help them, but she'll let him come here to work."

"But he's just a boy!" Tears welled up in her eyes.

"Do you really think I'm going to make him do all that

work?" He latched the stall and stood in front of her, a half smile on his face. "Buck does most of it, and Jim will just be his shadow. It won't hurt him a bit to gather eggs and tote water for your washing. And at the end of the day he can go home with a sackful of potatoes, some carrots, and a chicken now and then. By the end of summer, he'll know how to ride a horse. I can't just *give* him anything. Don't you see? His ma and pa have got to believe he's working for it."

Mariah's ire subsided. "I'm sorry. It's just that . . ." She trailed off, unwilling to admit that she'd thought the worst of him. Again. He was trying to do something for the boy's family, something they could accept without sacrificing their pride.

Lord knew she could relate to that.

"I'll take care of him." Slade tipped up her chin, the warmth of his touch twisting her stomach into knots. "I promise."

Sounds, movement, light all tilted into slow motion. Mariah's lips parted, and her senses raced to the spot where his fingers seared her skin. Her breath caught as his gaze tumbled to her lips. His hand moved along her jaw, cupped her head, and pulled her closer. She swayed toward him, unwilling and unable to do anything else.

"I'm ready when you are!" Jim raced into the barn, and Mariah's eyes popped open wide.

Slade's broad back shielded her from the boy. His heavy-lidded gaze held hers as he traced his thumb over her lips. She shuddered at the fleeting touch and the promise in his eyes.

He dropped his hand and turned to Jim. "All right, partner, let's get to work."

✻   ✻   ✻

The kitchen floor gleamed. Mariah tucked a lock of hair behind her ear and lifted the pail of dirty water. She surveyed the clean boards with satisfaction before lugging the bucket outside.

Her grandmother looked up from her rocker on the porch, a pile of mending in her lap. "Mariah, I wish you'd let me help with the cleaning. You're doing too much."

"I'm fine, Grandma." Mariah poured the water around the two rosebushes beside the porch. She snipped off three roses, savoring the sweet aroma cast by the deep-red petals. "I'd rather scrub floors and let you darn socks any day. You know I don't care much for chores where I have to sit down. I'd rather be up and about."

"It's just that I feel so useless." Her grandmother sighed.

"Grandma, just because you're weak and can't get around like you used to doesn't mean you're not doing your share. You do plenty—"

"Like what?"

"Like keeping me company and keeping watch on the stove when I'm outside, and shelling peas and beans and mending clothes. I don't how I'd get it all done without your help."

Her grandmother reached out a trembling hand and smoothed back Mariah's hair. Her eyes misted over, and she shook her head. "You're just saying that. I'm not—"

"Grandma, when I was a child, you did everything I'm doing now *and* saw after me and Amanda. Surely I can do it all now and take care of you too."

A wide smile creased her grandmother's weathered face. "You're just like your grandfather, Mariah. He always could turn things around to his way of thinking."

Mariah grinned. "Good. I'm glad you're seeing things my way."

She glanced up as Jimmy and Buck sauntered out of the barn and ambled over to the porch. Jim looked like he'd rolled in the muck. His straw-colored hair stuck out every which way, and big splotches of dirt and cobwebs, mixed with hay, clung to his threadbare clothes. Covered in grime and filth, you'd think he would be anything but happy. But the grin on his face told a different tale.

Her gaze met Buck's, and it was all she could do to keep from laughing. The twitching of his lips told her he was holding in his own laughter.

"Well, how did your first day on the job go, Jim?" she asked, remembering to use the more grown-up version of his name.

"Me and Buck got the corner stall cleaned out, and Buck said when I get my pony, I could put him in there."

"You didn't disturb the kittens, did you?"

"Oh no, ma'am. We left them alone." His face screwed up, looking apprehensive. "But Buck let me play with them."

"Good. They need a little boy to teach them the ways of the barn."

He grinned at her, then dug into his back pocket and pulled out a slingshot, handing it over. "Look what Mr. Slade made for me."

Mariah dutifully admired the slingshot. "That's a beauty. Think you can hit a rabbit with it?"

"Sure he can. He's just got to practice." Buck put one hand on Jim's shoulder. "Well, come on, kid, let's go down to the creek and get cleaned up. I promised Slade I'd bring you over to the west pasture so he could take you home."

Jim whooped and raced off.

"Come by the house before you leave," Mariah called after them. "I've got a sack of fresh potatoes for you to take to your mother."

"I'll say one thing," her grandmother said as they watched man and boy go over the rise toward the creek. "Giving that little feller a job was about the smartest thing Slade could have done. From what I've heard, the boy's pa is too much of a drunk to take care of his family, and his ma's too proud to take a handout."

"Slade said he wasn't going to make him work hard. Just enough so he'd be proud of himself and feel he'd earned his keep."

Her grandmother nodded. "That's as it should be." Her wise old eyes twinkled. "I seem to remember a girl about that age picking blackberries for two weeks to sell to the mercantile so she could save up for a doll."

"I did, didn't I?"

"Yes, you did. And it taught you the value of hard work and just plain doing something for yourself."

Mariah glanced out over the yard. "Grandma?"

"Hmm?"

"I know you and Grandpa taught Pa the same lessons you taught Amanda and me. And Pa worked hard and never did anybody wrong that I know of." Mariah picked up a shirt, smoothing out the wrinkles. "Why do you think he cheated Slade's father when he wasn't like that at all?"

Her grandmother dropped her darning in her lap and sighed. "I've wondered that very thing many a night since Seth told us what he had done. And to tell you the truth, I don't know. I just don't know."

CHAPTER FIFTEEN

"You wouldn't have believed it if you'd seen it. No way we could bring in that crazy mean bull. Heard he was loco or something."

Slade slouched in his saddle, trying to ignore Rio's incessant chatter. He'd make sure the kid rode fences with someone else from now on. He squinted at the sun hanging low over the horizon. They'd have to head back soon.

But first he wanted to check over the next rise. He eyed the grove of trees and nudged his horse up the draw. That'd be a good landmark to head for tomorrow.

Rio prattled on, his voice alternating from low to a squeaky high. Slade bit back a smile. Every so often Rio realized his voice had risen, and he'd lower it a couple of notches.

"... but I wasn't scared—" His tale stopped midsentence as they topped the rise.

The remains of a broken fence lay spread out before them. Mangled, twisted wire, posts pulled out of the ground, grass trampled flat, churned-up earth as fresh as a newly plowed field.

Slade pulled his horse up short. Rio did the same.

"What in holy smoke happened here?"

Slade had a sinking feeling he knew but didn't voice his opinion out loud. He dismounted. "Hold the horses. I'm going to scout around a bit."

"Need some help?" Rio stood in his stirrups to get a better view of the situation.

Slade eased away, studying the ground. "It's better if we don't mess up the tracks much till I have a look around."

"Okay, boss."

Leaving the youngster with the horses, Slade made his way around the perimeter of the broken fence, searching the ground for clues to what had happened. At the fence line, he picked up a strand of wire and pulled it hand over hand to the end. He clenched his jaw and carefully checked another strand. The sharp ends of the wire had been cut, not broken by a bunch of frightened cattle stampeding through.

He moved on, spotting a clear print of a cow's hoof here and there. He found what he was searching for when he saw the unmistakable trail of a shod horse, then another, both headed away from the Lazy M. Moving off to the side, he found a stretch of unmarred prints. He hunkered down and studied the tracks, cataloging the shape and size of each. At least three riders, probably more.

Frowning, he studied the tracks. One horse threw his left hind hoof out when he ran, making the dirt kick out to the side more than usual. He followed the tracks for a short distance. Sure enough, the hitch showed up consistently in almost every stride. The horse could have been tired or injured, but he tucked the information away, hoping it might come in handy someday.

He straightened, placed both hands on his hips, and gazed northward, trying to figure out who owned the land beyond the fence surrounding the Lazy M. He'd made it his business to learn the names of the ranchers in these parts, but this particular stretch could belong to Riker or Cooper.

Pushing his hat back, he swiped at his sweat-dampened forehead. Maybe there was a logical explanation for the broken fence, because the last thing he needed was a band of rustlers working the area. He walked back to where Rio waited with the horses.

"Is it rustlers?" The kid fidgeted, as excited as a banty rooster at a cockfight. "Can I look?"

Rio's enthusiasm made Slade chuckle, even under the circumstances. He waved him on. "Sure, go ahead. But be careful. And don't mess up the tracks."

"Sure thing, boss."

Slade shook his head as Rio bounded off like an excited

puppy, his loose-jointed frame flopping wildly. He let the kid go. Most of the evidence would be gone before the sheriff could check it out anyway, so Rio couldn't do too much damage even if he tried.

After Rio examined the site, they mounted up and headed for the barn. Slade waved in the direction the cows had gone. "Who owns the spread north of here?"

"Frederick Cooper. He bought the Roundup Ranch about the time Miss Mariah's pa took sick. Old man Crenshaw went bankrupt, and Cooper got the ranch for a song. He came to see Mariah the other day, remember? He's sweet on her, you know."

"Yeah, I know." Slade's stomach clenched at the reminder.

The sweet scent of baking cookies filled the kitchen as Mariah lifted a fresh batch of tea cakes onto a platter to cool.

She regarded the starburst pattern on top of each one. They were almost too pretty to eat. But Slade and Buck would inhale every one of them tonight, probably before supper if they could get away with it. Land sakes, but those two could put away the food.

Buck looked like he'd gained a few pounds lately, and she hoped her cooking had something to do with it. His slight muscles grew stronger every day. She'd discovered he liked potato soup, so she'd made a huge pot for tonight and a skillet of corn bread to go with it.

Slade enjoyed anything, but he favored tea cakes. Her

gaze fell on the still-warm cookies. Just when had pleasing Slade, or even Buck, become important to her?

She sank down onto one of the split-bottom chairs at the table. Slade had every intention of sending her and her grandmother packing as soon as his mother arrived. What did she care if he liked tea cakes or not?

A heavy weight descended on her. Slade cared about this ranch; even she could see that. He wanted it to prosper, and he worked harder than anybody else to make it happen.

Could that be why she felt so out of sorts? She hadn't been able to make the ranch flourish. Everything had been on a downhill slide ever since her father took sick and she had to make all the decisions. Every time Red had come to her with a report, he'd brought bad news of some sort. And it had gotten worse as time wore on and the doctor bills piled up.

She should've used a firmer hand with the men. Let them know who was boss. But she'd been so worried about her father that she'd let Red run the ranch as he saw fit. She'd trusted him to do his part since she'd had all she could do to tend the garden that fed the lot of them, take care of the house and her grandmother, launder everyone's clothes, and worry about Amanda. She'd thought she couldn't do much more.

But as owner, she should have done more, learned more, listened more.

In hindsight, she realized her grandmother and Cookie had tried to tell her. Her grandmother had never cared for some of the hands Red had hired, and Cookie had made a few remarks as well. But she'd told him to see Red, that he was in charge of the ranch hands. She hadn't wanted to deal with it. Hadn't really known how.

Red seemed like a good sort, eager to please most of the time. It hadn't occurred to Mariah that he might be shirking his duties. But looking back now, she could see where the ranch foreman and the hands had let things slide. She'd noticed a marked change for the better since Slade had taken over.

What if Slade had been the foreman when her father took sick? Would things have turned out differently? What if he hadn't come seeking revenge for her father's treachery?

What if . . . ?

There she went again, letting her thoughts wander down paths leading to nowhere except heartache. She picked up the tea cakes and carried them to the pie safe.

Her father had stolen Jack Donovan's hopes, his dreams. And when she'd written that letter, she'd given those dreams back to his son.

Nothing—not even wishing—would change that.

CHAPTER SIXTEEN

RED RODE WEST looking for Slade, dreading what he had to tell him.

Mile after mile of scruffy prairie grass stretched before him, beckoning. Not a cloud in the sky, so bright and blue he could almost reach out and touch it. The urge to keep riding hit him so hard his chest hurt and the burning in his gut intensified. He'd be long gone before anyone at the Lazy M realized it, and then it would be several more days before Emmit got word.

But he couldn't leave.

The image of Emmit's glazed expression when he realized he'd killed Slick haunted Red. For the past week, he had wrestled with his demons, trying to come up with a plan to save his brother, to save himself. Things had gone too far. Surely Emmit would see that now that he had blood on his hands.

Red spotted two horses loping toward him. Donovan and Rio. He reined in and waited. Rio spurred his mount and raced ahead to stop almost on top of Red. Red fought to hold his horse in check.

"You'll never guess what we found." Words shot from Rio's mouth, his excitement knowing no bounds. "A whole section of fence pulled down and a bunch of cattle gone. Could be rustlers."

Red's gut twisted in another round of fiery torment, and he wanted to bash something, namely Giff Kerchen's head. Did the idiot not realize that with Donovan ordering them to ride fences every day, somebody would find the mess he'd left when he moved the cattle? If Emmit hadn't asked Red to stick close to the ranch, he would've taken the cattle the long way around and then made sure the men repaired the fence afterward.

Maybe the news about Buck was a godsend.

What would be worse: getting fired for almost killing Donovan's brother or being hung for rustling?

Heart pounding, Slade jumped off his horse and headed straight for the bunkhouse.

Cookie met him at the door.

"Red said Buck was sick."

"Never should have gone off with that Giff Kerchen, I tell ya." His rheumy eyes held a steely glint.

"Giff? Where'd they go?" Slade frowned. He'd left Buck mucking stalls this morning.

Cookie lifted his chin a notch. "You'd better go ask Buck, I reckon. He didn't want you to know. Wouldn't even let me tell Mariah."

"Thanks, Cookie." Slade gave the old man a curt nod.

He hurried into the bunkhouse and made his way to the darkened corner Buck had claimed for his own. His brother lay in his bunk, his thin frame shaking even under a thick layer of blankets. Little Jim sat by his side, a bowl of water and a wet rag in his hand.

"Buck?"

His brother shifted, and his voice floated out from beneath the blankets. "I'll . . . be . . . all right. Just give . . . me . . . a little . . . time."

"What happened?"

"Noth . . . nothing."

"I know something happened. Cookie said you went off with Giff."

Buck shook his head, started to speak, but a round of coughing cut off his words.

Slade clenched both fists. "Stay with him, Jim. I'll be right back."

He stepped from the bunkhouse, quickly spotting Giff in a knot of men near the barn. The ranch hand leaned against the corral, and Red sat on a sawed-off log. A sharp bark of laughter rolled across the yard as Rio laughed at something one of the others had said.

"Giff."

"Yes, sir?" Giff answered, his tone anything but deferential.

"I want to know what you did to my brother today."

Giff's expression hardened. "Me? I didn't do nothing to that milk-faced boy. He just decided to go and help clean out the water hole. It ain't my fault the scrawny kid fell into the water."

White-hot anger surged through Slade. Getting chilled could bring on another round of pneumonia. And Giff had no excuse: he'd complained often enough that Buck's coughing spells kept him awake at night. The talk in front of the barn ceased and the men grew still. Cookie came to the door of the cookhouse, wiping his hands on his apron.

"That's the way of it, Donovan." Red stepped between them, hands out as if to ward off blows. "Your brother decided he was tired of lollygagging around here and volunteered to help clean out the water hole."

"That's not the way it happened," Cookie sputtered, "and you know it."

"Aw, shut up, old man. You don't know nothing." Red glared at Cookie.

"I won't shut up!" Cookie's voice shook with fury. "You let Giff goad that young feller into feeling guilty over being sick and all. You've seen his scars. He's been through more than either one of you could handle. Why, that mustang nearly stomped—"

"That's enough." Slade held up his hand.

A tense silence followed Cookie's outburst. Slade and Red eyed each other. Anger mottled Red's ruddy complexion. Slade took a deep breath. He'd known it was going to come to this the first day he'd squared off with the Lazy M foreman. Better to sever ties now with one fell swoop.

"Giff, I was willing to overlook the incident with the eggs, figuring you were just having a little fun with Buck, and that your temper got the best of you when Mariah dumped a basket of eggs on your head." His gaze included Red. "But in the weeks I've been here, neither one of you have shown any interest in doing your jobs. So maybe it's time y'all just pack up and head on out of here."

"Why you—" Giff's rage cut off in midsentence as he lunged.

Mariah heard a yell just as she took a second batch of tea cakes out of the oven. She glanced out the kitchen door and saw Giff ram Slade. The two men tumbled backward, rolled once, and sprang to their feet. Then they circled each other, looking like two mountain lions fighting over a fresh kill.

"Oh, my word." She lifted her skirts and raced across the barnyard to the ring of spectators standing around the two men. "Stop! Please stop!"

No one even glanced at her.

Slade threw a punch that sent Giff reeling backward. Giff recovered and came at Slade again. He swung, his fist grazing Slade's cheek.

Mariah pressed both hands to her mouth. *Lord, please don't let anybody pull a gun.*

Slade's fist slammed into Giff's stomach, and the other man staggered backward. Slade circled, keeping his eyes on his opponent.

When Giff's fist connected solidly with Slade's cheekbone, Mariah's stomach roiled as if she'd been hit herself. Slade stumbled, regained his footing, and came at the bigger man like an enraged bull.

"Hit him, Slade! Hit him hard." Mariah clamped her hand over her mouth again and cast a horrified glance around the group. Thankfully, they were all cheering the fighters on and hadn't heard her. She hopped from one foot to the other, moaning with each punch but keeping her hands over her mouth.

When she thought she couldn't stand it any longer, Slade rammed his left fist into Giff's stomach and followed with a hard right-handed uppercut that connected with Giff's chin.

Giff stopped dead in his tracks. Eyelids fluttering, he sank to the ground like a stone to the bottom of the creek.

The sound of Slade's harsh breathing filled the sudden silence around the barnyard. He staggered to the watering trough and picked up a bucket. He filled it with water, then dumped it on Giff's head. As the man sputtered and rolled over, Slade turned to Red.

"Get out," he said, his low voice brooking no argument. "Both of you."

"What about our pay?"

"You got paid Saturday. That's enough."

Red looked like he would argue, but instead he helped Giff to his feet. Giff gave Slade a hard-eyed glare.

They moved away and Rio broke into a big grin. "Did you see that, Cookie? Mr. Donovan knocked him out cold. Wait till I tell the boys in town about this."

Slade splashed water over his face while the men recounted each punch thrown.

Mariah picked up Slade's hat from the dust and waited until the men drifted away before she approached him.

"Come into the kitchen. I've got some salve that will help."

He glanced at her, one eye already beginning to swell and a cut on his right cheek trickling blood. He shrugged. "I'll be all right. I've had worse."

Tentatively she touched his arm. "Please."

He stared at her a moment before nodding. "All right. But I need to check on Buck first."

"It won't do your brother any good to see you all beat up like that," Cookie growled. "Go on and get cleaned up."

"He's right." She tugged on Slade's arm. "Come on."

Mariah tossed Slade's hat on the kitchen table and rummaged in the cabinets for the salve. Slade hiked one hip onto the table, boot swaying back and forth. Finally she located the stuff and set it on the table, then poured some clean water into a small bowl and dampened a piece of cloth.

She moved closer until she stood within inches of him. Trying to ignore the pressure of her full skirt brushing against his legs, she reached out to clean the area around the cut and found his blue gaze watching her steadily. Casting about for something to ease the tension, she asked, "What happened?"

He shoved one hand through his hair only to have the too-long strands tumble right back onto his forehead.

"Giff convinced Buck to go clean out the water hole today. Somehow Buck fell in the water." His jaw tightened. "Or Giff pushed him."

"Oh no. Is Buck all right?"

"As long as he doesn't take pneumonia again, he'll be fine."

She pushed his hair out of the way, swallowing as the silky strands tangled about her fingers. "This might sting."

His lips twitched. "I'll try not to yell."

She frowned at him and gently dabbed at a cut over his eye, the cloth soaking up the blood. He smelled of horses, leather, sweat, and a trace of the soap he'd washed up with earlier. "Giff's a bully, running roughshod over anyone weaker than he is."

His jaw hardened. "Red should've put a stop to it."

"He's always let Giff get away with more than he should." She swiped at the cut on his cheekbone, the rasp of the cloth against his skin breaking the silence.

When she'd cleaned the cuts, she dipped a finger in the salve and spread it across each injury, her stomach clenching. Thank goodness Giff hadn't broken his nose. His cheekbone felt hard and smooth against her fingertip and slightly cool to her touch. She let her finger glide upward, relishing the contact.

She smoothed his hair back and touched the gash over his eye, gently coating the area with salve. "Do you want this one bandaged?"

"No," he rasped out, sounding half-strangled.

Her startled gaze collided with his, lids half-cast as he watched her every move. She swallowed, jerked her hand away, and concentrated on screwing the lid back on the salve.

He reached out, capturing a lock of her hair between his thumb and forefinger. Mariah found herself rooted to the spot, mesmerized by the intensity in his blue eyes. His hooded gaze moved leisurely from hers, over her cheekbones to her lips.

Mariah's breath lodged in her throat.

Tucking the hair behind her ear, he slid his hand behind her head and pulled her toward him. Before she could form a protest, his mouth slanted over hers.

With a soft moan, he wrapped both arms around her, drawing her closer, capturing her mouth more fully. The sweet softness of his lips skimmed along hers. She sighed, letting her hands glide up and over his shoulders, drinking in the taste of him. All too soon, he eased away, putting some distance between them.

Her attention riveted on his chin, zeroing in on another bruise put there by that brute Giff Kerchen. She had a sudden urge to kiss it, somehow make it better.

His fingers moved along her jaw down to her chin. Slowly he cupped her face and tilted her chin up, and she focused on his lips again. A half smile played around them. Her stomach did a delicious little roll of delight.

"I heard you out there."

She blinked. "Heard what?" Her voice sounded weak and breathless.

"Were you afraid Giff might win?"

"Of course not." A hot flush crept up her neck.

His eyes twinkled with laughter and something else, and she wondered if he might kiss her again.

"Hmm." He slid one thumb across her parted lips. "Thank you for your vote of confidence, Mariah," he whispered. "That last punch was for you."

He pressed another gentle kiss to the corner of her mouth and reached for his hat. Placing it securely on his head, he grabbed a handful of her freshly baked tea cakes and walked out of the kitchen, leaving her feeling as if she'd been kicked in the stomach by a day-old colt.

CHAPTER SEVENTEEN

THE NEXT MORNING, Slade reported the rustling incident to Sheriff Dawson, and the lawman promised to ask around. See if any of the other ranchers had noticed anything suspicious. There wasn't much to go on, but at least he'd filed a formal complaint. On the way back to the Lazy M, he stopped by the Riker homestead. Riker's operation was small compared to the Lazy M and Cooper's Roundup, so if the rustlers hit him, they could wipe him out in one night. The news spurred Riker into action, and he and his boys were throwing leather on their horses before Slade even left their homestead.

It was after noon when Slade made it to Frederick Cooper's

Roundup Ranch. He surveyed his surroundings, carefully taking in the bunkhouse and the large barn nestled in a grove of trees a bow-shot from the house. A couple of the horses in the corral looked vaguely familiar. One big roan, even from this distance, favored Giff Kerchen's horse. Had Giff already hired on with Cooper?

He turned his attention to the ranch house. Big and imposing, with an elegant wraparound porch, it was out of place on the outskirts of a one-horse town like Wisdom. Rio had said Cooper bought the place after the bank foreclosed on the previous owner. Slade wondered which one had built such a monstrosity of a house and for what purpose?

Cooper stepped out onto the porch, sporting a shiny vest and matching black coat and pants. Slade frowned. Cooper looked more like a slick gambler than a rancher. A man didn't dress like that for a day of punching cows and fixing fences.

"Donovan." His hand swung out in a grand gesture, a sardonic smile on his face. "What brings you to my humble abode?"

Slade dismounted, wondering if he'd get any satisfaction from the other man. He'd worked for many men like Cooper. Kings of their own spreads, they paid little attention to the smaller ranchers around them or the problems they faced. But even though he'd gotten off on the wrong foot with Cooper concerning Mariah, if rustlers were stealing cattle in the area, they'd do well to put aside their differences and work together.

"Someone cut the fence between the Lazy M and the Roundup and took off with a couple hundred cows."

"Mine or Mariah's?"

"Mine." Slade didn't acknowledge the intended reference to the cattle belonging to Mariah.

Cooper reached into his pocket and withdrew a fat cigar, taking his time snipping off the end and lighting it. His gaze flickered over Slade's face, but he didn't ask about the cuts and bruises. "I haven't lost any cattle to rustling."

"The cattle were driven onto Roundup land. I'd like to take a look, see what direction they went after that."

"A friendly warning." Cooper puffed on his cigar. "My men have instructions to shoot and then ask questions, so I'd be careful if I were you."

Slade went still, eyes narrowed on his neighbor.

One wrong word and they'd have a fight on their hands. He'd seen feuds between two ranches escalate from something as simple as a dead skunk in a water hole, and the resulting bloodbaths stunk to high heaven with many innocent ranch hands caught in the middle. He'd hoped it wouldn't be that way here in Wisdom, but he should have known better.

Men were men, but greedy men were insatiable in their thirst for power. And Cooper struck him as a greedy man. He didn't like Cooper, and he certainly didn't trust him, but he didn't want to say the wrong thing and start a feud.

Not until he had a better grip on the lay of the land.

"I'll watch my back." He gathered up his reins and swung into the saddle. "The same goes for Roundup men. Keep away from me and mine, and we'll get along just fine."

"Does that include Mariah?" Cooper snubbed out his

cigar on the pristine white porch railing, the only evidence Slade's words had burrowed under his skin. "I plan to marry her, you know."

Slade leaned on the saddle horn, studying Cooper. The man seemed almighty sure of himself given the fact that Mariah had refused him—more than once from what Slade gathered. The taste of her kiss lingered in his mind, and he had a sudden urge to keep Cooper as far away from her as possible.

"I suggest you stay away from her, too. With rustlers on the prowl, I can't be responsible for what might happen to anyone who sets foot on the Lazy M." He paused. "As you said, we'll shoot and ask questions later."

"Rustlers?" Mariah crossed her arms and glared at Slade. He wanted to believe her ire was directed at Buck, too, but her flashing brown eyes zeroed in on him, leaving Buck in the clear. "When were you going to tell me?"

"I was getting around to it."

Slade glanced at Buck. His brother gave a helpless shrug, his split-bottom chair tipped back against the front of the barn. He'd recovered from his drenching without contracting pneumonia, but he was still weak as water.

"It happened two days ago. It's all the men are talking about. Grandma heard it from Cookie, and I got the whole story out of Rio this morning."

"I'll let you two hash this out on your own." Buck

smothered a cough and tipped his chair forward, the two front legs plunking into the dirt with a solid thunk. Without another word, he slipped away into the barn.

Slade watched him go, then turned his attention to Mariah. "We found the fence the same day Buck fell in the water hole."

"Oh." Her face flamed, and instantly he was transported back to the fight, Mariah applying salve to his cuts, and then the moment he'd kissed her. And from the look on her face, she was thinking the same thing.

"So you know as much as I do." He pointed a finger at her. "But I don't want you riding off by yourself. Not until we know what we're dealing with."

Her concerned gaze met his, and his fingers itched to smooth the line of worry between her beautiful brown eyes. "Do you think they've been working this area before? Maybe that's why the Lazy M has been doing so poorly the last couple of years."

"I don't know. Riker said he hadn't seen any evidence of rustlers before now, and I didn't get much out of Cooper."

"Frederick hasn't been in the cattle business long enough to know, really. He just bought the Crenshaw place and started stocking it two summers ago." She chewed her fingernail, eyes wide. "What are we going to do?"

Slade noticed how she referred to the ranch as if she were still involved. Somehow hearing Mariah lay claim to ownership didn't prick him nearly as much as when Cooper had needled him.

"We'll keep a close watch and report anything suspicious to the sheriff. That's all we can do right now."

A plume of dust rose in the distance, and the rattle and creak of a buggy reached their ears. Slade straightened. "Somebody's coming."

Mariah shaded her eyes and smiled. "It's Sally and Reverend Winston."

As the buggy pulled up in front of the barn, Slade took hold of the harness.

"Good afternoon, Mr. Donovan. Mariah." Sally Winston offered them a bright, bubbly smile.

Slade shook his head as the tall, lanky preacher helped his short, plump wife down from the buggy. He'd never seen a more unevenly matched pair. He shrugged off the thought. What he knew about matched pairs when it came to happily married folks would fit in his back pocket with room to spare.

While Mariah hugged the preacher's wife, the preacher took Slade's hand in a firm handshake. "Afternoon, Donovan."

"Afternoon."

Sally Winston gave him a once-over. "Goodness gracious. What happened to your face?"

"I had a run-in with one of the hands. Nothing serious."

"Well." She pursed her lips. "I certainly hope everything turned out all right in the end."

"It did." Slade nodded.

"It's so good to see you both." Mariah hugged her friend again. "What brings you out this way?"

"What's this I hear about rustlers?" The preacher caught

Slade's eye. "I was over at the jail having coffee with Sheriff Dawson this morning, and he told me all about it."

"Not much to tell. We found some broken fence, and some cattle are missing."

Sally lifted a basket from the back of the buggy. "When I heard, I wanted to check on Ma and Pa and stop by here, but George wouldn't hear of me coming out here by myself. Said it was too dangerous."

"Did your pa find anything yet?" Slade squinted at the preacher's wife.

"Nothing yet."

"Maybe they've already left the area, then."

"We can hope and pray." The preacher's wife patted the basket. "I brought your grandmother some fig preserves."

"Oh, thank you. She'll be thrilled." Mariah looped her arm through Sally's. "You will stay for supper, won't you?"

The words had no sooner left her mouth before she turned toward Slade, eyes wide and questioning. "I'm sorry. Is that all right with you?"

Slade frowned. His mother rarely had company over, and it hadn't even occurred to him to invite the preacher and his wife for supper. He wiped the scowl off his face in case they took it the wrong way. "Of course it's all right. Glad to have you."

"Good, it's settled then." Mariah smiled. "Let's go see if Grandma's up from her nap. She'll be happy to have company." The women moved toward the house, Mariah chattering like an excited magpie.

Slade headed to the barn, already thinking up excuses to get out of eating supper with their visitors.

"Do you mind if I tag along, Donovan?" Reverend Winston fell into step beside him. "I like to look at a good horse now and then."

"Sure." He didn't see any way of getting rid of the preacher.

"I heard you were making some improvements around here." Reverend Winston appraised the recently repaired corral and the new roof on the bunkhouse. "You'll have this place in tip-top shape in no time."

They meandered into the barn and studied Duncan's lame horse. "That brother of yours must be a miracle worker. I heard how he helped my father-in-law the other day with his prize bull."

"He's no miracle worker, but he has a way with animals. Treats them like he'd want to be treated." Slade rested his elbows on a stall and squinted at the reverend, putting two and two together. "John Riker is your wife's pa?"

"Yes. I never thought I'd almost be as old as my father-in-law." The preacher tugged on his earlobe with his thumb and forefinger, a flush deepening his features. A wry smile slashed across his lean face. "Or have a wife as young and full of life as Sally. Don't know what she saw in me."

Slade didn't know what to say. He'd never understand women. He frowned. Why had his ma married his pa? Had he been different when they were young, before Malone shot him? Had it been a love match, or had she married him out of necessity? All of a sudden he realized he'd never asked.

Someday he'd ask his mother how she met his father. He cast about for something to say. "Maybe she liked your preaching."

The preacher chuckled. "There is that. Why don't you and your brother come to church? It's the fastest way that I know of to get acquainted with your neighbors. And we have a church social once a month. Every fourth Sunday. You'll want to attend that for sure. Our church ladies cook some of the best victuals you ever put in your mouth."

After eating Mariah's cooking for the last few weeks, Slade didn't doubt it. "Thank you. I'll pass the invite along to Buck."

But he wouldn't be attending church, no matter how friendly Reverend Winston and his plump little wife were. Church had been off-limits for a number of years, and he preferred to keep it that way.

Mariah welcomed Sally's help in the kitchen but craved the chatter even more. She could depend on Sally to lighten anybody's mood with her cheerful attitude.

"How are you feeling these days?" With Sally's slightly rounded frame, it would be a while before most people noticed that she was in the family way.

Sally placed one hand over her stomach and smiled. "Better. The morning sickness is waning."

"Glad to hear it." Mariah took the plates out of the pie safe and started setting the table. "I've heard it lasts for several months with some women."

"It does. You remember Emily Baxter? She had her second

child, a boy, a couple of months ago, and she told me that she stayed sick the entire time."

Mariah shuddered. "It's a good thing I'm not married or expecting. Being sick for nine months doesn't sound appealing at all."

"Oh, but there's so much more to it than being sick, Mariah. Just think. In a few months, I'll hold my very own baby in my arms. If it's a boy, he might have George's hair and eyes." A dreamy look stole over Sally's face.

Mariah smiled. She wouldn't exactly wish Reverend Winston's features on any child, but she wouldn't tell Sally that. When the middle-aged, widowed Reverend George Winston had accepted the pastorate in Wisdom seven years ago, it had never occurred to her that her best friend would end up married to the preacher. But anybody with a lick of sense could tell they were happy. And that's what mattered.

"If you say so."

"Just wait and see. When you fall in love and get married, you'll long to have children of your own, children who will be the spitting image of their father." Sally hugged her. "Trust me on this one."

Mariah turned away to hide the blush staining her cheeks as images of little dark-haired, blue-eyed babies danced in her imagination.

Slade slid into his chair at the table beside Reverend Winston. Showing the man around hadn't been half as bad as he'd expected. A friendly man and easy to talk to, the preacher knew horses and a bit about ranching, and he'd done a smattering of carpentry over the years to supplement his income. He was a jack-of-all-trades but not a know-it-all by any means. Slade liked that in a man.

In the last hour, the preacher revealed that he'd grown up dirt-poor in Alabama, and his first wife had died in childbirth several years ago. He'd left Alabama, working his way west, preaching here and there until finally settling in Wisdom. After spending some time in Winston's company, Slade felt at ease with the amiable preacher.

He let his gaze travel around the table to the Winstons and Mrs. Malone before settling on Mariah. The sparkle in her eyes held him mesmerized as she laughed at something Sally said. For once he'd be able to watch her unobserved while her attention was focused on entertaining her friends.

She'd changed from her everyday dress into that brown outfit she wore to church and had swirled her thick mane of golden-brown hair up on top of her head. He stared at her hair, realizing the style was fancier than the way she fixed it day in and day out, but he had no clue how she'd accomplished the feat. As usual, several strands had escaped to tickle her high-necked shirtwaist. Even her cheeks had more of a rosy glow than usual. He supposed the heat of the kitchen and the excitement of having company had done that to her.

The women had outdone themselves with supper. The table fairly groaned under the weight of a thick chicken stew, new potatoes fresh from the garden, bright-green string beans, and lightly browned corn bread straight from the oven. And judging by the aroma wafting from the warming oven, somebody had whipped up a blackberry cobbler. His mouth watered in anticipation of the sweet, tart dessert.

"More potatoes, Reverend Winston?" Mariah asked, her gentle voice brushing like silk across his attentive ears.

"Yes, thank you. Everything is delicious as always, Mariah."

"Thank you." She reached out and clasped Sally's hand. "It was a pleasure to have Sally in the kitchen with me. Together, we're tempted to cook enough for an army."

"I'd say the two of you came close to achieving your goal."

"Save room for dessert." Mariah's eyes twinkled. "Blackberry cobbler."

"Oh, I think I'll have room." Sally pressed a hand to her stomach and laughed. "What about you, George?"

"I've always got room for Mariah's cooking. It's second only to yours, dear."

Mrs. Malone cackled. "Spoken like a man who knows which side his bread is buttered on."

Slade found himself enjoying the friendly banter between the Malones and the Winstons. Mariah's soft laughter filled the kitchen, brightening it, and her happy responses to Sally's questions filled the space with joy. Mrs. Malone chatted with Reverend Winston, finding out about each and every family who lived in Wisdom—who'd married, who'd died, who'd moved away, and who'd moved to town. The woman didn't leave one stone unturned.

Over dessert, Mariah and Sally moved on to discussing the church picnic.

Could this be what it felt like to be part of a real family? To invite the neighbors to supper every now and then? To talk about the recent rain and the threat of summer drought? To plan a church picnic?

To have someone to come home to every night. Someone to be the mother of his children. Someone to grow old with.

Mariah's laughter tugged at him, and he glanced toward her.

Someone like Mariah.

Stunned, he jerked his attention to the bowl of steaming cobbler in front of him. Where had that thought come from? He'd seen Mariah's hand tremble when she'd given him the deed to the Lazy M. She would never consider staying and becoming his wife, even if he asked her.

Which he wasn't going to do anyway.

No way on God's green earth could he forget what her father had done to his. Malone had shot Slade's father, leaving him for dead, and the bullet lodged in his pa's brain had tormented him until the day he died. The only thing that dulled the pain and the headaches was whiskey. And when he couldn't get his hands on whiskey, he'd found other outlets for his pain.

His fists.

Slade shook his head, blocking thoughts of his father from his mind. Now wasn't the time to start thinking about the past.

"Mariah, have you heard from Amanda lately?" Sally asked.

Mariah threw Slade a quick glance, and the excitement in her eyes dimmed slightly. He frowned. Even though he didn't care for her sister's selfishness, it didn't bother him if Mariah talked about her.

"Yes. I got another letter the other day. She's doing well."

"How does she like it in Philadelphia?" Reverend Winston asked. "I'd think it would be kind of difficult for her, in her condition and all."

Her condition? Slade sent Mariah a questioning glance. What did Reverend Winston mean by that remark?

"It's not really that difficult." Mariah fiddled with her napkin. "Well, I suppose it was at first. But then, once she realized they were there to help her, she got accustomed to it."

"Is it true that she had to learn how to do all those things for herself? Like cooking and cleaning and such?"

Slade sipped his coffee, trying to remember what Mariah had said about her sister. He couldn't recall if he'd ever heard Amanda's age. He'd never asked, and she'd never told him. As a matter of fact, every discussion they'd ever had about her sister had ended badly.

Mariah nodded. "It's true; she had to learn those things. Not at first, though. They spent several weeks teaching her how many steps it took to reach the kitchen and the linen closet, which door led to the washroom—things like that. Once she became comfortable with her surroundings, they started teaching her how to care for a home."

Mariah's grandmother spoke up, her feeble voice laced with pride. "Amanda's smart as a whip, Reverend Winston. And she's got spunk. She'll pass with flying colors."

"No doubt about that." The reverend chuckled. "I remember passing by the schoolhouse during recess. Didn't matter if they were playing chase or hide-and-seek or even climbing trees. She'd be right in the thick of things."

Slade shook his head. What were they talking about?

Sally sighed and reached over to pat Mariah's hand. "We're all so blessed," she murmured, a hint of moisture in her eyes. "Just think how hard it would be to go through life not being able to see the ones you love, the color of a sunset, or the blue in the sky. Amanda is truly a special young lady. Not many blind people have the opportunities you've given her, Mariah."

Slade sat there staring at Mariah in shocked silence as the truth sank in.

Her sister was blind.

CHAPTER EIGHTEEN

"Why didn't you tell me?"

Reverend Winston and Sally had long since gone. Mariah put her grandmother to bed, only to find Slade still waiting for her when she returned to the kitchen.

He stared at her over the rim of his coffee cup, his gaze simmering with something she couldn't quite identify. Anger? Remorse? Pity?

She started clearing the table. "You never gave me the chance." She picked up another plate. "You drew your own conclusions."

"Did you think me that coldhearted, that I wouldn't listen?"

"At first I did." She paused, studying him. "You didn't exactly show up here with my family's welfare in mind."

"I didn't know what I would find when I got here."

"We'll manage." She lifted her chin. "We always have."

"How?" A muscle jumped in his clenched jaw, the blue and purple bruises making his scowl even more ominous. "There's no way you can keep sending your sister to school on what I agreed to pay you. Schools like that aren't cheap."

"I'll get a better job when I get to Philadelphia."

"It won't be enough either." He scowled. "Maybe you and your grandmother should stay here."

And do what? Where would they live? *How* would they live? Slade couldn't afford to pay her a living wage forever.

Nothing had changed.

"It's too late for that."

"Why?" His brows drew together in a concentrated frown, daring her to explain.

Because I'm falling in love with you.

A love that was doomed because of the past. Instead of addressing the way she felt about him, she focused on his feelings. "Can you honestly say you've forgiven my father for what he did?" Her question hung in the air between them.

He didn't answer, and for a wild moment Mariah hoped he'd take her in his arms and tell her he loved her, that he'd forgiven her father, that he'd take care of her and never let her go. But he didn't. He just sat there, brow furrowed as if the whole conversation gave him a headache. Turning away, she dumped the dishes in the sink and poured hot water over them, her heart clamped tight around an aching sorrow.

"I can't stay. There's nothing here for me anymore."

"If that's what you want."

It's not what I want, she wanted to scream at him. But she kept silent, fighting back tears.

She heard him move, heard the scrape of his boots as he walked across the floor, the click of the door as he let himself out.

A single tear plopped into the hot, soapy dishwater.

"What do you think?" Mariah held up the flour-sack pinafore she'd made for Jim's younger sister.

Her grandmother smiled. "It's perfect. A bit of the old, made new. I can't see how Mrs. Denton could turn it down."

"That's what I'm praying for. I made Becky another pinafore and a long-sleeved dress too. It didn't take much cloth since she's so small."

She reached for the shirt she'd cut down from one of her father's better ones. "This should be just about right for Jim, don't you think? The other day when he let me mend the rip in his shirt, I cut a paper pattern from it."

"I hope you allowed plenty extra. That boy's growing like a ragweed." Her grandmother shook her head.

"I did." She examined a tear along the hem of one of her grandmother's nightgowns. Threading her needle, she stitched up the rip.

Slade rode into the yard and called for Jim. "Afternoon, ladies."

Mariah nodded, then pretended to be engrossed in her sewing. They'd said all that needed saying last night.

Her grandmother plucked a worn shirt off her pile of darning and eyed it critically. "Slade, this shirt is so far gone, I'm not sure if I'll be able to mend it properly."

"That's fine, ma'am. It's old as the hills." He shifted in the saddle.

She nodded at the folded stack in the basket beside her. "And your blue one's not much better. Mariah would be glad to make you up a couple of shirts if you'd like."

Mariah refused to look up, but her heart pounded. *Please refuse the offer.*

"I don't want to be a bother, ma'am. I'll just pick up a shirt or two next time I'm in the mercantile."

Mariah jabbed a needle into the nightgown in her lap. Bother indeed. He just didn't want to be beholden to her.

Jim came running out of the barn straight toward the porch. It hadn't taken him long to figure out that she'd have something waiting for him every day before he went home. He skidded to a stop near the steps.

"You've been working a full week now, Jim. How does it feel?" She put the last of Becky's new clothes in the bag and moved to the edge of the porch.

The boy glanced at Slade, clearly anxious for his approval. "Me and Buck got the stables all cleaned out, and next week we're going to start on the tack room."

"Good for you." She handed over the sack. "Here's

something to take home to your mother. And there's something extra on top for you and your sister."

Jim looked at her quizzically. "Miss Mariah, this ain't charity, is it? Pa says I can't accept charity."

Mariah silently asked for wisdom before she sat down on the steps. "Jim, do you know what charity is?"

"It's when somebody is poor, and other people feel sorry for 'em and give 'em stuff."

"Hmm. Well, that's sort of right. The Bible tells us that charity is love. And when we love people, we want to help them." She reached out and pushed his too-long bangs out of his face. "Since I love you and your family, I want to help you. I don't want you and your mother and sister to go to bed hungry. I want you to have clean clothes to wear and money to buy shoes. Because I love you. Because God loves you. That's what charity is."

He cocked his head to one side. "It don't sound to me like taking charity is such a bad thing, is it?"

Mariah shook her head. "It isn't. Because you know what? Someday you'll be able to help somebody. Then you'll be giving charity instead of receiving it. And that's what makes the world go round."

His face brightened. "I've got an old slingshot that I don't need since Mr. Slade made me a new one. Do you think I could give it to somebody who needs a slingshot?"

"I think that's a wonderful idea." She ruffled his hair.

He grinned, looking pleased that he'd found a way to help someone else. "Thanks, Miss Mariah."

*   *   *

"Ma." Jim hopped off the back of the horse and raced toward the cabin. "Ma."

Mrs. Denton hurried out to the front porch, sidestepping a rotten board between the door and the steps. The concern on her face softened, and a tiny smile flitted across her features. "Jimmy, quit your hollering. For a minute, I thought something was wrong." She glanced at Slade and nodded. "Evening, Mr. Donovan."

"Evening, ma'am."

"Look, Ma." Jim held out the sack.

A red flush crept up Mrs. Denton's face. "Mr. Donovan, I appreciate the job you've given Jimmy, but we can't accept charity. Please take these things back to Miss Malone with my apologies."

Slade shifted in the saddle, trying to think of a way to convince her to keep the food and the clothes.

"Oh, but, Ma, it's not charity." Jim pulled his new slingshot out of his back pocket. "Mr. Slade made me this slingshot. And now that I've got two, I can give my old one to someone who needs one. That way, I'm giving something too."

"Jimmy—"

"Please, Ma."

She glanced at Slade, clearly helpless in the face of his logic.

He shrugged. "He's got a point."

She plopped her hands on her hips and shook her head. "Oh, all right. Just this once, mind you."

"I'd better be getting on, ma'am. Got some errands to run in town." He tipped his hat. "I'll see you tomorrow, Jim."

Slade rode straight to the post office and picked up the mail. There was a letter for Mariah from her sister and one from his mother saying they were finally on their way. Mr. Thompkins had already turned out the lights by the time he made it to the mercantile, but the man wasn't one to refuse a customer. He invited Slade in with open arms.

Slade rode back toward the Lazy M, thinking about what Mariah had said to Jim about giving and receiving charity. He grinned as he fingered the brown paper-wrapped parcel tied to his saddle. Would she accept the same logic when he gave her the package he'd picked up especially for her?

Somehow he doubted it.

CHAPTER NINETEEN

"You didn't have to kill him."

"He knew too much." Emmit gave Red the same scowl his stepfather used to give him when he was being thickheaded. "And besides, I needed to make an example of him."

Red frowned. His brother had killed Slick to keep the others in line? When had he become so cold-blooded? He eyed Emmit, searching for some sign that killing Slick bothered him at all. On the one hand, he wanted to ask him, get it out in the open, but on the other, he was afraid of what Emmit might say.

Did he have any regrets about pulling the trigger? Had watching the man die kept him awake at night like it had

Red? Emmit looked the same as always. He went about his business same as usual. As if the incident were no more than butchering a hog on a cold winter's day.

While Red hadn't had a decent night's sleep in a week.

They were already skating on the outside of the law by stealing cattle. It was one thing to kill to defend yourself or your family, but to just shoot someone down in cold blood? Red's stomach pain returned full force, and he grimaced.

"One killing will lead to more. I don't like it."

"You knew the dangers when you agreed to work for Malone in the first place."

Red glared at Emmit. "Once, you said. We were gonna hit them once and then move on."

"Don't be stupid. Until Donovan came along, you were plenty happy to play ranch foreman and turn a blind eye to the rustling going on right beneath your nose."

Emmit was right. It had been so easy to get sucked deeper and deeper into his brother's scheme, and now there didn't seem to be any way out without killing or being killed.

He *had* been stupid.

Stupid for letting Emmit talk him into skimming cattle from the Malones in the first place. Stupid for not standing up for what was right. Stupid for not riding away long before now.

Emmit stared at him, his face hard and unreadable. "There are only two ways to get ahead in this world, Red. You either work for what you want, or you take it." He jammed his hat on his head. "I plan to take it."

✯　✯　✯

"Is she going to foal tonight?" a wide-eyed Jim asked, a kitten nestled in his arms.

Mariah and Jim watched Buck examine the mare.

"She might." Buck patted Dusty's bulging side before stepping out of the stall and latching the gate behind him. The mare stuck her head over the top and whinnied. "Her milk's come in, and she's been mighty fidgety all day."

Jim hung his head. "I wish I could stay here and help you, Buck."

"Don't worry, kid. She'll be fine." Buck gently slapped the boy on the back. "I bet you'll get to see a pretty little foal in the morning."

Jim's face brightened.

Mariah strode to the wall and pulled a lead rope from one of the pegs. "I'm going riding today, Buck. It's been ages since I've been out."

"I don't think that's a good idea. Not until the sheriff catches those rustlers."

"I imagine whoever stole those cattle are long gone."

"But until we know for sure—"

"Why don't you ride into town with me and Slade?" Jim interrupted, the kitten still clasped tightly in his arms.

"I don't know." Mariah doubted Slade would want her along. "Slade might be in a hurry, and I wanted to ride down the creek a ways before coming back."

"I'm not in any hurry."

She whirled around, her heart lurching at the sight of Slade's tall, broad-shouldered frame silhouetted in the barn door. She licked her lips. "I don't want to be a bother."

"You won't be. And like Buck said, I'd rather you ride along with us anyway."

"I'll get your horse." Jim took the kitten back to its mother and raced outside to the corral. He returned with her favorite horse.

Instead of heading directly into town, Slade led the way along the creek bank. They rode slowly, enjoying a cool breeze that had sprung up. About a mile from the ranch, they came to a grove of trees clustered on the banks of the creek.

"This has always been my favorite spot," Mariah said. "We used to have picnics here all the time. If Amanda and I didn't show up for supper, Grandma would know where to find us."

"You don't come here anymore?"

"Not very often." She let her gaze rove across the tranquil scene. "It's just not the same."

Soon the three of them arrived in town, Jim talking non-stop. They rode down Wisdom's main street as most of the shops closed up for the day. Mariah waved at Mr. Benedict and Mr. Tisdale as they locked up the bank. They passed the church, crossed the railroad tracks, and headed out of town.

Jim pointed toward a run-down shack in a grove of cottonwoods. "That's where I live, Miss Mariah."

Mariah stared in dismay at the weathered building—the chimney that tilted dangerously to one side, the broken windows, and the torn and patched roof. "That's the old Hancock place, Jim. Nobody's lived there in years."

"I know." He grinned. "But Mr. Tisdale at the bank said we could live here until Pa got back on his feet. And he ain't charging us rent either."

"I would hope not," Mariah said under her breath.

"It's better than living in the tent," Jim prattled on. "The tent leaks awful bad when it rains."

She gazed at the broken-down home, thankful for Mr. Tisdale's generous heart. "You're right, Jim. It *is* better."

Jim slid off Slade's horse. "I'll tell Ma you're here." He raced toward the house.

Mariah looked at Slade. A muscle jumped in his cheek, and she wondered if his own poverty-stricken childhood came to mind.

"I can't believe they're living in this . . . this—" she searched for the right word—"hovel."

Slade's mouth thinned into a harsh line.

"I wish you'd told me." She sighed. "I could have done something. More."

"You're doing all you can for now." He turned toward her, raw pain reflected in the depths of his blue eyes. "They're proud. Too much and they'd refuse to let Jim come out to the ranch. Then you couldn't help at all."

She nodded. What else could they do? *Help me, Lord,* she prayed silently. *Help me to say the right thing. To do the right thing. I don't want to offend Jim's parents, but they need more help than I'm giving.*

Jim came out on the porch followed by his mother. His sister clung shyly to her mother's skirts, watching them curiously. In spite of the poor condition of the house, the woman's patched dress was clean. It pleased Mariah to see that Becky wore one of the dresses she'd sent with Jim.

"Ma, this is Miss Mariah. She's the one who made Becky's dress." Jim grinned from ear to ear, proud to introduce them to his mother.

Mariah couldn't help but stare. The tired-looking young woman with wheat-colored hair didn't seem old enough to be Jim's mother. Mariah smiled. "Pleased to meet you, Mrs. Denton."

"Miss Malone." Her eyes darted toward the door of the cabin.

"Please, call me Mariah."

"I'm—Elizabeth. Thank you for the clothes and potatoes," she said, her voice barely above a whisper. She placed a hand on Jim's shoulder, a look of love softening her features. "I'm right proud of Jimmy."

"He's a hard worker, ma'am," Slade said.

Mariah bit back a smile as Jim squirmed with pleasure. "He's been a big help out at the ranch." Her gaze swung to Becky. "I'd love for you and Becky to visit sometime. My grandmother doesn't get out much nowadays and loves having company stop by."

Jim's mother shook her head. "Thank you, but I couldn't—"

A dark-haired man lurched into the doorway of the cabin,

216

and it seemed as if Jim, his mother, and his sister all shrank within themselves at the sight of him.

"What's all this yakking about?" he asked, his unkempt beard and hair sticking out in every direction. His stained undershirt appeared to have been slept in for several days. About the same age as Slade, he might have been handsome once, but hard drinking had taken its toll.

"James, Mr. Donovan brought Jim home."

The man scowled. "Get in the house."

Mariah watched helplessly as Jim's mother hurried the children inside, leaving her husband weaving drunkenly on the porch. He fixed his bleary gaze on Slade. "You treatin' my boy right, Donovan? He's doin' a man's job, ain't he?" he asked. "I'll take a switch to 'im if he ain't."

Mariah gritted her teeth. He wouldn't work but expected Jim to do a man's job. She wanted to tell the lazy drunkard what she thought of him, but a sharp glance from Slade warned her to hold her tongue. She hid her clenched fists in her skirts.

"He's doing a good job, Denton," Slade answered, his voice calm and even. He didn't sound the least bit angry. "He's turning out to be a hard worker."

"Ain't it about time he got paid?" The man rubbed his hands expectantly down his filthy undershirt and licked his lips. "He's been working out there at that ranch over a week now."

"I expect you're right. I don't have much money on me, though." Slade considered him. "Tell you what. How about

I give you a small portion of his wages? I'll make up the rest later, along with vegetables from the garden out at the ranch."

The man's eyes narrowed. Finally he reached up and scratched his chin through his scraggly beard. "How much you going to give me now?"

Mariah balled her fists more tightly.

"A nickel," Slade drawled.

Denton grunted. "T'ain't much."

"It's all I've got on me."

"All right. I reckon that'll have to do." He held out a grubby hand.

Slade rode forward and handed him the money. "I'll be here in the morning to pick up Jim."

He reined his horse around. The moment they were out of sight, Mariah hissed, "You know good and well he's not going to keep that money. He'll drink it up before morning."

"I know."

"Why did you give it to him, then?"

"If I had refused to give him a bit of money, he wouldn't let Jim come back. And worse, he would take his anger out on his wife and kids."

Fear clutched at Mariah. "You don't think he'd hurt them, do you?"

Slade pulled his horse to a stop. Mariah did the same, scanning his face.

"You saw how scared they were. He won't hesitate to hit them if he thinks it will make him feel better." He pushed his hat back and rested his forearm on the pommel of his saddle, his face level with hers. "But he won't feel any better. Not until he can control his drinking. He's too much of a coward to take care of his family and too ashamed of himself to let someone else do it. Of course, he won't admit that. He hides behind the fact that he's the head of the house, and they've got to do exactly as he says."

"Isn't there something we can do?"

"Not much more than we already are." He straightened. "Denton's in control here. He's calling the shots."

"We can pray." Mariah blinked away the sting of hot tears.

Slade's jaw hardened, and he gathered up his reins. "You can pray. Pray that Jim's pa will let him keep working. Pray that his guilty conscience won't get in the way of putting food on the table for his family. Pray that he doesn't decide to up and move before Mrs. Denton can save up a nest egg for herself and the children. You can pray, Mariah, but it won't do any good." He jerked his head back toward the run-down shack hidden in the grove of trees. "His kind don't respond to prayers."

"That's not true, Slade. They will if we don't give up on them." She could see the pain in his eyes, hear it in his voice.

"Pa didn't." His gaze bored into hers. "Ma prayed for him for years. He laughed at her. If he found out she'd taken us to church, he'd beat the living daylights out of her—and us, too."

"It doesn't have to be that way."

Suddenly the fight went out of him, and he shook his head. "I'm telling you it won't do any good, but you just keep on praying. In the end, it won't make any difference."

✳   ✳   ✳

Sorrow etched itself across Mariah's heart. She lay in bed, staring at the ceiling and pondering the situation with the Dentons. Surely she could do something more for Jim's family.

Imagine being afraid of your own father! The one man who should love and protect you. She couldn't make sense of it. She wanted to fix the problem but didn't know how.

What would she have done if her father had been like James Denton or Slade's father? Even though her mother had died when she was small, her father and grandmother had showered her and Amanda with love and affection all their lives. She'd never been afraid of either one of them.

"Lord," she whispered, "please take care of Elizabeth Denton and her children. Protect them and provide for them. And help James Denton to see the error of his ways. His family needs him. They need a godly man to be a husband and father. Help that family, Lord, in Jesus' name I pray. . . . And, Lord, help Slade see that people can change. Just because his father never turned his life over to You doesn't mean Jim's father won't. I'm trusting in You, Lord. Amen."

She'd ask Reverend Winston and Sally to spend extra time in prayer for the Dentons. And she'd enlist her grandmother's prayers as well. Where two or three agreed, God would intervene.

Rolling over, she stared out the window. She stilled as she heard the creak of the barn door. Frowning, she threw back the covers and padded to the window. Light shone through the cracks in the barn door.

Dusty. Buck had said she'd probably foal tonight. A bubble of excitement tingled through her. Without bothering to light a lantern, she found a heavy wrap and headed toward the barn, braiding her hair as she went. She eased the door open, its creak announcing her arrival. She spotted Slade leaning over Dusty's stall. He glanced around, an eyebrow quirked in question.

"Dusty?"

He nodded.

Easing inside, Mariah moved closer. "How's she doing?" She spoke softly, careful not to disturb the mare.

Slade left his position and eased over to where she stood. Resting his hands on his hips, he glanced back at the stall as Dusty whinnied. "She's getting there. Buck says we should have a foal before long."

"Wonderful. Jim's going to be so happy when he gets here in the morning." She gestured toward the barn door. "I'll make some coffee."

Slade squinted at her. "We didn't wake you, did we?"

"No. I wasn't asleep." She chewed her lip. "Worrying and praying about the Dentons."

Surprise registered on his face, but he only nodded.

A scrambling and a heave came from the stall. Slade turned away. "What's she doing?"

"Just standing up. Restless." Buck's calm, soothing voice wafted toward them. "Easy, girl. It's all right."

Mariah touched his arm. "I'll be back soon with that coffee."

He winked at her, and her stomach flipped. "Thanks. Looks like we're going to need it."

Slade watched as Mariah lifted the voluminous folds of her heavy wrapper and picked her way across the open space between the barn and the house. She hadn't bothered to lace up her boots, and they flopped around her ankles. She teetered, one boot almost slipping off, before she regained her footing.

He grinned, thinking of the package stored under his bunk. He'd meant to give it to her tonight after supper, but he'd lost track of time, and then Buck had called him to the barn to see about Dusty.

He'd take care of it tomorrow for sure—before he lost his nerve.

She stepped onto the porch, her long braid swinging across her back. He wondered what her hair would look like unbound and cascading over her shoulders, how it would feel to run his fingers through the thick, lustrous mass.

He jerked his mind back to the task at hand as she slipped through the kitchen door. Mariah wasn't that kind of woman. He'd never see her that way unless they were married. And with their past, it was unlikely that would ever happen.

Buck eased out of the stall. "Just giving her a little room. She'll settle down and have this foal a lot faster if we don't crowd her." He glanced at Slade. "What did Mariah want?"

"She saw us out here and figured out what we were doing. She's gone to make coffee."

"Sounds good. I could sure use a cup."

They waited in companionable silence. Dusty sniffed at some hay and started nibbling at it like having a foal was the last thing on her mind. In a few minutes, she grew restless again. She groaned and lay back down, stretching out on her side. When the contraction passed, she sat up but didn't try to stand again.

Slade sat on an old split-bottom chair and tilted it back against a post. Buck crouched down near the stall where he could keep watch on the mare.

Slade's thoughts went back to earlier in the day when he and Mariah had taken Jim home. "I've been thinking about offering James Denton a job. You think he'd take it?"

Buck squinted at him in the dim light cast by the three lanterns they'd lit. "Don't know. But it's worth a shot."

The mare whinnied and Buck stood, peering into the stall. "Her pains are coming a lot closer than before. It shouldn't be long now."

Dusty had stood, turned, and endured another round of pains by the time Mariah returned. She carried several mugs and a pot of coffee wrapped in a towel. Doling out the cups, she poured.

The barn door opened and Duncan stepped inside. "How's it going?"

Buck shook his head, a worried frown creasing his forehead. Dusty lay on her side, breathing heavily. "Not good. She should have had that foal long before now. Something's not right. If she doesn't give birth soon, we might have to help her."

Slade had already come to that conclusion but had decided to let Buck make the call. His brother had a sixth sense about these things.

"Oh no. I hope the foal's all right." Mariah flicked her nail against her teeth.

Dusty had another contraction. Buck set his mug on a post and went back to the stall. "Duncan, bring a couple of ropes and hobble her. Mariah, hold the lantern."

Duncan grabbed the ropes and did as Buck instructed. Then he held on to the halter and tried to keep the horse calm. They waited in tense silence as Buck examined the mare. She strained as another pain hit. Finally Buck glanced up at Slade. "I've got one foreleg. It's in position, but from the feel of it, it's big."

Dusty heaved as if to sit up, and Slade patted her neck, ready to help Duncan hold her down, or Buck if he needed more muscle for the pull. "Easy, girl. Easy." She lay back, panting, her nostrils quivering, eyes wide and frightened.

Buck worked to secure a rope around the foal's front feet, stopping each time Dusty had a contraction. "Okay, I've got it."

On the next pain, Buck pulled and the mare strained. Sweat drenched Buck, running down his forehead. He swiped it away.

"Any progress? Can you see the hooves?" Slade asked.

"Not yet," Buck panted. "It's stuck in there. There she goes again."

"Lord, help us."

A coughing spell hit Buck, and Slade scrambled to help. His brother wasn't strong enough to pull the foal by himself, and if they didn't do something, they'd lose both animals. "Here, let me."

"Oh, Lord, save this baby." Mariah's whispered prayers floated over the rustling, heaving tension.

Buck handed the ropes to Slade as Dusty groaned and gave a mighty push. Slade braced his boot against the mare and pulled, hoping the foal would ease out of the birth canal. He felt a slight movement, but not the easy one he expected.

Dusty relaxed and Slade let the ropes hang slack, gathering his strength for the next contraction.

"Please, Jesus."

"Get ready," Buck muttered, hands on the mare's distended stomach.

As soon as the mare groaned and pushed, Slade took a deep breath and pulled with the contraction. Finally he felt the foal start to move. He kept pulling, sweat dripping from the end of his nose.

"Is it coming?" Mariah asked.

Slade gritted his teeth. "Yes."

"Praise the Lord!"

Slade didn't slack up. With the foal halfway out of the birth canal, it was now or never. Buck joined him and the two of them gave one more heave, and the foal slipped right on out.

For a moment, no one moved, and the sounds of heavy breathing filled the barn. Buck cleared the foal's nostrils, and it lay prostrate for a moment, then shuddered, taking a deep breath.

Mariah broke the silence, her voice trembling. "It's breathing. Thank You, Jesus."

"What a beauty. No telling what he weighs." Duncan sounded relieved. They all were.

Dusty heaved herself up into a sitting position, and Buck started pulling the ropes off the colt. "Untie her. I think she can take it from here."

They stepped out of the stall as Dusty stood on trembling legs and turned to her baby. Nature took over, and she started taking care of business as if she'd done it a hundred times before.

Mariah gathered up the coffeepot and the mugs and stepped outside, Slade at her side. Buck and Duncan stayed inside, admiring the healthy colt.

As they breathed in the fresh night air, Mariah sighed. "I'm glad that's over. For a minute there, I thought we were going to lose both of them."

"We came close." Slade studied her. "You'll pray for just about anything, won't you?"

She appeared startled. "What do you mean?"

He jerked his head toward the barn. "You were praying to beat sixty in there."

"What else could I do? Just stand there and hope the foal would survive? The Bible says God sees the sparrows when they fall. I think He'd be concerned about a mare and her foal."

"Sorry, Mariah; I didn't mean any offense." He smiled. "I reckon you did the right thing. Your prayers might have saved them both. Who knows?"

"God knows." She returned his smile, then glanced away. "I'd better turn in. Good night."

"Good night. And thanks for the coffee."

Slade watched until Mariah was safely inside the house; then he looked up, his gaze focused on a distant star. Could her prayers have made a difference tonight? Did God really care about horses and see every sparrow that fell from the sky? If God loved that much, then maybe He cared for Slade as well.

He squinted at the star. A thought worth pondering.

CHAPTER TWENTY

Jim squirmed, tilting his head away. Mariah followed with her scissors, determined to get the lank mass out of his face.

"Hold still." She snipped several strands of his straw-colored hair.

He eased to the edge of the chair as if preparing to bolt any minute.

"Don't you dare get out of that chair, young man," she warned as she walked around to snip away at the bangs straggling over his eyes.

"It hurts." He gave her a sad puppy-dog look.

She frowned at him. "Now, Jim, you know good and well it doesn't hurt."

"But it does!" He looked ready to cry.

"What's all this caterwauling about?" Slade stepped out of the barn.

Jim whipped around. "Miss Mariah's trying to scalp me!"

Mariah placed both hands on her hips, trying not to grin. "Jim, you should be ashamed. I'm just trying to help you look better. Your hair is way too long."

Jim gestured at Slade. "Why don't you cut his hair? It's even longer than mine."

Mariah's gaze met Slade's amused one.

"Why don't you, Mariah?" he drawled.

"Because—because you're much too busy." She adjusted the sheet around Jim's shoulders, heart pounding. "Maybe some other time."

"I'm too busy too, Mariah. Buck said I could pet Midnight if I got my chores done." Jim tried to stand.

Mariah pushed him back down and grasped him by the chin. "Not so fast. Now, hold still. There'll be plenty of time to pet the colt before you leave."

"Aw, Miss Mariah."

"So you finally settled on a name, huh?" Maybe talking about the colt would keep him still for a few minutes longer.

"Buck let me choose." Jim grinned. "You like it?"

"Midnight." Mariah let the word roll around on her tongue. "It's a perfect name for a colt born in the middle of the night."

She snipped at his bangs until her handiwork satisfied her. Giving him a careful once-over, she pulled the sheet from his shoulders, ruffled his freshly cut hair, and smiled. "All right. Go."

He shot out of the chair so fast it tipped over. Without a backward glance, he raced toward the barn. Mariah shook her head and laughed. She reached for the chair, but Slade's big, callused hand closed over hers.

"You're scared."

She raised her gaze to his, pretending she didn't know what he meant. "Scared?"

He grinned. "Yeah. You're scared to cut my hair."

"I am not." Her heart fluttered and her laugh sounded shaky.

In one smooth movement, he turned the chair around, straddled it, and took off his hat. "All right. Cut away."

"You should be the one who's afraid." She snapped the sheet, letting the wind blow Jim's hair away on the breeze. "Afraid I'll cut off your ear."

"You won't."

She draped the sheet around his shoulders and stared at the back of his head, her fingers itching to touch the dark, curly strands of hair that reached to his collar. Slowly she reached out and let the thick, lustrous strands wrap themselves beguilingly around her fingers. She bit back a groan. He'd be lucky if she didn't shear him bald.

Resolutely she first ran a wide-toothed comb through his hair and then started snipping. She shaped up the back, thankful the mistakes her trembling fingers made would be hidden in the tumbling waves. Satisfied with the back of his head, she eased around to one side. He sat as still as a statue, his eyes closed, looking relaxed.

Her gaze traveled across his smooth forehead, over his dark, curving eyebrows, to the deep-brown lashes sweeping against his dusky skin. Tiny lines, formed from squinting against the sun, feathered out from his eyes, and a small scar graced his cheek. The bruises from his fight with Giff were still visible up close, but fading fast. Her heart gave an alarming tumble when her searching gaze landed on his lips, and she jerked her attention back to the job at hand.

It would never do to let her thoughts wander, or he might end up with a clipped ear after all.

Finally happy with her work over his ears, she moved in front and started on the hair falling over his forehead. He usually kept the wavy strands pushed back underneath his hat, but when she pulled them out straight with the comb, they were almost as long as Jim's had been.

She carefully combed and trimmed until the results pleased her. She combed his hair again and the wavy strands fell hither and thither. A snip here, one there. More on the left. She was so caught up in playing with his hair, she didn't realize he'd opened his eyes to tiny slits and was watching her.

She stared into his heavy-lidded gaze for a long, drawn-out moment, reliving the kiss they'd shared in the kitchen. Finally she found her voice. "I'm done."

"I'm not bleeding?" he asked, his voice a lazy drawl.

"No," she managed on a strangled laugh.

He straightened and stood, his broad back to the barn and any prying eyes. He closed the short distance between them, his gaze locked on hers. Her stomach flipped at the half wink he threw her way.

"Thank you for the haircut, Mariah. I think I enjoyed it as much as you did."

"Oh!" For a flustered moment, she almost wished she *had* cut off his ear.

Slade must have taken her grandmother's advice and bought some shirts. The haphazardly wrapped package he dropped by the kitchen door could only be Mr. Thompkins's handiwork. Mariah could always tell the difference in his wrapping and his wife's. Mrs. Thompkins tied pretty bows on her packages, while her husband just threw something together as fast as he could.

Hopefully the shirts would fit. Mr. Thompkins wasn't any better at sizing up his customers than he was at wrapping.

She carried the potatoes to the table, checking to make sure she hadn't left anything in the warming oven.

When Buck reached for a biscuit, Mariah slapped his hand. "Buck! That's not polite. Sit down and I'll have everything on the table shortly."

"But, Mariah, I'm starving."

"Well, you'll just have to starve until we say the blessing." Mariah brushed past him, placing the plate of biscuits on the table.

Mariah's grandmother came in, and Buck helped her to the table.

She patted his arm. "Thank you, young man. You'll make a fine husband to some lucky young woman one day."

Buck grimaced. He glanced up, and Mariah glimpsed the pain on his face. "No girl would have me, Mrs. Malone."

"You'd be surprised, Buck Donovan. You'd be surprised." Her grandmother smiled in a knowing way.

Mariah glanced at Slade, trying not to notice how nice his freshly cut hair looked in the lamplight. If she did say so herself, she'd done a fine job. "Did Jim make it home all right?"

The slight quirk of Slade's lips sent a spiraling warmness through her. "He was asleep before we got halfway to town. I had to carry him in front of me so he wouldn't fall off the horse." He swatted Buck's shoulder. "You shouldn't have worked the poor kid so hard, Buck."

"Me? The kid rushed from job to job all day. Wore me out trying to keep up. Wanted to get done so he could pet Midnight."

"What did his mother say about the canned beans?" Mariah asked.

"I told her they were in payment of a day's work well done. She didn't say anything, but I think she's getting used to the idea."

"Good. I'd hoped she'd take it that way. At least they'll have something to go with the rabbit Jim killed with his slingshot."

She glanced around, making sure she had everything on the table. "Supper's ready. Grandma, would you say the blessing, please?"

During the meal, Buck and Slade talked about the progress the men were making around the ranch.

Mariah poured coffee. "Has Sheriff Dawson said anything about the rustlers?"

"No." Slade shook his head. "I stopped in the other day, and he said no one had seen a thing. We won't know how many head we lost until the fall roundup."

"So you think whoever it was is long gone."

Slade took a bite of biscuit and chewed for a minute. "I don't know. But we can hope so."

"Buck, you up for another game of checkers?" her grandmother challenged.

"Yes, ma'am. Tonight's my night. I can feel it."

When they were finished, Mariah started clearing the table. Checkers had become a nightly ritual for the two of them. She was glad that Buck enjoyed spending time with her grandmother, but it left her more time alone with Slade. And that made her uncomfortable. She'd pulled away from him, guarding her heart and biding her time until she had to leave.

As Buck and her grandmother headed to the parlor, her grandmother's taunt floated back to her. "You know I'm going to beat your socks off."

Her gaze slid to where Slade slouched at the table, nursing a cup of coffee, one arm slung over the back of his chair.

When he glanced up and caught her staring at him, she lowered her head and continued clearing the table, careful not to look at him again.

If she did, he'd see in her eyes what she was too afraid to say. Her heart ached. This crazy longing would lead nowhere. She didn't have a future here. She didn't have a future with him. He felt sorry for Mariah and her family; that's why he'd asked them to stay.

Slade stood and moved toward the door. "I went by the mercantile."

"Yes, I saw your package." She wiped her hands on her apron. "Did Mr. Thompkins get the size wrong?"

He picked up the bulky parcel and turned to her, one eyebrow cocked, looking amused. And a little surprised. "Ma'am?"

"Your shirts. Mr. Thompkins never gets anybody's sizes right."

His mouth twitched. "He doesn't?"

"I guess they need altering. Just a word of warning. Make sure Mrs. Thompkins is in the store next time. She'll find you a better fit. I'll get my measuring tape." She hurried from the kitchen. As she rummaged in her sewing basket, she muttered, "What have I gotten myself into this time?"

When she'd so heedlessly volunteered to alter Slade's new shirts, it had not even crossed her mind that she'd have to touch him. Her trembling fingers clutched the measuring tape, and she pulled it out of the basket. She could do this. It would be simple. She'd done it lots of times before. First for her father, then for Cookie, Rio, and Jim. Measuring Slade shouldn't be any different.

Resolutely she marched back into the kitchen to find Slade leaning against the table, the package lying by his side.

She held up the tape. "What first? Your arms?"

He shrugged. "I suppose. You know what you're doing."

"All right. Hold out your arm."

He held it up, his elbow bent at an angle.

"No. Like this." She reached over and straightened his arm so that it stuck out level and true. "Now, hold still."

She took one end of the measuring tape and held it securely against his shoulder, unable to ignore the warmth that shot from underneath his cotton shirt into her fingertips.

Feeling his gaze on her, she peered at him from under her lashes. His gaze moved lazily over her face, and his arm drooped downward.

Mariah's thoughts came back to the matter at hand. "Hold your arm up."

Obediently he straightened it. "Yes, ma'am."

She walked her fingers down his shirtsleeve and across his muscled forearm, holding the tape in place. Her fingers slipped off the edge of his cuff, and the dark hairs at his wrist tickled her fingers. She stared at the contrasting texture of his tanned skin against hers. "Thirty-four inches."

"I could have told you that." His breath stirred the tendrils of hair at her temple.

She jerked the measuring tape away. "Why didn't you, then?"

He shrugged, a crooked grin on his face. "You didn't ask."

Mariah bit her lip. "You're right. I just assumed you wouldn't know."

"Just like you assumed this package is for me." He reached for the parcel.

Her gaze dropped to the bundle, face flaming. She'd made a complete fool of herself. "It's not?"

He shook his head.

She brightened. "It's for Jimmy. You bought Jimmy some new clothes."

"No."

"Buck?"

"No."

She frowned.

He held out the parcel. "You."

"I don't know what to say." Her wide-eyed gaze skipped from the parcel to meet his head-on.

He pushed the package toward her. "Say 'thank you' and open it."

"You shouldn't have."

"Mariah." He arched a brow at her, still holding the parcel out.

"Thank you." Hesitantly she took the bundle, laid it on the table, and reached for the string holding the brown paper together.

The wrapping rattled loudly in the silent kitchen. Slowly

she peeled back the layers, revealing a pair of brown leather boots.

"Oh, Slade, they're beautiful."

The leather gleamed, sparkling when she turned the boot in the lamplight. Twin rows of hooks marched downward in unison, the laces ready and waiting for the job of tightly securing the boots around her ankles.

"Did Mr. Thompkins get the size right?"

Her fingers trembled. "I think so."

She ran one finger along the intricate stitching, mentally calculating how much the boots cost and how long the money would keep Amanda in school. "I can't take these. They're too expensive."

He crossed his arms, determination in the set of his jaw. "I bought them because you need them, and I'm not taking them back."

"Slade—"

"Just take them," he cut her off, his voice low and husky. "Don't argue. Please. This once. Don't argue. You hear?"

Mariah fingered the boots. "I hear," she whispered. A tear escaped and rolled down her cheek.

Slade cupped her face in both hands, wiping her tears away with his thumbs. His eyes darkened as he slowly lowered his head to hers.

She couldn't breathe. If he let go, she'd melt into a puddle at his feet.

His lips brushed softly against hers, and her world spiraled out of control.

*　　*　　*

The moon reflected off the creek. Slade stared at the water, wondering how he'd gotten himself into such a mess. How could he want to send Mariah away from the Lazy M but at the same time be unable to resist the sweet temptation of her lips?

He jerked his hat off and raked a hand through his hair. What was it about her that drew him so? Her brown eyes sparkling like live coals when she grew angry or excited? Or how she bundled up goodies for Jim to take home every afternoon? Or how she fed that crazy cat day after day, hoping he'd let her pet him?

Or maybe the fact that she'd sacrificed her own comfort and the good of the ranch for her sister? It still rankled when he thought of how he'd talked about Amanda, only to discover that Mariah's sister couldn't see.

Blind! And he'd thought Amanda a selfish young woman who'd left Mariah to eke out a living while she flitted about in Philadelphia.

The land. That's all he'd ever wanted or needed. All her life, his mother had scraped by, struggling to provide the basic necessities for her children, living from hand to mouth. He'd grown up determined to make life easier for her and his sisters. If he had the land, he could accomplish the rest through hard work and sheer determination.

He jammed his hat back on his head. When he'd made up his mind to claim the Lazy M for his own, he hadn't given any thought to how Seth Malone would take care of his family. So when he'd arrived to find the man dead and his daughter left to care for her sister and an elderly grand-mother, he'd needed to adjust his thinking.

Now he found himself drowning in the depths of a pair of dark-chocolate eyes and lips as sweet as honey . . . and a desire to toss caution to the wind and protect her and her family as if they were his.

CHAPTER TWENTY-ONE

"JUST A LITTLE CLOSER," Giff whispered, a bloodthirsty tinge in his voice.

"Giff." Red glanced between the riders in the distance and Giff sighting along the barrel of his rifle.

"Buck's mine." Giff hunkered down, his rifle braced against a rock. "You take Slade. If they find these cattle, we're done for."

Stomach churning, Red slid his rifle out and settled into position, squinting along the barrel, bringing Slade into his sights. He didn't want to be any part of this, but he didn't have any choice. He'd made his decision when he'd let Emmit talk him into this foolhardy scheme in the first place.

The minutes ticked by. Sweat dripped down his face and his palms grew slick.

He prayed the cattle wouldn't stir. The time of day and the heat worked in their favor. Midafternoon and the cattle dozed in what little shade they could find in the box canyon behind Red and Giff. One movement, though—one bellow from a cow calling for her calf—and the Donovans would come investigate.

And Giff would start shooting.

"Easy. They're too far away." He swallowed, mouth dry as a tumbleweed in the dead of winter.

"Come on, Buck Donovan. I owe you."

Please, Giff, don't get trigger-happy now.

Red's hands trembled. Could he shoot a man in cold blood? He wouldn't have another option if Giff squeezed off a shot. He'd have to take out Slade before the man dove for cover or, worse yet, got away and rode for help. Fifty feet and they'd be within range.

He struggled to keep his gun steady as his finger tightened on the trigger.

Twenty-five feet.

The riders turned and followed the fence as it marched over the next hill and veered away from the canyon. Red's pounding heart slowed to a crawl as he watched them ride out of sight, saving their own lives and his sanity. He closed his eyes as relief washed over him.

Giff cursed.

Red glared at him. "Keep watch. I'm going to check on the cattle."

He walked away on unsteady legs, horrified at what he'd almost done. God wouldn't answer any prayer of his, but if He'd have mercy, Red prayed those brands had healed so they could get out of here before the choices in his past forced him to kill somebody.

*   *   *

"Miss Mariah!" Jim ran full tilt down the lane toward the porch, his legs and arms pumping as if a rabid coyote chased him. Mariah put her mending to the side and stood, moving to the edge of the porch.

"Who is it?" Her grandmother shaded her eyes against the afternoon sun.

"It's Jim." As he neared, his tear-streaked face came into view. A prickle of fear stabbed at her. "Oh, mercy, something's happened."

She picked up her skirts and ran to meet him. He fell into her arms, sobbing.

"Jim. Jimmy?" She held him at arm's length, her gaze raking him from head to toe. No blood. Arms and legs intact. "What's wrong?"

He took in great gulping breaths of air.

She knelt in the dirt and wiped his face with her apron. "What's happened? Is it your ma? Becky? What is it, sweetheart?"

Fresh tears filled his red-rimmed eyes as he flung himself

at her again and wrapped his thin arms around her neck. "It's Becky! Pa ran over Becky with a wagon—"

Fear pierced her heart. "Oh, Lord, help us. Where are they, Jim?"

"At Doc Sorenson's place, in town." He clung to her, his hoarse words muffled against her. "I don't want her to die, Miss Mariah. She can't die."

Mariah hugged him close. "Hush, Jim. It'll be all right. You'll see."

She rocked him back and forth in the dirt, praying that it *would* be all right.

✶   ✶   ✶

Slade saw Mariah and Jim huddled together the moment he and Buck topped the rise behind the barn. His heart slammed against his rib cage, and he kicked his mount into a hard gallop.

He slid off his horse before the animal came to a complete stop.

Jim flew at him, and Slade grabbed the boy. Jim cried so hard, Slade couldn't make out the hiccuping words tumbling out of him. He glanced at Mariah. She stood and swiped at the tears on her cheeks.

"It's Becky." Her chin trembled. "Their pa ran over her with a wagon."

Slade hugged Jim closer, searching Mariah's face. "Is she—?"

"They don't know yet. She's with the doctor."

Slade held Jim away from him, hunkering down to eye

level. "I want you to stay here with Buck, okay? I'll go into town and see how Becky is. Promise me you'll stay here?"

"Don't let her die, Mr. Slade. Please don't let her die." Tears cascaded down his cheeks.

Slade clutched the frantic child to his chest once more, fighting tears of his own. "I won't, Jimmy. I won't."

He handed Jim over to Buck.

Mariah touched his arm. "I'm going with you."

"All right." He took in her determined, tearstained face. "Take Buck's horse."

They rode hard and fast and arrived at Doc Sorenson's to find Elizabeth Denton hysterical and James Denton staring at the blood on his hands. Doc Sorenson immediately pulled Mariah into the back room and shut the door.

The moans finally subsided late into the night, but Slade didn't know which was worse: hearing Becky alive and in pain or not hearing any sound from beyond the closed door of Doc Sorenson's back room and fearing the worst. Mariah emerged several times to heat water or collect clean bandages, linens, whatever the doctor needed, before disappearing into the back room again. Her pale face and bloodless lips told him it was bad.

He forced himself to lean against the wall, out of the way but close by in case the doc needed him.

A lone lantern on the table cast an eerie glow around the kitchen. Elizabeth Denton slumped with her head pillowed in her arms on the hardwood table. She'd finally cried herself to sleep.

James Denton sat on a straight-back chair in the corner, his head cradled in his hands. His own moans of despair had echoed around the room every time the sound of Becky's pain drifted through the door.

Slade couldn't find it in himself to feel sorry for Jim's pa. Instead, he wanted to give the man a good beating. They'd finally pieced together why Denton had been driving a wagon in the first place. He'd scraped together a few dollars doing odd jobs around town and had spent it all at the local saloon. The saloonkeeper had kicked him out as soon as he ran out of money, and he'd taken off in the first wagon he found tied up at the mercantile.

The low murmur of Doc Sorenson's voice reached them from beyond the closed door. A whimper of pain followed. Becky's whimpers brought back painful memories of his own childhood, of his sisters' cries after their pa had taken his anger out on all of them. Unable to stand it anymore, he bolted for the front porch.

Outside, he took huge gulps of the fresh night air, trying to understand why God allowed this to happen. That little girl shouldn't have to suffer the consequences of her father's actions. Three or four years old at the most, she'd never done anything wrong.

He gripped the porch railing.

The door opened, and James Denton lurched outside and down the porch steps. But this time grief, not whiskey, made his steps haphazard. Too weary to move, Slade stayed slumped against the porch.

Denton moved out into the yard and raked both hands through his hair. He stood for a moment with his head bowed before raising his face to the darkened sky. A shaft of moonlight played across his bearded jaw, and the wetness of tears glittered on his cheeks.

"Oh, God," he rasped, "I'm sorry. Lord, You tried to tell me. You warned me over and over to stop drinkin'. Lord, I'm tired of runnin'. Tired of drinkin'. Tired of seeing Elizabeth working so hard to make ends meet."

His hoarse voice thickened with emotion until Slade could barely make out his words.

"Please, Lord. Just make Becky well. I'll do whatever You want. I'll quit drinkin', Lord. I'll go to church. I'll do anything if You'll heal my baby. I'm so sorry, Lord. Please forgive me."

Sobbing, Denton slumped to his knees and bowed his forehead to the ground, begging God to spare his daughter's life—the life he'd almost snuffed out in his drunken stupor.

Slade turned away and ran a weary hand over his own face. He stared out into the night, a curtain of dread sweeping over him.

What would James Denton do with his promises if Becky died?

CHAPTER TWENTY-TWO

THE PINK HUE of the rising sun peeked over the horizon as Slade made his way back into the doctor's kitchen. Mariah turned from the stove, coffeepot in hand. Dark circles under her eyes made them look bigger and more vulnerable than ever.

"Coffee?" she asked, her voice not much more than a raspy whisper.

He accepted the cup she offered. "How's she doing?" he asked, sitting down and sipping the bitter brew.

She sank into one of the chairs beside him, shoulders slumped, exhaustion in every line of her body. None of them had slept. Who could sleep when a child's life hung in the balance?

"Doc let James and Elizabeth in to see her a few moments ago. She doesn't even know they're there, but at least they can touch her, know she's alive." Her tear-filled gaze met his. "She's so tiny. I don't think she'll make it. The wagon wheel went across her chest, over one shoulder, and grazed the side of her head. Doc thinks she might have some broken ribs, maybe even a broken collarbone—"

Tears overflowed, running down her cheeks, and she reached up to wipe them away with her apron. A vise squeezed his chest at the anguish on her face. Great, gulping sobs spilled out of her as she released the tension and fear she'd bottled up through the long, dark night.

Slade stood, pulled her from the chair and into his arms, his hands splayed across her back, willing his own strength to shore her up. A tight desire to take away her pain gripped his chest. But there wasn't anything more they could do. Only time would tell if Becky would live. He closed his eyes, breathing in the sweet aroma of Mariah's rose-scented hair, and let her cry enough tears for both of them.

Slowly her sobs subsided. A weary sigh escaped her, and she whispered against his shirt, "I've prayed and prayed for the Lord to spare her. I don't have any strength left to pray."

Slade stared at a spot on the wall, his hand stilled against her back, trying to make sense of the thoughts swirling in his head. James had prayed for his daughter. Mariah was praying. Half the town, those who'd heard, would be praying.

But he hadn't uttered one single, solitary prayer.

"If God cares about Becky, why'd He let Denton run over her in the first place?"

She pulled away and wiped at her cheeks. A sad little smile turned up the corners of her mouth. "God doesn't keep us from trouble; He keeps us through it."

"Not always."

"No, not always. I don't know if He'll heal Becky or take her on to be with Him. All I can do is pray He spares her. But if He does take her, I'll keep praying. Only then I'll be praying for Elizabeth and James and Jim."

Slade shook his head, trying to make sense of her logic. He latched on to the one thing that didn't make any sense at all. "James? How can you pray for him? All this is his fault."

"Can't you see how he's hurting? He'd do anything to undo what he's done."

"Right now he feels that way. But when she's better, he'll go right back to his drinking."

"Maybe. Maybe not. If we help him, pray for him, and come alongside him in his time of trouble, who knows what good can come of this?"

Slade wanted to argue with her. He wanted to tell her she prayed for something that could never be. But he didn't. He saw the exhaustion in her face, and why argue when Becky lay in the next room, fighting for her life? He clenched his jaw and kept his thoughts to himself.

When Doc Sorenson walked out of the sickroom, they both looked up. The doctor took off his horn-rimmed glasses and ran a hand over his face before pinning his gaze on Mariah. "Is that coffee I smell?"

Mariah started toward the stove, but Slade pushed her into a chair. "Sit. I'll get it."

"How's Becky?" Slade poured the doctor a cup of coffee and handed it over.

"She made it through the night. As always, that's a good sign. If there isn't any internal damage, she might make it now."

"Praise the Lord," Mariah said.

The doctor glanced at Slade. "Mr. Donovan, could you head over to the parsonage and let Reverend Winston know what happened? I imagine he'll want to pray for the girl and her parents."

"Be glad to." Slade reached for his hat.

"I'm going to try to get some sleep. Can you stay awhile longer, Mariah? I don't want to leave the Dentons alone with Becky."

"Of course."

"Wake me if there's any change." He took another sip of his coffee and shuffled toward the stairs leading to his bedroom.

✷　　✷　　✷

"Mr. Donovan! This is a surprise. Come in." Reverend Winston held the door wide.

Slade nodded. "Reverend."

"What can I do for you this early?"

"Doc Sorenson sent me over. James Denton ran over

his little girl with a wagon yesterday, and Doc thought you might want to know."

"I heard. I was on my way over there." The reverend grabbed his hat and stepped outside. "You headed back to Doc's?"

Slade nodded.

"I'll walk with you."

Some of the residents of the small town began to stir as Slade and the preacher headed toward the doctor's. Several men loitered outside the sawmill, Slaughter among them. Slade nodded at the sawmill owner.

"Howdy, Reverend," one of the men called out.

"Morning, Sam." Reverend Winston shook the man's hand and dipped his head in greeting at the others.

"Reverend, you hear about that poor little girl over at Doc's?" Sam scratched his leathery cheek and squinted at the pastor. "The one whose pa ran over her with a wagon?"

Reverend Winston nodded. "I'm on my way over there now to see if there's anything I can do. But I'm afraid all any of us can do is pray. The rest is up to the Lord and Doc Sorenson's skilled hand."

"But, Reverend, a man like that oughta be run out of this town. Wasn't he drunk at the time?"

"Stays drunk all the time," someone else volunteered.

"He ain't fit to raise young'uns." Sam spit a stream of tobacco juice, an angry glint in his eye. "And I heard he's been beating on his wife and the young'uns too."

A murmur of assent ground out among the men present.

Slade sized up Sam. Clearly he cared more about creating trouble than finding a solution to the problem. "And what's going to happen to Mrs. Denton and the children if you run James Denton off?"

Sam puffed out his chest. "And who might you be?"

Reverend Winston stepped in. "Excuse me, Sam. I didn't know you two hadn't met. This is Slade Donovan, the new owner out at the Lazy M. Mr. Donovan, this is Sam Butterton."

"I heard Mariah sold out. Probably the best thing that could happen. Ain't no woman can run a ranch properly."

"You didn't answer my question."

Butterton scowled. "About the woman and her kids?"

Slade gave a short nod.

"How should I know?" The man's face grew flustered. "I've got my own family. I can't be running off seeing about somebody else's."

"You'd all do well to remember that, if you decide to run somebody out of town." Slade let his gaze roam around the body of men before he stalked away. Reverend Winston fell into step beside him.

"Well done, Donovan. Sometimes people get carried away trying to do what they think is right, and they don't even realize what they're saying. Not that I agree with Denton's drinking and all. But I'd like to help the man, not try to railroad him out of town."

"People like Butterton aren't interested in helping people. They'd rather shift 'em off on down the line and let somebody else deal with them. Once they're out of sight, they're out of mind, and good citizens don't have to worry about them anymore."

Reverend Winston glanced at him. "You sound as if you've had some experience with that type before."

"You might say that." He rubbed the back of his neck. "Is Wisdom wrapped up with folks like that?"

It would be too much to hope he'd left that kind back in Galveston.

"We have our share. But mostly they're good Christian folks. Folks who want to do right by their neighbors. Even if you hadn't spoken up, cooler heads would have convinced Butterton that running Denton out of town wasn't the way to solve the problem. He goes off half-cocked sometimes, but once he's on your side, you've got a friend for life." The preacher slapped him on the shoulder. "You'll be glad you put down roots here, I promise."

The brisk walk to the doctor's house cooled Slade's anger. He didn't regret speaking his mind and giving Butterton something to chew on, and he'd never been known to skirt around an issue. Maybe the reverend was right and folks here did know how to show compassion and give someone a hand up when they needed it.

Mariah and Mrs. Malone hadn't turned their backs on the Dentons. They'd done all they could to help. He'd thought it was just because of Jim and Becky. Most people would go out of their way to help a child. But Mariah had said she was praying for James Denton, too, the very man who'd caused all the trouble to start with. But James had asked forgiveness for what he'd done, so could there be hope for him after all?

"Reverend? There's something you should know." Slade frowned, thinking about Denton's prayer during the middle of the night. "Last night, Denton promised God he'd stop drinking if God would save his daughter's life."

A smile creased Reverend Winston's face. "That's a start. But it might not be enough."

"Why?" Slade stopped, his attention focused on the preacher. Was the man thinking what he'd been thinking?

"Will Denton keep his promise if Becky dies, or will he be worse than before? I've seen folks grow bitter when God doesn't answer their prayers just the way they see fit. If she dies, he might even blame God instead of himself, when the whole thing was his fault. Making promises like that isn't a good idea for a saint or a sinner. Because when they backfire, even a saint can feel like God has let them down."

The preacher's words landed like well-placed blows to Slade's midsection.

He'd done that. He'd blamed God and Mariah's father for every ill that had ever befallen his family. Each catastrophe had been one more nail in the coffin that buried his faith and trust in God. He'd hardened his heart against God as his father's drinking grew worse. He'd determined to stand up for himself and not depend on anyone when he couldn't protect his mother from his father's fists. He'd turned his back on his mother's teaching when he found his father dead in an alley in Galveston.

God didn't care about them, wasn't going to take care of them, and they'd had way too few of the good folks of Galveston to lend a helping hand. No, if anybody was going to see that they survived and prospered, it would be Slade himself. So he'd blamed God at every turn.

Buck didn't die.

Slade's steps faltered, and he hung back, letting Reverend Winston go inside.

It had never occurred to him to thank the Lord that Buck's life had been spared, that he'd lived. He knew without a shadow of a doubt that if his brother had died, he would have rushed head over heels to *blame* God.

How could he be so quick to cast blame when he'd never even considered giving thanks?

Slade and Mariah headed back to the ranch as soon as Sally arrived and took Elizabeth Denton under her wing. Becky had regained consciousness and asked for her ma, and Doc Sorenson had hopes she'd make a full recovery. But it was still going to be touch and go for several days.

Slade kept his attention on Mariah as she swayed in the saddle. She'd been up all night and could barely stay awake. He hadn't slept any either, but he was used to long days and nights without sleep.

Her lashes fluttered against her cheeks.

"Mariah?"

"What?" She jumped. "What's wrong?"

"Nothing." He pulled her horse to a stop and tilted her chin up, forcing her to look him in the face. "Do you think you can make it home?"

She nodded, eyes heavy-lidded, weariness evident. She shook her head and blinked several times. "I'll be fine. I need to check on Grandma, and we need to let Jim know how Becky is doing."

"All right. Just hold on. We'll be home soon."

Slade set a slow, steady pace the rest of the way home. He caught Mariah smothering yawns, but she managed to stay awake until they got there.

Mrs. Malone waited on the porch. Slade helped Mariah dismount, and her grandmother embraced her, worry written all over her lined face. He figured she'd spent a sleepless night along with the rest of them.

"How's Becky?"

"Better. Doc thinks she's going to be all right."

"Praise the Lord. I've been praying for that child all night."

"Where's Jim?"

She motioned toward the creek. "Down there. Poor boy. Buck and I couldn't get him to eat a bite of breakfast."

Slade found Jim seated on the creek bank, his knees drawn up to his chin and his scrawny arms wrapped tightly around his legs. Early morning sunlight filtered through the trees. Shadows danced across the water, and a slight breeze ruffled the leaves overhead. But Jim stared straight ahead, not seeming to notice his surroundings. Slade hunkered down beside him.

"I think Becky's going to be all right. Doc's taking good care of her."

Jim flung a rock into the creek. "I hate my pa."

Slade sighed. "Don't hate him. It's not worth it. Hate will just eat you up inside, and you'll only become bitter."

"But it's never going to get any better. Pa is just going to keep on drinking and being mean and hurting Becky and Ma. I wish he was dead." Jim swiped at his face, smearing dirt and tears across his cheeks.

Slade's heart twisted. He'd said much the same thing to Mariah only hours before. He could see so much of himself in Jim's face, in his words. Many times he'd wanted his own father dead. But when he *had* died, Slade wanted him back. No matter how mean when drinking, the man had still been his father.

"No, Jim, you don't. Your pa prayed last night. He said he wasn't going to drink anymore. He told God he would do better."

Jim sniffed. "Do you think he means it?"

Slade shrugged. "Miss Mariah thinks he does. And Reverend Winston's praying for him too."

"Do you think he'll do better?"

Slade scraped a hand over his mouth. How could he tell the boy what he thought when he didn't even know himself? "I think your pa can do better if we help him."

"Could we pray for Becky and my pa?"

A hollow spot of dread bottomed out in Slade's stomach. "I'm not much of a praying man, Jim, but if you want to, I'll stand by you."

"Will you say something?" Jim hung his head. "I don't know how to pray."

Me neither.

But if one simple prayer would help the boy get through this, Slade would attempt it. For Jim's sake. He stared at the rippling creek, his heart hammering with what he was about to do. "Lord, Jim and I aren't very good at this, so we ask that You forgive us if we don't do it right. We're asking You to heal Jim's little sister, Becky. And also, Lord, Jim's pa promised he'd stop drinking. Show us what to do to help him keep his promise. Amen."

Jim squinted up at Slade. "Do you think I should say something too?"

Heart still pounding from the first real prayer he'd said in years, Slade nodded. "If you want to."

"I think I'd better," Jim whispered. He bowed his head. "Lord, this is Jimmy Denton. I know You've heard about how sick my little sister is, and I don't want her to die. Can You please help her to get well? And help my pa, too. He's not so bad when he's sober, but he's powerful mean when he's been drinking. Help me to be good so he won't get mad and want a drink. I reckon that's about all, Lord. Amen." Jimmy peered at Slade, his tearful gaze unsure. "How'd I do?"

"I think you said a mighty fine prayer." Slade stood. "Now, how about some breakfast? Mrs. Malone said you hadn't eaten anything, and the last thing Becky needs is for you to get sick."

"Okay. I feel a lot better now that I've prayed, don't you?"

"I sure do." He ruffled the boy's hair. "Come on, let's go get something to eat."

Jim raced on ahead, Slade right on his heels.

Halfway up the path, Slade turned. Nothing had changed. Sunlight still danced across the water, a bird twittered in the trees somewhere off to his right, and a breeze stirred the leaves over his head. Nothing had changed, but somehow everything had changed.

He bowed his head.

I'm a little late doing this, Lord, but thank You for sparing my brother's life.

CHAPTER TWENTY-THREE

Five days after Becky's accident, Jim skidded to a stop outside the barn door. "Miss Mariah said I could go to the church picnic today."

"That sounds like a good idea." Slade threw a forkful of hay into one of the stalls and moved on to the next. A quick glance revealed that Buck had cleaned that one and left a bucket of water inside.

"You going?" Jim cocked his head to one side, chewing his bottom lip.

"To the picnic?"

"Nah. To church."

"Hadn't planned to."

"Please?"

"You scared?" Slade leaned on the pitchfork and eyed the boy.

"Yeah." He scuffed the dirt. "I've never been to church. Pa wouldn't ever let us go."

The barbed memory of his own father pricked Slade. "Why not?"

"Dunno." The boy shrugged. "But he said he'd better not catch us in church. He'd wallop us good if he did."

Slade forked some hay into the last stall. "I don't think your pa would mind now that Becky's been hurt. I think he'd be mighty pleased if you went."

"But will you go too?" Jim asked. "Please."

He studied the boy for a moment before putting the pitchfork up. "All right. I guess it won't hurt."

In the bunkhouse, Slade grabbed his only good shirt and shook out the wrinkles. It had been years since he'd been in church. And he wouldn't be going today if Jim's pleading hadn't been his undoing.

His pa had beaten the desire to attend church out of him much the same as Jim's father had done. A hot flash of anger swept over him, and he jerked the shirt on, buttoning it with quick, determined moves. His father had been dead for years. If he wanted to go to church, it was nobody's business but his own.

Jim stuck his head in the bunkhouse and hollered, "You coming? Everybody's ready and waiting."

"I'm coming."

He strode across the wide expanse of swept dirt toward the wagon waiting in front of the house. Cookie stepped off the porch, carrying one of the rockers. Slade almost laughed out loud. Cookie wore black pants, a white shirt, and a black string tie.

The cook scowled at him. "What's so funny?"

"Nothing." He motioned to the rocker. "What's that for?"

"Mrs. Malone likes to have her rocker at the picnic. Not anyplace for her to sit."

Slade took the rocker and put it in the buckboard.

Cookie hefted himself into the driver's seat. "Help the ladies, you young whippersnapper, and we'll be on our way."

"Yes, sir."

Slade helped Mrs. Malone up onto the seat beside Cookie, then handed Mariah up next to her. It was a tight squeeze with all three of them on the seat, but Mrs. Malone and Mariah were both small boned. Slade sat on the back of the wagon, and Jim hopped up beside him.

Mrs. Malone kept up her usual monologue all the way into town, so Slade let his mind wander. Why had his father been so intent on keeping them out of church? Because the preacher spoke out against drinking, and his pa hadn't been willing to quit? Or had there been something more?

His mother always said she'd found peace and safety in church. Slade could understand that. She'd had precious little peace or safety at home when his father was alive.

All too soon, they drew up in front of the whitewashed church, the boards gleaming in the bright sunshine. Slade hopped down and helped the ladies from the wagon. Cookie clambered to the ground and offered his arm to Mariah. Slade held out his arm to Mrs. Malone. Jim stood beside Mariah, being properly quiet and respectful.

"You coming inside today?" Mrs. Malone asked Slade as they walked slowly toward the church, Cookie, Mariah, and Jim trailing behind them.

"I thought I might." He cleared his throat. "Jim wanted to come, but he was a little scared." He didn't tell her he was pretty nervous himself.

"'And a little child shall lead them.'"

"What was that, ma'am?"

"Nothing." She smiled. "Just something out of the Bible."

Mrs. Malone dragged him down the aisle halfway to the front of the church. The farther they walked, the more self-conscious he became. Glancing around, he couldn't figure out what had made his mother feel better. Sure, the church smelled nice and clean, and somebody had put a bouquet of wildflowers on a table up front. But other than that, he didn't feel any different than he did on the outside.

If anything, he felt a sight worse.

He settled in, ignoring the curious stares of the congregation, his eyes straight ahead, focused on the front. By the time they'd made it through the opening prayer and two congregational hymns, his heart had stopped its vicious pounding in his chest.

Mrs. Winston motioned to the song leader from her perch on the piano stool and whispered something to him.

The man turned toward the congregation. "Mariah, it's been requested that you honor us with a song this morning."

Mariah rose from the seat and glided toward the piano, her skirts swishing against the pews as she passed. She faced the crowd, her attention focused over Slade's head, toward the back door. Mrs. Winston played the opening strains of a vaguely familiar hymn, and Mariah started singing.

A hush fell over the congregation.

The preacher's wife had been right. Mariah *could* sing. She stood beside the piano, her dark-brown skirt and cream-colored blouse showing off the light-brown hair she'd swept to the top of her head.

Jim leaned over and whispered, "She sure can sing, can't she?"

Slade nodded.

Her gaze met his, and she tripped over the words for a moment but then caught herself and finished without another flaw. As she made her way back to the pew, she wouldn't even look at him. Why? She'd been wonderful. Had the slight mishap at the end embarrassed her that much? When she sat down between Jim and her grandmother, Slade stole another glance at her.

She faced forward as if unaware of his attention. He studied the side of her face, the way her hair flowed smoothly back from her temples, the tiny jut of her eyebrows, then the gentle tilt of her nose, on down to her full lips.

As he watched, a tint of red crept up from her high lace neckline and covered her cheeks. He bit back a grin and faced forward, amused that it took so little to bring that blush to her cheeks.

Reverend Winston stood behind the pulpit, and Slade tried to concentrate on the preacher. Maybe the sermon was what made his mother enjoy church so much.

"I'm going to take my text from Luke 6:37 today. 'Judge not, and ye shall not be judged: condemn not, and ye shall not be condemned: forgive, and ye shall be forgiven.'"

The preacher placed his hands on either side of the podium and regarded the congregation. Slade swore the reverend's attention lingered on him longer than on anybody else.

The nervous tic in Slade's jaw started. Had Reverend Winston decided to preach this sermon on forgiveness because Slade had come to church this morning? Did he know about what had happened between the Malones and the Donovans? After all, Mariah and Sally Winston were good friends. Had Mariah confided in the preacher and his wife, even though she'd made him promise not to slander her father's memory?

Reverend Winston slapped the podium with his open hand and Slade jumped. "I tell you, if you're not willing to forgive those who wrong you, you are none of His."

Was Reverend Winston asking him to forgive Mariah's father? And what if he did? The direct result of forgiveness would be to turn the ranch back over to Mariah and her grandmother and walk away.

He crossed his arms and glared at the preacher, letting Reverend Winston make his case.

* * *

After church, the entire assembly headed to the creek for the picnic. Cookie rode with Doc Sorenson in the doctor's buggy, and Slade drove the team. As he slapped the reins against the horses' backs, Slade considered all the preacher had said. And realized none of it mattered now. He couldn't change his mind if he wanted to. Not with his mother and sisters just days away from arriving.

He hauled back on the reins, and the wagon jolted to a stop. He set the brake and jumped to the ground. Jim tumbled out of the back.

"Here, young man, help me down from this contraption." Mrs. Malone held out one hand to Jim. The boy looked at Slade, and he nodded permission.

Once on solid ground, she pointed with her walking stick. "Put my rocking chair over there under that tree. After they say the blessing, you can bring me a plate. Mariah will fix it. And I want some of Gertrude Riker's lemonade."

Slade escorted Mrs. Malone across the uneven ground to where Jim placed the rocker.

Jim fidgeted. "Can I go now?"

Mrs. Malone sank into her rocker and shook her cane at him. "You can, but don't forget about me."

While Jim raced off to join a couple of other boys, Slade moved toward the wagon, intent on seeing to the horses.

"Slade?"

"Ma'am?"

She gave him that peculiar look of hers that said she was old enough to say what she wanted and get away with it. "Reverend Winston's sermon on forgiveness shook you up pretty good, didn't it?"

He flushed.

"No use denying it." She waved a bony hand at him. "You squirmed like a bug caught in a jug of syrup all morning. I declare, I reckon you were more fidgety than little Jim."

Slade couldn't disprove what she said, so he just stood there, watching the women as they hurried back and forth toting baskets of food and arranging it all on makeshift tables made out of boards placed on sawhorses.

"You know, when you showed up demanding the entire ranch, I told Mariah the land legally belonged to you and your family, and we just had to accept that fact. But in my heart, I questioned why God would let something like this happen to our family."

"Mrs. Malone—"

"No, let me finish. I've come to realize that possessions aren't everything. But souls are." She held his gaze, her expression intent. "Maybe the Lord sent you here for a reason. Maybe He wanted you to find peace with Him and accept Him as your Savior."

His heart jumped at the very words he'd been contemplating all morning. *How do I find that peace?* he wanted to ask. Instead, he tucked the still, small voice inside. "I don't think the Lord has any use for someone like me, Mrs. Malone."

"The Lord has use for everybody. That's why He died on

the cross for our sins. He loves us all, no matter what we've done or who we are. All you have to do is ask Him to forgive you for your sins and ask Him into your heart. He's the only one we can trust to never betray us or fail us." She paused. "You remember that, son."

"All right, ma'am, I will."

"Now, go on. I plan to sit right here in the shade and take a little nap before Mariah catches me."

Slade walked away and watched from a distance as the church ladies spread out platter after platter of fried chicken, salted ham, vegetables, biscuits, corn bread, cakes, and pies, laughing and talking among themselves.

The men stood around in small groups, talking about ranching and farming or anything else that came to mind, while children's laughter rang out from the shallows of the nearby creek.

Cookie stood off to the side, speaking with a plump older woman. He held himself erect as if his neck and back didn't bother him a bit. Slade grunted. The Lazy M cook might be more spry than he'd let on.

Slade wondered if he could ever feel a part of the people of Wisdom, if he would ever belong. Reverend Winston, Doc Sorenson, and John Riker had made him welcome. But he still felt like an outsider.

Maybe he needed that peace Mrs. Malone talked about. Peace that no matter what happened, everything would be all right. That God loved him even though Slade had turned his back on Him all these years.

He sought out Mariah. She reached up and tucked a strand of hair behind one ear. Somebody said something, and a round of merriment burst from the group. Tightness gripped his chest at the carefree look of happiness on Mariah's face. Would she find that kind of happiness when she left here? Would she find friends somewhere else she could laugh with so freely?

And would his own family ever be accepted so fully into this community? His mother and sisters would attend church, and eventually they'd be accepted. But what about Buck and himself? Both loners, they'd never felt at home in Galveston because of their father's reputation. Would it be any different here?

His roaming gaze collided with Mariah's. Her eyes sparkled with mirth, and her face had the rosy glow of simple contentment. But then her smile shimmered and died, and she turned away.

A gut-wrenching sadness filled him.

He'd done that to her. He'd taken away her smile. Every time she saw him, his presence reminded her of her loss. And how much more she'd lose when she left.

His jaw clenched.

The ranch belonged to him and his family. He couldn't help it if her father had stolen the gold that bought the land. And he wouldn't let some two-bit preacher or a woman with hair like molasses make him feel guilty for claiming something that belonged to him.

The camaraderie of the close-knit community closed in

on him, and he pivoted, taking long strides toward a gap in the trees that led to the creek. He shouldn't have come. He didn't need to get closer to Mariah, close to these people who loved her, or close to God, who demanded he forgive.

Because forgiveness might force him to give back the ranch and ride off. And he didn't know if he was strong enough to do that.

Mariah watched Slade disappear into the shadows, an aching hurt in her chest. Why did things have to be this way? Why hadn't he come to Wisdom as an ordinary cowhand? Why couldn't she have fallen in love with him without the bitterness and hurt from the past?

She sighed. He wouldn't have come here at all if not for revenge. Revenge against her father and her family.

Reverend Winston clapped his hands and gained everyone's attention. "Well, the ladies have put on a mighty fine spread, and I for one can't wait to get started." Laughter rolled through the crowd. "Brother Slaughter, could you say the blessing, please?"

Mariah bowed her head.

"Our Father in heaven, we thank You for this day You've given us and for this food we are about to partake. Bless the hands that prepared it. Amen."

Mariah poured lemonade until most of the crowd had filled their plates and moved out of the way. Then she fixed something for her grandmother and carried it to her.

"Here you go, Grandma. Sally made her chicken and dumplings. One of your favorites."

"Thank you, Mariah. Where's Jim? I told him to bring me something to eat."

Mariah glanced at the creek. "He's off with the other boys and forgot all about us."

"Well, he has to eat."

"They'll come whooping up here before long. Don't worry about those boys. They'll take care of themselves when they're good and ready." She turned away.

"Mariah."

"Yes, ma'am?"

"Can you fix Slade a plate?"

Mariah glanced in the direction Slade had gone. "He's a grown man. He can get his own food."

"He's a stranger to most of these folks, and he feels uncomfortable."

"Grandma."

"It would be the neighborly thing to do. After all, Slade did come to church with us this morning. It's the least you can do."

"Yes, ma'am."

Mariah trudged back to the tables. A nervous flutter found its way into her stomach. She didn't want to fix Slade a plate and then take it to him like some kind of peace offering. He'd made her so nervous this morning she could barely carry a tune.

Halfway down the table, she ran into Sally. "Gracious, Mariah, whose plate is that?"

Mariah glanced down. Maybe she'd overdone it. She'd piled the plate high with all of Slade's favorites. "Grandma insisted I fix Slade a plate since he wouldn't do it for himself."

"I'm glad he came to church today."

"Of course you are." Mariah glared at her friend. "It gave you an excuse to ask me to sing."

Sally laughed. "You enjoyed every minute of it."

"I did not," Mariah sputtered. "You embarrassed me. We both know you only asked me to sing so he could hear me."

"Yep."

"Sally Riker Winston." Mariah shook her head. "What am I going to do with you?"

"Nothing. You're going to take that monstrous helping down to the creek and give it to that handsome man who can't keep his eyes off you." Sally shoved another plate of food into her hand. "Here. Take this with you. It would be rude to leave him to eat by himself."

Hands full, Mariah quipped, "Well, if I only had two more hands, I could carry some lemonade."

"The kids are headed this way. I'll send one of them down to the creek with lemonade. Now scat." Sally gave her a gentle push toward the tree line and the gurgling creek. "And don't come back, or I'll make you regret it."

"Sally!" But Sally had already abandoned her, her laughter lingering as she made a beeline for the dessert table.

Mariah skirted the crowd and slipped among the trees where she'd last seen Slade. Picking her way carefully down the path leading to the creek, she found him chucking rocks into the water. He glanced up as she approached, and his gaze went to the food. His eyebrow quirked upward.

"Grandma and Sally insisted." She shrugged.

She held out the heavily laden plate. After a moment of hesitation, he took it from her.

Jim came racing down the path, a quart jar of lemonade in his hand. "Mrs. Winston said to bring this to you."

He handed the jar to Slade and took off downstream.

"Jim, get back here," Slade called after him. "Where are you going?"

"To catch frogs."

Slade jerked his head toward the picnic area. "Get on up there and eat. The women aren't going to leave all that food out there till you boys decide you're hungry. Now get."

"Yes, sir." He took off up the hill, running full speed.

Mariah watched him go. "He'll probably grab a chicken leg and keep running."

"Probably. But at least he'll have something in his stomach."

She stood uncertainly. What would Sally do if she returned? Say something about Slade in front of the other women? She could skirt around the tables and join her grandmother under the trees. Then Sally would be none the wiser. "Well, I'd better—"

Slade motioned to the tangled roots jutting out from a tree. "That looks like a level enough place to sit. Can you manage?"

As soon as she was settled, he hunkered down and leaned

against the tree, his plate balanced on one knee. He set the jar on the ground between them. "We'll have to share the lemonade."

Mariah swallowed a dumpling. "You might not want to share when you taste it. Sally's mother makes the best lemonade in the country."

They ate in silence, listening to the murmur of the townspeople on the knoll above them. A soft breeze ruffled the leaves overhead, and a squirrel chattered at them from across the creek.

Slade took a long drink of lemonade. She arched a brow. "Well?"

He closed his eyes, his mouth puckering as he savored the taste. Mariah's stomach did a slow flop as he licked the sweet, tart liquid off his lips. He considered the jar and tossed her a wink. "Best stuff I ever tasted."

Then he turned up the jar and started guzzling it down.

"Hey, stop that. You're supposed to share." Mariah lunged for the lemonade. She squealed as she pitched over a root as big as her leg, dumping the rest of her lunch onto the ground.

Slade's arm snaked out, and he snagged her before she fell headlong into the dirt. He held the jar out of her reach, laughing. "Hey, watch out; you almost spilled the lemonade."

His laughter did funny things to her insides, and to cover her embarrassment, she adopted an imperious attitude and held out a hand. "The lemonade."

"Nope. You're not getting it." He dangled the jar over her head. "But I will let you have a sip."

His smile faded as he lowered the jar. Her world tipped into slow motion. Mariah cupped both hands around his and took a sip. When she finished, he drank from the other side, never taking his eyes from hers. He leaned over, pressing her gently against the tree. His mouth slanted across hers, and she savored the sweetness of his kiss.

He moved back slightly and smiled. "You taste like lemonade."

Her gaze flickered to his lips—so soft, yet so firm. "You do too," she whispered.

Unable to resist, she closed the short distance between them and kissed the corner of his mouth. With a low groan, he turned his head and slanted his mouth against hers, deepening the kiss.

They pulled apart as squeals of laughter spilled over the quiet solitude. A half-dozen boys, Jim included, rounded the bend and raced by on their way to the creek.

CHAPTER TWENTY-FOUR

WHILE MARIAH GATHERED THE EGGS, the chickens pecked at the corn she'd scattered on the ground. Her basket full, she left the chicken coop, latching the gate securely behind her. As she rounded the corner of the barn, Slade and Jim rode into the barnyard.

Her knees turned to jelly when Slade's gaze rested on her lips and a ghost of a smile flitted across his face. Her own face grew hot as she remembered their kiss from yesterday. She forced her thoughts away from the kiss they'd shared and smiled at Jim.

"Good morning, Jim."

The boy grinned as he slid from the back of Slade's horse and ran to her. "Guess what?"

"What?"

"Pa's going to come work for the Lazy M. Mr. Slade asked him this morning, and he said yes." The boy fairly danced with excitement.

"That's wonderful news." She tousled his hair.

"I gotta go tell Buck. Won't he be surprised?" Jim whirled around and raced away.

"That's one happy little boy." Mariah smiled at his enthusiasm and headed toward the house. Slade fell into step beside her.

"I know. He nearly talked my head off all the way back this morning. I asked Denton if they'd like to move into that old cabin down by the road. I know it's not much, but it's better than what they're living in now. And I thought you'd enjoy having another woman around."

"I'd like that." A warm glow started somewhere in the pit of her stomach and spread outward before reality returned to snuff it out. Slade spoke as if she would be here to enjoy another woman's company. Had he forgotten that she'd be leaving soon?

He gave her a crooked little smile, touched the tips of two fingers to his hat, and turned away.

"When are they coming?" she remembered to ask.

"Denton said they would have to take it easy on the way out here because of Becky, so it'll be late afternoon, I imagine."

"Late afternoon?" Mariah gasped. "Today? Oh, my goodness, I've got to get the cabin aired out."

Slade laughed. "Elizabeth can help you."

"No, it'll never work." She shook her head. "Becky shouldn't be around all that dust and dirt." She thrust the basket of eggs at him. "Here. Put these in the kitchen. I've got to get some buckets."

She hurried toward the barn, already making a mental list of what she'd need. "Jim!"

"Yes, ma'am." He skidded out of the barn.

"I need your help. We've got to get that cabin cleaned up before your ma and pa get here."

Mariah bustled about, gathering cleaning supplies. At the last minute, she hurried back inside and put together the makings of stew for supper. No telling how long it would take to clean the cabin, and the stew could simmer on low heat while she was gone. Within the hour, she and Jim headed toward the cabin.

Jim explored every nook and cranny when they reached the cabin.

"Did you know this was where my parents lived when Papa bought the Lazy M?" Mariah swept the worst of the debris out the door.

"Really?" Jim grinned. "I like it. I hope Pa decides to stay here a long, long time."

Mariah laughed. "Me too, Jim. Me too."

Two hours later, she sloshed another bucket of water onto the wooden floor of the old cabin. "Men," she muttered.

"To think they wanted to bring that little girl into this filthy place."

She'd long ago given up trying to keep her skirt from getting soaked. She grabbed her scrub brush and got down on her knees, attacking the boards with a vengeance.

Thankfully, the stream was close by, and she'd enlisted Jim to carry bucket after bucket of water for her. He'd been more than willing at first, bounding around like an excited puppy. She couldn't count the times he'd climbed the ladder to the cozy niche tucked under the eaves, which he'd claimed as his very own room.

But he'd grown restless during the last half hour.

She spotted Jim returning from the creek and smiled. He trudged up the path, his little body swaying from side to side as he concentrated on keeping his balance and saving as much water as he could.

Mariah stood and arched her back before walking out to the porch. She reached for the bucket. "It's getting on toward noon, Jim. Why don't you run up to the house and get something to eat?"

Relief flashed across his sun-kissed face. "You coming?"

"Later." She glanced around. "I'd like to finish here first. Go on. I think I've got enough water now."

Jim whooped and raced toward the house. She shook her head. One minute he'd been all tuckered out, the next full of energy.

She picked up the nearest bucket and toted it inside, then bent to her task again.

*　　*　　*

Slade sauntered down the road toward the cabin, a burlap bundle in one hand and a jar of cold water in the other. He heard humming and stopped outside to listen.

Mariah hummed some tune that sounded like one of the hymns they'd sung in church on Sunday. He studied the peaceful little house nestled beneath a stand of oaks, the stream gurgling not a hundred yards away.

The creek supplied plenty of fresh water, and the trees offered fuel for a fire, protection from the wind, and shade from the sun. Mariah's father had chosen this spot with care. Slade stepped onto the low porch and peered inside. Mariah knelt on the floor, her back to him, scrubbing hard. Her hair resembled a cross between a rat's nest and a cobweb, and her skirt looked like she'd tossed herself in the creek, then rolled in the dirt.

And she was still beautiful.

He cleared his throat.

She whirled. Her foot caught the bucket of water and knocked it over. Most of it soaked into her skirt where she knelt on the floor. She groaned.

He laughed.

"It's not funny." She tossed her scrub brush at him and swiped a hand at the wisps of hair that had escaped her bun. "My skirt's so wet I'm not even sure I can make it back to the house. I'm a mess."

He crouched down beside her, letting his gaze travel over

her face. At his perusal, her eyes softened and her lips parted, and if anything, the rosy hue of her cheeks turned pinker. He reached out and plucked the spiderwebs from her hair, smoothing her golden-brown tresses back. "You look fine," he murmured, his words tinged with laughter.

His hand stilled as their eyes met. As slow as molasses, he eased his hand behind her head and drew her toward him. His lips touched hers, and he felt himself falling . . . falling . . . falling . . . right onto the wet, slippery hardwood floor of the cabin.

As he lay on his back, he heard a giggle, then another. She sat in the middle of the puddle of water, both hands clapped over her mouth, trying to hold back her amusement. Her laughter subsided, and she bit her bottom lip. Then slowly, ever so gently, she leaned over and let her lips touch the corner of his, as light as the brush of butterfly wings.

He claimed her mouth fully, his arms going around her, pulling her down beside him. For a long, breathtaking moment, she kissed him back with a sweetness that left him reeling.

A murmured protest reminded Slade that he'd better slow down. They were traveling a dangerous path. He caressed her lips one last time and pulled away.

"Enough," he rasped out.

Her eyes blinked open, a bemused expression of contentment in their depths.

He swallowed and gently ran his fingers through her hair, smoothing the wayward strands into place, knowing he had to get up before he gave in to the temptation to kiss her again.

Standing, he helped her to her feet. "We need to clean up this mess."

He searched for a corn-husk mop or a brush broom or anything. Anything to keep his mind—and his hands—off her. Grabbing the first thing that came handy, he took the broom and started to sweep the puddled water out of the cabin.

✳   ✳   ✳

They ate lunch by the creek, the sun drying their damp clothes. Birds sang in harmony with the gurgling stream, and Mariah wanted to sing along with them.

Slade cared for her. She knew he did. Why else would he kiss her? Why else would he help her mop up the water she'd spilled in the cabin? Why else would he buy her a new pair of boots?

And he'd gone to church yesterday. That counted for something, didn't it? A warm glow engulfed her. They could take one step at a time. Maybe—just maybe—she wouldn't have to leave the Lazy M after all.

A niggling worry about what her father had done hovered on the fringes of her mind, but she pushed the thought away. For this one day, she didn't want to think about her father, the gold, or the ranch.

She watched as Slade walked to the creek to refill the jar with water. Her heart filled to overflowing as he hunkered down on the creek bank.

His shoulders strained at the fabric of his work shirt as he leaned over and held the jar beneath the surface of the cool, sweet water.

He returned, and she drank her fill. "Thank you for bringing me something to eat."

"You're welcome." He slid down the tree and leaned against it, relaxed. "It wasn't much."

"One of Cookie's ham-filled biscuits is plenty, thank you."

"He does make good biscuits. Reminds me of Ma's."

"Tell me about your mother and your sisters." She held her breath, half-afraid he wouldn't. He'd never talked much about his life before he'd come here, except that time at the bank. Would he open up to her today?

"My mother's a lot like you. She'd go to the ends of the earth to help someone in trouble. I think you'll like her."

Mariah leaned back against the tree, her eyes closed, and listened to the sound of his voice. "And your sisters?"

He chuckled. "Katherine and Cassandra. They're a little younger than you are. Most people can't tell them apart—"

"Twins?"

"Yes."

"I didn't know that." She laughed. "I'll bet they're both beautiful—blue eyes and dark hair. Am I right?"

He nodded. "They look alike, but they're different on the inside. Kat has a streak of wildness in her a mile wide. Loves horses. Given half a chance, she could give Buck a run for his money in breaking them. I guess her name suits her. But Cassie wouldn't dream of doing anything unladylike. She enjoys helping Ma in the house, while Kat can't stand to be cooped up inside."

"Kat sounds a lot like Amanda."

"Really? I wouldn't have thought that, not with her being blind and all."

"Oh, she's not afraid of anything. I've spent many a day just trailing after her to make sure she didn't get into something. That's one reason I've worried so about her in Philadelphia."

"What happened?"

She'd wondered if he'd ever ask about Amanda's blindness. Now the question took away some of the magic of the day. "She was three years old, and it was my job to watch her. The garden had come in, and Grandma had her hands full."

Talking about it brought back the painful memories of her part in the accident. She pleated her skirt between her fingers, then smoothed the still-damp material. "I left Amanda while I went inside to get my doll. When I came outside, I couldn't find her. She'd climbed up into the hayloft of the barn. Nobody really knows what happened, but somehow she slipped and fell out of the loft. Doc says she must have hit her head, and she lost her sight. Nothing could be done for her."

"And you felt responsible?"

"Yes."

"That's why you want her to have a better chance. To be able to make something of her life. You think it's your fault she's blind." He studied her as if he knew exactly how she felt.

Her father and grandmother had never really understood the depth of her guilt.

"It is—it was. I shouldn't have left her." Tears pricked her eyes. "If I'd been there, she wouldn't have climbed into the loft and fallen."

Mariah stared at the creek, thinking back to that horrible day. After all these years, she could still see Amanda lying there on the ground like a broken doll, bloody and still. And ultimately—permanently—blind.

Slade reached out and captured her hand, and she felt the warmth of his fingers, the calluses on his palm. She laced her fingers through his, liking the feel of her hand engulfed in his larger one.

"I'm sure she doesn't blame you."

"She doesn't. But I blame myself."

CHAPTER TWENTY-FIVE

LATE AFTERNOON saw the arrival of the Denton family. Slade caught a glimpse of little Becky bundled up in a ragged quilt. Mariah had been right to insist on cleaning before the Dentons arrived. What had he been thinking when he'd suggested they move right in? He should have realized the cabin would need a good scrubbing first.

Slade and James moved the family's meager belongings inside, and Mariah brought a pot of stew and a pan of corn bread to welcome the family.

Elizabeth could hardly contain her excitement. James carried Becky inside and placed her on the bed they'd set up on one side of the room. Jim watched everything from his perch in the loft.

The men walked down to the creek so James could water the horse he'd borrowed from Mr. Tisdale. Slade started to offer the use of one of the horses on the ranch but decided not to mention it yet. Denton would have to earn the right to a horse.

The man had shaved off his beard and started the day in clean clothes. "This is a nice place."

"It's not much."

As the horse drank, James's attention wandered to his wife, chatting with Mariah on the porch. "It's better'n where we were." He cleared his throat, his gaze raking Slade's before he looked down and toed the dirt with his boot. "I can't thank you enough for all you've done, Donovan. First for Jim an' Becky, and now offering me a job and a place to stay."

"Think nothing of it." Slade shrugged, uncomfortable with the man's thanks.

"But I need to get this off my chest. I know I've been a terrible father the last few years. I stayed drunk more'n I stayed sober. And God forgive me for treating Elizabeth and the kids like I have." He sighed. "I told God I'd do better if he'd heal Becky. She's far from well, but she's on the mend, and I give God the glory for that."

"I'm glad she's going to be okay."

"God could've taken her, and it would've been what I deserved." Denton glanced at him. "I've been running from God for a long time."

A shiver rolled over Slade. "God wouldn't take your daughter's life to punish you, would He?"

Denton shrugged. "Who knows the mind of God? But I'll tell you this. If she had died, it would have been my fault completely. That's enough to make me determined to turn over a new leaf. I promise I won't let you down, Mr. Donovan."

Slade clapped his hand on Denton's shoulder as they headed back toward the cabin. "I'm going to hold you to that promise."

✶   ✶   ✶

Mariah heard a knock at the door. She left supper on the stove and peeked through the window. Frederick stood on the porch. She'd forgotten all about him what with Becky getting hurt, the picnic, and then the Dentons moving out to the ranch.

"Frederick." She motioned him in, surprised at his appearance. He wore a dusty suit coat, rumpled as if he might have slept in it, and mud-spattered pants and boots. Frederick prided himself on being neat, clean, and perfectly groomed at all times.

A little too neat, as a matter of fact. Made her feel dowdy by comparison.

"Frederick, is everything all right?"

"Everything's fine. Just had a little mishap with my horse, that's all."

She led the way into the parlor, still as old and worn as it had been the last time he came, but this time, she didn't think it would matter. She pushed back the curtains to allow more light into the room. A sunbeam played across Frederick's face, revealing dark circles under his eyes and sunken cheeks. It wasn't like him to be so disheveled. He must have come straight to see her on his way home from Laramie.

"I'm sorry I missed the picnic," he said. "I got tied up in Laramie."

"I understand." She bit her lip. What would he say if she told him she hadn't missed him at all?

A door slammed, and running feet clattered down the hall. Frederick jumped. "What was that?"

"That's Jim. His pa is working at the Lazy M now, and he pretty much has the run of the place." Mariah frowned. "Are you sure you're all right?"

"Just tired." A tight smile creased his face.

"Let me get you something to drink." She moved toward the door. "There's some of Mrs. Riker's lemonade left from the picnic if you'd like."

"I'm not thirsty." He stopped her with a hand on her arm. "You know why I'm here."

"Yes—"

"Say you'll marry me, Mariah—soon. We can leave today and go straight to Philadelphia. You could be with Amanda in a matter of days."

To be able to see Amanda was tempting, but not tempting enough to say yes to his proposal. She looked at his mussed hair, the carefully controlled facade that had slipped, his disheveled clothes, and decided she liked him better now than when he'd been the perfectly coiffed, impeccably dressed gentleman so out of place in Wisdom.

She pulled away. To her relief, he let her go. She walked across the room and turned to face him. Had she done something, said something in the past to make him think she loved him?

"Frederick, I've prayed about your proposal, but I just can't marry you."

"You've said that before—"

"Please. Let me finish." Her stomach roiled at what she was about to say. "To be honest, since you've been gone, I considered accepting, but not for the reason you'd expect."

He strode toward her, a pleased smile on his face. He took her by the shoulders. "Mariah, I don't care what your reason is, as long as you say yes."

"I'm sorry; I'm making a mess of this. I considered accepting your offer after you told me that you plan to sell out and move back east. It would be the obvious solution, since my grandmother and I are penniless—"

"What did you say?"

She frowned. "I said since you wanted to move back east, and we'll be going to Philadelphia—"

"No, the other part." His hands tightened on her shoulders.

"Frederick, you're hurting me. Let me go."

"Not until you explain yourself." His face had gone pale, and his eyes glittered dangerously. "What do you mean, you're penniless?"

His fingers dug into her arms, and she winced. "I said there isn't any money. I owed some debts—"

* * *

The unfamiliar horse tied to the hitching rail had been ridden long and hard. Lather coated the underside of the animal's belly where the girth rested. Frowning, Slade made his way around to the back porch and washed up for supper. The visitor could have at least seen to his horse.

Supper simmered on the stove in the quiet kitchen. Enticing aromas wafted throughout the room. He walked over to the stove to investigate. Peas, corn bread, and thick slices of fried ham. He grinned and reached for a piece of meat. Mariah would have his hide if she knew he'd snitched food before supper, but what Mariah didn't know wouldn't hurt her.

His hand paused in midair when voices from the parlor reached him.

"Do you mean to tell me you didn't get a dime from Donovan?"

"Let me go. You're hurting me."

Cooper.

White-hot anger exploded inside Slade, and he hurried down the hall toward the parlor.

"That money was the only reason I came back." Cooper laughed, a harsh bark devoid of humor. "If it hadn't been for the money, I would've been clear across the country by now."

"What are you talking about?" Confusion laced Mariah's words.

Slade shoved against the parlor door, not caring that it crashed against the wall. Cooper whirled to face him. "Get out."

Cooper's gaze slid from Slade to Mariah, a knowing smirk on his face. "Well, Donovan, it didn't take you long to sweet-talk Mariah into handing over everything here at the Lazy M—lock, stock, and barrel."

Slade clenched his fist and took a step toward the two-bit scum. If he said one more word . . . "I won't tell you again."

"Don't worry. I'm going." He glanced at Mariah, his face twisted with hatred, no longer trying to hide behind his suave good looks and debonair charm. "I wasted enough time here anyway."

"I'm warning you, Cooper."

Cooper held up both hands and backed away.

The front door slammed, and Slade turned to Mariah. She stood with both arms wrapped tightly around her waist, her face pale as death.

He should have decked Cooper on the spot.

"Are you all right?" He took a step toward her.

"I believed him. I thought he cared about me, but he wanted the ranch; then after he thought I'd sold it, he wanted the money."

She laughed, the sound bitter. "How long will what my father did haunt me? It seems everywhere I turn, every decision I try to make, the consequences of my father's actions are staring me in the face. Even you . . . ." She took a deep breath. "Even you're here because of the gold my father stole."

He reached for her. He wanted to tell her that everything would be all right. That what her father had done didn't matter anymore. "Mariah—"

"No." She held up her hands, palms out. "Don't touch me. I . . . I need time to think."

She fled the room.

Something cold and hard twisted in Slade's gut as he watched her go. He couldn't undo what her father had done, couldn't undo what Cooper had done.

And God help him, he couldn't undo what he'd done.

Mariah spent a sleepless night tossing and turning. Dawn found her in the kitchen fixing breakfast for her grandmother and herself, but her thoughts weren't on the task at hand.

Instead, she found herself thinking about Frederick. It appalled her that she had misread him so completely. Admittedly, she had never loved him—and hadn't misled him to the contrary—but she'd honestly thought he loved her.

And Slade?

A sick feeling coiled in her stomach. Did he care for her, or had he been toying with her affections much the same way Frederick had? But for what gain? He already had everything he'd come here for.

But one glance from Slade had her melting inside while Frederick's touch left her as cold as a Wyoming winter storm.

Her mind whirled. What should she do now? If she stayed any longer, her heart would be so tied to Slade that she wasn't sure if she would be able to leave. Could she do it even now? She had to. Otherwise, she risked loving a man she could never have. Yes, he'd softened toward her and her family, and he felt sorry for Amanda, but that didn't mean there could ever be anything else between them.

The pounding of hooves drew her out of her reverie, and she paused to listen. From the sound of it, several horses had thundered into the yard. She frowned and hurried toward the front door, wiping her hands on her apron as she went.

Her grandmother tottered down the hall. "What's all this commotion?"

"I don't know."

They stepped out onto the front porch to find the sheriff surrounded by a dozen men or more, none of whom she recognized.

Slade came out of the cookhouse, followed by Rio, Buck, and the rest of the men.

"Morning, folks," Sheriff Dawson drawled.

"Morning." Slade nodded. "What can we do for you, Sheriff?"

The sheriff thumbed toward a man on his left. "This is Sheriff Warner from Laramie. They're looking for a man named Emmit Frederick. The description of the fellow fits Frederick Cooper. Seems he had a run-in with some men on Saturday night at a saloon in Laramie. A couple of them accused him of cheating at cards, and he pulled a gun."

Mariah bit back a gasp.

Sheriff Dawson's gaze rested on her for a moment.

Rio spoke up, his voice laced with excitement. "Anybody killed?"

"One dead, another in pretty bad shape." He shifted,

and his saddle creaked in the early morning stillness. Horses stomped and snorted, anxious to be on their way. "I understand Cooper's sweet on Miss Malone. I'd like to have a word with her."

Slade stepped forward. "That won't be necessary, Sheriff. Cooper stopped by last night, and I stood there as he said his good-byes to Miss Malone. I don't think he'll be back." He pushed back his hat. "At the time, we didn't know there'd been any trouble."

The sheriff turned to Mariah. "Is that right, Miss Malone?"

Heat seared Mariah's face as all eyes came to rest on her. "Yes, Sheriff, that's right."

Sheriff Dawson nodded. "I reckon I can take your word for it. We'll be on our way."

"Do you need more men?" Slade said.

"No, you folks stay here and keep a lookout. Now that Cooper's on the run, there's no telling what he's liable to do."

Mariah's appetite rode out with the posse. She stood in the kitchen, her mind and hands finishing their tasks by rote. She took the biscuits out of the oven and forked the ham out of the skillet. Her grandmother sat at the table, nursing a cup of coffee.

"I can't believe Frederick shot a man." Her grandmother shook her head. "Makes me wonder if we ever truly knew him at all."

Mariah placed the biscuits on the table and sat, a cup of coffee in her hand, thinking about Frederick's visit last night. He'd shown his true colors to her more than to her grandmother, but she was still shocked to find out he'd killed a man. She shuddered. Figuratively speaking, he'd had blood on his hands when he stopped by yesterday afternoon. He'd sat in her parlor, touched her. She'd even considered marrying him, though for the wrong reasons.

"How well do we ever know anybody?"

Tears pricked her eyes as she thought of what her father had done. And now Frederick. Her conscience stung. She'd betrayed her family and friends too. No, she hadn't stolen anything or killed anybody, but she'd kept secrets from Amanda and the good people of Wisdom. All to salvage her foolish pride.

Needing time alone to think, she put the leftovers in the pie safe and carried a few pieces of bread and pan drippings out to the cats. The yellow tomcat nibbled at the food. She watched the cat, thinking about his life.

So much simpler than hers.

He didn't have to worry about money, rustling, gambling, pride, or greed. As long as he had scraps of food and the barn had mice, there was nothing for him to worry about.

She reached out a hand. To her surprise, he let her fingers touch his back before he darted away. "It's okay, Yellow. I won't hurt you. Here, kitty, kitty, kitty," she whispered.

He inched back to the tin plate and started eating again.

Mariah waited patiently. Slowly she reached out and ran her hand down his back. He arched into her hand before skittering away once again. A feeling of accomplishment surged through her.

She smiled through her tears. "Someday you'll beg me to pet you, Yellow. You just wait and see."

Her elation popped like a soap bubble when she remembered. In a few days, she wouldn't be here to tame Yellow. She needed to leave as soon as she could make arrangements. She had to go now, before Slade took her heart and trampled it completely. She stood and turned toward the house.

Her heart lurched when she spotted him leaning against the porch.

"You're making progress." Slade nodded toward the cat.

"Yes." She moved toward him.

He dropped down on the second step, his boots braced against the ground, arms dangling loosely between his knees. "What's the point?"

While Mariah pondered his question, she gathered her skirts and sat next to him. She glanced to where she'd fed Yellow, but he'd already left, running off as soon as Slade spoke.

"I don't really know." She shrugged. "I hate to see him so lonely, and I want to be his friend."

Silence fell between them, but it wasn't entirely uncomfortable. Mariah sighed, too tired to wonder why his nearness didn't send her heart rate soaring. Lack of sleep? Or maybe her encounter with Frederick, Sheriff Dawson, and the posse from Laramie had dulled her senses. Whatever the reason, she wanted to go back to bed and curl up for the rest of the day.

"Are you ready to talk about Frederick?"

She shrugged. "There's nothing to talk about really. I guess it's a blessing I didn't have any money. Or I might be Mrs. Frederick E. Cooper by now. Well, that or whatever Sheriff Dawson said his real name is."

"Uh-huh."

She plopped her chin in her hands. "Do you think he wanted the ranch to settle his gambling debts?"

"Sounds like it."

"And I believed him. I thought he cared for me."

"He put on a convincing act."

Mariah stared at the woodpile. *But not convincing enough. He couldn't make me love him, no matter how hard he tried.* Her eyes filled with tears. "I'd better go. I need to see about Grandma."

She gathered her skirts to stand, but he reached out and gently closed his hand around her wrist. Shivers of delight shot up her arm and straight to her heart.

He moved his hand to cup her face. She relished the feel of his rough palm against her cheek.

"I'm glad you're not going to be Mrs. Frederick E. Cooper."

She stared, drowning in his blue gaze shadowed beneath the brim of his hat.

Kiss me.

She touched his lips with the tips of her fingers, letting her touch convey what she was unwilling to say with words. Just once more. Something she could hold close to her heart in the long, lonely years to come. Maybe he only played with her heart and these kisses meant nothing to him, but they mattered to *her*. Right now, she wanted to feel his arms around her one last time, his lips caressing hers.

He leaned toward her, his attention zeroing in on her mouth. A tingle of expectation spiraled through her. His hooded gaze moved slowly over her face before he claimed her lips with his own.

She sighed as he slipped his hand around the nape of her neck and pulled her closer. He tasted as good as she remembered. He pulled back, his fingertips caressing her cheek. She shivered, opened her eyes, and smiled up at him.

"I love you." The words popped out. She hadn't meant to say anything, anything at all. For a moment in time, her world stopped spinning as she realized all she'd laid bare.

Slade's heart hammered against his rib cage. He searched her face, lingering on her eyes, filled with love but overshadowed with uncertainty.

The realization that he loved her too hit him square in his chest and exploded into a million glittering pieces, but guilt held him back from confessing it.

What had he done?

How could she love him when they shared such a bitter past? His heart pounded out a rhythm of fear, his thoughts churning like a bucking bronco. How could he make it up to her?

Suddenly everything became crystal clear.

He shook his head, amazed he hadn't thought of it sooner.

They'd get married and share the ranch. The past didn't matter. But the love in her eyes did.

But first, there was something he had to do. He had to ask her forgiveness for what he'd done to her and her family.

"Mariah, I need—"

Before he could speak, she pulled away and stood in one jerky movement. "You don't have to answer. I know you can't forgive my father for what he did. And you can't forgive me either." Her face turned to stone. "Please, just forget I said anything."

"Wait—"

She fled, leaving him on the porch with his apology and declaration of love unspoken.

CHAPTER TWENTY-SIX

Dear Amanda,

    I hope this letter finds you well. There have been some changes here at the ranch. I don't know how to tell you everything that has happened, so I'll start at the beginning.

Mariah let the letter flutter to her lap and leaned against the tree.

The gurgling creek did its best to soothe her wounded spirit, but nothing could, not even the scent of budding wildflowers drifting by on the breeze, or the steady chomping as her horse nibbled grass, or the *swish-slap* of the mare's tail swatting flies.

Her gaze wandered over the smooth stones, and she recalled the laughter as her grandmother, Amanda, and she had picnicked in this very spot. She remembered times her father had ridden by and stopped to sample their fried chicken and take a sip of lemonade before rushing off to tend to some chore on the ranch.

Once he'd even removed his boots, taken Amanda in his arms, and waded in the shallows. Amanda had squealed with delight. Mariah sighed, the long-ago memories filled with love and laughter and family. When her father was alive, she didn't think anything would ever change. The ranch made a profit. They were happy. They had hopes and dreams for Amanda.

And what about her? She frowned. She'd assumed she'd marry some rancher or someone from Wisdom and her life would continue as it always had.

But then her father had gotten sick. She'd spent so much time taking care of him that she hadn't had time to worry about a family of her own. After he died, more than one man had asked for her hand, but it was obvious they'd set their sights on the ranch and she was just window dressing.

Frederick had seemed different. He'd bought the old Crenshaw place not long before her father took sick. He'd been so nice and helpful during that time, even recommending Red to her father. And he hadn't pressured her about marriage—until recently.

She shuddered. How could she have been so naive? How could she not have known he only wanted the ranch? Or the money it would bring? At least Slade hadn't pretended to be something he wasn't. He'd been honest with her from the beginning.

A pang of regret shot through her at the thought of Slade. She'd written the letter that had brought him to the Lazy M, and that same letter would send her away.

He would never forgive her father for what he'd done. He'd proven that this morning when she'd told him she loved him. An empty ache hollowed the spot between her heart and her stomach as she remembered the look on his face.

Surprise, shock, disbelief, guilt, maybe even pity.

Mariah blinked back the tears and picked up her letter. She wanted Amanda to know she and her grandmother would be arriving in Philadelphia. It was time to go. Slade could manage the house however he saw fit until his mother came.

It is impossible for me to remain in Wisdom. I . . . I have given my heart to someone who cares nothing for me, and I cannot bear the pain any longer. It is much too complicated to pen here, so I won't try. Be assured I will explain all when I arrive in Philadelphia.

Amanda, please forgive me for not telling you what Father did all those years ago. I only did what I thought best. We will survive somehow; I promise you that, dear heart.

She glanced up at the late-afternoon sky. Time to head home and start supper. Then she'd begin packing. She folded the letter and placed it in the small leather bag she carried. She'd mail it tomorrow and hope it arrived in Philadelphia before she did. She stood and brushed off her skirt before she turned toward her horse.

And came face-to-face with Giff Kerchen.

He grinned. "Well, well, well, what do we have here?"

"Let me pass." She lifted her chin.

"I don't think so, pretty boss lady."

Giff scared her spitless, but she tried not to let her fear show. "They'll be expecting me back at the ranch soon."

He leered at her. "You mean Donovan will be expecting you? Well, he'll just have to wait . . . maybe for a very long time. I'm taking you with me."

Mariah threw the bag at him, hiked her skirts, and raced toward her horse. But she didn't get far. Giff grabbed at her from behind, and she went sprawling on the ground. The fall knocked the breath out of her, but she came up swinging. Her nails raked Giff's face, and he howled with fury.

He wrapped one arm tight around her waist, the other twisting in her hair. "You do that one more time, and I'll slit your pretty little throat."

Tears sprang to her eyes, but she blinked them back, refusing to let him see her cry.

"Donovan and Bucky-boy aren't here to take up for you now, so I'll just have a little fun. Come on."

Mariah clenched her teeth as he dragged her toward her horse. *Lord, please help me.* She could barely think the words, let alone pray. Where was he taking her? Bile rose in her throat as terrifying images of what Giff planned to do ricocheted through her mind.

He jerked her hands together and tied them with a piece of rope. "Mount up. And don't try anything stupid."

She heaved herself into the saddle and watched with mounting panic as Giff reached for the trailing reins. Raw desperation clawed at her. She grabbed the pommel and kicked him as hard as she could.

When he doubled over in pain, she jabbed her horse with her heels, ducking low as the mare scrambled through the trees toward the open grassland away from the creek.

Her horse flew past trees, branches clawing and grabbing at her hair, ripping the pins loose. Mariah hung on, praying her horse wouldn't step on the reins and Giff wouldn't catch up to her before she could make it back to the ranch.

"Jim said you wanted to see me."

"It's Mariah." Mrs. Malone looked up from her rocking chair, her face lined with worry. "She went riding several hours ago, and I haven't seen her since. I checked with Jim, and he said she headed downstream. I'm afraid something's happened. It's unlike her to be gone so long, especially as it's getting on toward time to fix supper."

A knot of fear lodged in Slade's chest, but he tamped it down. He didn't want to worry Mrs. Malone any worse than she already was. "It's probably nothing. The days are getting longer, and the time probably slipped away from her. I'll go look for her. Any place in particular she likes to go?"

Mrs. Malone's hands fluttered. "Several spots along the creek where she likes to sit and think. One in particular is about a mile downstream. We used to have picnics there all the time when the girls were small."

"I know the spot."

Her troubled brown eyes gazed up at him. "Please find her, Slade."

"I will." He patted her veined hand.

"I'll be praying."

Slade headed downstream. No more than a quarter of a mile from the house, he cupped his hands around his mouth and called out, "Mariah!"

No one answered.

Maybe she'd passed him and gone back to the ranch. Or maybe she'd gone in a different direction when she'd ridden out earlier. But Jim said she'd gone downstream, so he'd have to keep looking. Hopefully he'd find her at the family's picnic spot.

He rode slowly, searching for signs. Anything. A broken limb. A hoofprint. Finally he came to the copse of trees Mariah had shown him the day they'd taken Jim home. He glanced around, noting the sunlight filtering through the willows, the water gurgling along to his left.

He listened. No sounds at all. The hair stood up on the back of his neck. Something had happened here, though; he could feel it. He dismounted and walked in an ever-widening circle, his gaze eventually landing on a small leather bag on the ground. His heart jumped in his chest as he hurried to the bag and picked it up.

Inside, he found Mariah's letter to Amanda. He skimmed it, a dull ache forming in his chest when he read that she intended to leave Wisdom immediately without giving him a chance to make things right between them. He looked up from the letter, knowing she wouldn't have deliberately left it behind.

He searched every square inch of the leaf-strewn ground surrounding the spot where he'd discovered the leather pouch. Minutes later, he found what he was looking for: the prints of a small boot and a much-larger boot heel.

He followed the prints, trying to see where they led. Then, mixed in with the boot prints, he found two sets of hoofprints. First, a jumble of tracks, smudged markings of boot heels, a scuffle, then running horses. He tamped down rising panic, his gaze on the tracks, trying to find something, anything, that could identify the other rider. And when he did, his heart nearly stopped.

The second horse threw its left hind hoof out when he ran. Just like the horse one of the rustlers had ridden.

He wanted to run, to hurry, to save Mariah.

But he took his time, doggedly following the trail that led away from the Lazy M.

"So you thought you could get away from me, huh?"

Giff jerked the rope tied around Mariah's wrists. It cut

into her skin, and she almost cried out from the searing pain. He tied her bound hands to the pommel of the saddle and then tied a lead rope to her horse. There would be no escaping this time.

"This is payback for those eggs you dumped on me."

Mariah glared at him.

Giff set a fast pace. Hope of rescue fell with the encroaching darkness and every mile he put between them and home. *Oh, God, please help Slade find me.*

Her fingers had grown numb by the time a shack came into view. Giff untied her and yanked her off her horse. She landed with a thud against him and would have fallen to the ground if he hadn't grabbed her by the arm and held her upright.

Inside, she blinked at the light spilling from a lantern.

"Look what I found wandering around all by herself."

The sound of chair legs crashed to the floor. "Giff, what have you gone and done now?"

Mariah jerked her head up at the familiar voice.

Frederick moved out of the shadows, the smooth, gentlemanly demeanor completely gone. In its place stood a haggard man, his once-white ruffled shirt sweat-stained and dirty. His cold eyes raked her from head to toe, and she shivered. Then he turned to Giff.

"Have you completely lost your mind?"

"She deserved it. Always staring down her nose at me. Thinking she was too good for everybody."

"After all I've worked for, you had to pull a stupid stunt

like this." The deadly calm in Frederick's voice snaked down Mariah's spine. "Do you realize everybody within miles of Wisdom will be after us now? You could hang."

Giff shrugged. "I could hang for rus—"

"Shut up."

Mariah's gaze swung between Frederick and Giff as the pieces all clicked into place. These two were involved with the rustlers. She searched the shadows, and her heart sank as she recognized Red's big, rawboned frame. She'd know him anywhere.

Frederick leaned against the table and reached for a cigar. "Yes, we were doing quite well for ourselves until Donovan came along. I thought it would all work out, but then you let him swindle you out of the entire ranch."

"I wasn't swindled."

He raised an eyebrow. "Then how else do you explain handing the Lazy M over to him?"

Mariah lifted her chin.

He shrugged. "It doesn't really matter, I suppose. After tonight, Donovan won't have enough cattle to stay in business anyway."

"You can't get away with this." Mariah speared him with a glare.

"I can, and I will." He puffed on the cigar and studied her, face devoid of emotion. She shuddered. How had he fooled her so completely? "You know, Giff, now that I think about it, you might have done me a favor by bringing pretty Miss Malone along for the ride."

Giff looked pleased. "I did?"

"Maybe. All right, you both know what to do. Round up the others and head out. I'll meet you in Cheyenne. And, Giff, I need your horse. That old nag I picked up in Laramie is just about done for. You can switch horses when you get to the canyon."

"What about her?" Giff asked.

Frederick snubbed the cigar out on the table. "She's going with me."

CHAPTER TWENTY-SEVEN

"You didn't find her?" The lantern in Buck's hand cast eerie shadows on the barn walls.

"No." Slade shook his head. "I tracked as far as I could before it got dark."

"Did you find anything? Any sign?" Mrs. Malone stood beside Buck, wrapped in a thick shawl. Her quavery voice had taken on a strong, determined cast.

Slade glanced at Buck.

She straightened, the backbone that had seen her through an entire lifetime of trouble surfacing. "Slade, I've been through Indian raids, droughts, tornadoes, and more fires than a body can count. I buried three children and my husband. Don't hold anything back."

"All right. She'd been down by the creek just like you said. But somebody else had been there too. Looked like a scuffle; then she got away."

"Frederick?" Mrs. Malone's chin trembled.

"I don't think so. It's a big man, and he rides a horse that has a hitch in its stride."

Buck frowned. "What kind of hitch?"

"The horse throws out its left hind hoof when it runs."

"That's Giff Kerchen's horse."

"How do you know?"

"I noticed it the day Giff and I went to the water hole."

"I saw those same tracks when Rio and I found the broken fence. Giff must have been involved in the rustling. As soon as I get a fresh mount, I'm going to head out again."

Mrs. Malone put a hand on his arm. "You can't find her in the dark."

"She's right," Buck said. "You'll have to wait until daylight."

A hollow feeling washed over him. "What if—?" He couldn't say it out loud. What if Giff violated Mariah? He couldn't stand to sit here and wait. He shook his head. "No, I have to go now."

"Please, Slade. You've done all you can tonight."

Slade knew he wouldn't sleep, so he nursed a cup of coffee in the cookhouse all night. Several times he stopped himself short of jumping up and running to the corral. He'd saddle his horse and hunt Giff Kerchen down. He'd take Mariah back by force.

But reason kept him from running off into the night

without a hope of finding her. Reason and the niggling thought that he needed to ask God to help him. He stood and raked a hand through his hair before pacing back and forth across the room. What had Mrs. Malone said that day at the picnic? That God was the only one he could depend on? That God would never betray him?

What else had she said? He couldn't remember, but he did know he needed God's help in the worst way. He *wanted* God's help. He stopped pacing and braced himself against the sturdy oak table in the center of the room, hands splayed across the rough surface.

"I'm not exactly sure how to go about this, Lord, but I need You to help me find Mariah." He gritted his teeth, desperate to find the right words. "Lord, I want to believe in You like Mrs. Malone does and like James Denton is learning to do. What I'm trying to say is that I'd like You to come into my heart and life. I'm tired of trying to figure it all out on my own."

He stood silent and still, waiting. Nothing happened. What had he expected? Trumpets? Angels? He didn't know. But he'd expected . . . something.

He stood like that for a long time, braced and waiting.

Cookie shuffled in long before dawn and started preparing breakfast. One by one the other hands joined them, silent and anxious.

Rio looked solemn. "I want to go with you."

"You and Cookie stay here and watch after Mrs. Malone."

The kid's face fell, but for once he didn't argue. "Yes, sir."

Cookie rattled pots and pans. "I don't need any help taking care of Mrs. Malone. Been doing it for years. Why, the day you rode in, you young whippersnapper, I had you in my sights the whole time."

Slade had no doubt Cookie would have shot him, but where the lead went would be anybody's guess. "Why didn't you shoot me then, Cookie?"

The old man snorted. "Miss Mariah didn't give me the go-ahead, and I figured you might come in handy." He smiled—thin and grim. "Seems I was right."

Soon Cookie had an early breakfast on the table so the men could eat. No one had much of an appetite, except for Rio, the bottomless ravine.

Cookie offered Slade a bundle wrapped in cheesecloth. Slade shook his head. Food would just churn in his belly.

"Take it. For Mariah." Cookie cleared his throat and pushed the bundle toward him before turning quickly away.

Slade grabbed the bundle and pushed back his chair. "Buck, go on down to the Dentons' and see if Elizabeth can come stay with Mrs. Malone. Duncan, you ride into town and tell Sheriff Dawson what's happened. I'm going to see if Mrs. Malone is up."

"She's up, mark my words," Cookie said.

"I'll saddle your horse," Rio volunteered.

Slade tossed him the bundle of food. "Put that in my saddlebags."

He found Mariah's grandmother in the kitchen, trying to make a pot of coffee. Her gnarled hands trembled, and dark circles shadowed her eyes.

"Here, let me do that." He moved forward.

"I'm just a useless old woman. Can't even make a pot of coffee on my own."

Slade stoked the fire until a good blaze roared. "You're not useless, and you know it."

"When are you leaving?"

"Soon as the men get saddled up. Buck's going to fetch Elizabeth. And I'm leaving Cookie and Rio here, in case you need anything."

"We'll be fine. You just find my girl." Tears shimmered in her eyes.

"I'll find her." The aroma of coffee wafted from the pot, and he reached for a mug.

"You love her, don't you?"

How had she guessed? He'd only recently admitted it to himself.

"She'll never forgive me for what I've done." His gut churned.

"Have you asked her?"

"No." He glanced out the window. "It'll be daylight soon. I've got to go."

"I'll be praying for you, Slade. And I'll be praying that you find Mariah safe and sound."

"Thank you, ma'am."

He stepped out on the porch and breathed in the damp

air. A faint glow lit up the eastern sky. It would be light enough to track Giff and Mariah within the hour. Somehow knowing Mrs. Malone would be praying made the task ahead a little less fearsome.

Daylight found Slade and Buck on the trail where Slade had left off the night before. But it was painstakingly slow. They lost the trail twice and had to backtrack to find it again.

They topped a rise and reached the edge of Lazy M land. An expanse of barbed wire had been cut. Slade calculated the distance. Several hundred feet. Posts just pulled up out of the ground and tossed aside like driftwood. Slowly he rode down the steep incline, squinting at the churned-up earth. Cows, hundreds of them, had passed this way during the night. His jaw clenched. These men had made a run at the cattle too.

A piece of cloth fluttered in the wind a hundred yards to the right. He rode over and plucked it from the fence. A small square of brown cotton from Mariah's skirt.

Dread clutched at his stomach as he scanned the horizon. One—no, two pieces of cloth waved in the distance. There wasn't any need to even search for tracks.

The rustlers had gone in one direction.

Mariah and Giff in another.

"What do you make of it?" Buck asked.

"They're offering me a choice. Go after Mariah or save the herd."

"That's no choice." Buck scowled, pointing his horse toward the cloth flags waving in the distance.

"Buck, find Duncan and the sheriff. Tell 'em not to worry about the cows. Mariah's safety comes first."

"All right." Buck paused. "What are you going to do?"

"I'm going after Mariah."

✻   ✻   ✻

"Do you think he'll come after you?" Frederick asked.

Mariah ignored him.

"It doesn't really matter." He laughed. "We've got a good head start, and we'll be in Cheyenne long before he catches up with us."

"Then what?" She dreaded asking but needed to know.

"As soon as Red wires me that the cows have been sold and we're in the clear, I won't need you anymore."

Mariah stared at his cold-blooded eyes, knowing he wasn't going to let her go. She shuddered and looked away. What if Slade chose to go after the herd? What if he didn't come after her?

No, he wouldn't do that. Slade would come. She was sure of it. *God, protect him. Don't let Frederick kill him.*

Even though she'd put on a brave face in front of Frederick, inside she was terrified. She didn't know what he was capable of, and she didn't want to find out.

She bowed her head and prayed silently. *Lord, help me to be strong. I accept Your will for my life, Lord.* A vise squeezed her chest as she thought of her grandmother. *Please give*

Grandma strength to face whatever happens. And keep Slade, Buck, and the rest of the men safe. Help them to seek Your will and to make the right decisions.

Mariah continued her litany of prayers as Frederick led them farther and farther away from home and all she held dear.

Noon passed, and the sun marched resolutely across the sky, marking time. Mariah squinted against the glare. By her calculations, they had another two to three hours of daylight left. Frederick stopped and fear kicked her hard in the stomach. Without a word, he uncapped his canteen and took a long swig.

She licked her lips and swallowed, trying to bring a little moisture into her mouth. Would he offer her water? She wouldn't beg. Panic bubbled up as she realized that she might have to. If no one came, she'd be forced to plead for water—for her very life, even.

"May I have some water?" She croaked out the words, the request almost choking her.

Frederick considered her, then rode close and tipped the canteen into her mouth. Only a swallow, but it was enough. For now.

He capped the canteen and started off again, the ground sloping upward at a sharp angle. Mariah braced her feet in the stirrups and attempted to hold on to the pommel, but it didn't do any good: her hands had gone numb hours ago.

Suddenly Mariah's horse stumbled, and she screamed.

*   *   *

Mariah's horse had gone lame.

Slade breathed a prayer of thanks for the chance it gave him to catch up. He topped a rise, his heart thudding in his chest when he spotted two horses ground-hitched in a copse of trees. He slowed, eyes squinted, searching the area for Mariah and Giff.

A man moved out from behind the horses, arm wrapped around Mariah, holding her tight in front of him, a pistol at her head. Slade kneed his horse closer, blood curdling in his veins.

"Donovan!"

The shock of hearing Cooper's voice, not Giff's, brought him up short.

"Ride in slowly, hands up. And don't try anything foolish."

He drew closer, his hands where Cooper could see them, but he had eyes only for Mariah. Her wide, terrified gaze met his. Her thick mane of hair had come undone and flowed unchecked down her back and over her shoulders, but other than a rumpled, grass-stained dress, she looked unharmed . . . and just as beautiful as ever. He shifted his attention to Cooper, his gut twisting with rage. If he could get his hands on the snake, he'd kill him.

"Stop right there. Get off your horse, and drop your gun." The cold, no-nonsense tone convinced Slade that Cooper would shoot first and ask questions later.

He did as he was told, holding both hands up. "I should have known you were involved."

Suddenly it all made sense. Cooper recommending Red when Mariah's father got sick. The slow siphoning of cattle a few at a time, so nobody would get suspicious.

"I guess you know about the cows?"

Slade knew enough. "What does that have to do with Mariah?"

Cooper smiled. "Yeah, Giff did me a favor by grabbing Mariah."

"You won't get away with this."

Cooper laughed, a sharp bark of amusement that grated down Slade's spine. "Of course I will. Why do you think I'm riding Giff's horse?"

Slade tried to think of a plan, anything to get Mariah away from Cooper. But he came up empty. He looked deep into her eyes and saw fear there, but he glimpsed trust shining in their depths too. Fear squeezed the air right out of his chest—the pain so hard and brittle, he felt like he'd shatter if he took another breath.

Save her, God. Whatever it takes, keep her alive. Let me die in her place if need be.

He inched one foot forward, his only hope to distract Cooper and gain the upper hand.

Cooper thumbed the hammer back, the ominous click loud in the tense silence.

Slade froze, his senses attuned to Cooper's every move. The twitch of his eye, the subtle flex of his arm wrapped around Mariah's neck, the telltale sign of when he was about to turn the gun on Slade.

Because he would shoot Slade first, possibly keep Mariah for insurance until he got to where he was going. Slade might get shot, might even get killed, but it was a chance he was willing to take.

The thundering sound of a horse's hooves registered just as Cooper's gaze shifted and focused over Slade's shoulder. Hope beat anew in Slade's chest as the rider drew near, but the gun at Mariah's temple kept him frozen in place. Something akin to anger flashed across Cooper's face, then was gone. His gaze flicked back to Slade, steady and relentless in his purpose.

Slade's brief flash of hope died a quick death.

The man's reaction made clear whose side the rider was on.

A tear trickled down Mariah's cheek. There was nothing he could do to reassure her.

Not one blasted thing.

The rider pulled his horse to a stop a few feet to Slade's right. Slade slowly turned his head, not giving Cooper any reason to fire, and spotted Red, his face streaked with dirt, clothes dusty and sweat-stained. Haunted eyes met Slade's for a split second before focusing on Cooper.

"This has gone far enough, Emmit."

Emmit? Slade studied the two men, eyes narrowed. How long had Red known that Cooper and Emmit Frederick were one and the same?

"What are you doing here?" Cooper scowled.

"I can't let you do this." Red kneed his horse forward.

Slade shifted one foot farther, taking advantage of the distraction and closing the distance between himself and Cooper.

"It's too late. They know too much."

"I won't let you do this. Think about what it will do to Ma."

"Ma's dead." Cooper laughed. "Has been for months."

"Dead?" Red's voice cracked on the word. "How?" The silence thickened as he stared at Cooper, the man he'd called Emmit. "What . . . what happened?"

"It doesn't matter. She's gone, so you can stop worrying about what she'd think or what she'd say. We've got a job to do."

The words flung between the two men barely registered as Slade focused on Cooper and the gun. He'd only get one opportunity to save Mariah, and he'd better make it count.

"It does matter." Red flushed. "Tell me."

"All right. She broke her leg. Gangrene set in, and she didn't make it." Cooper's flat black eyes bored into Red. "Satisfied?"

"Gangrene?" Red's face turned pasty white. "You knew, and you didn't tell me?"

"What good would it have done?"

Red's horse sidestepped, and Slade took his chance, diving behind the nervous animal. Cooper twisted, jerked Mariah to the side, his pistol swiveling toward Slade. The discharge blasted through the air as the bullet plowed into Red's chest. His horse reared, and Red toppled to the ground.

Slade scrambled for his own gun, got his hand wrapped around the grip, and rolled just as Cooper's pistol blasted again, the bullet kicking up dirt inches from his face, spraying him in the eyes.

Somewhere he could hear Mariah screaming his name.

He blinked.

Once. Twice.

Then he took aim.

CHAPTER TWENTY-EIGHT

SLADE'S SHOT DRILLED through Cooper's shoulder but didn't bring him down. Cooper aimed again, black eyes narrowed with an intent to kill.

Slade's finger tightened on the trigger.

Mariah threw herself at Cooper, swinging a chunk of wood at his head. Slade jerked the tip of his pistol up just in time. His shot went wild.

Cooper's next shot sent Slade's pistol flying. A white-hot burn clawed at his right arm.

Then the earth tilted into slow motion as Cooper slapped Mariah away like a rag doll. Slade launched himself forward, growling. He'd kill the snake with his bare hands.

Cooper drew down on him, so close Slade could see the rage in his eyes. The blast nearly deafened him, but he didn't feel a thing. Had Cooper missed? At this distance?

Cooper looked away from Slade and down to where blood pumped through a hole in his chest. He lifted his gaze past Slade, horror-struck shock on his face. "Red?"

His eyes glazed over, and he fell and lay still.

Slade spun toward Red, who lay on his side, staring at Cooper. Blood coated his shirt and his breathing came in shallow, raspy gasps. Slade put his hand on Red's shoulder, his touch conveying his gratitude for what Red had done.

Red held out his gun, butt first, then nodded in Mariah's direction. "Go. Take care of her."

Slade took the gun from Red's unresisting fingers, then strode to Cooper and kicked his gun away. But there was no need to be cautious with Cooper. He wouldn't bother any of them anymore.

Mariah threw herself into Slade's arms. He held on tight, never wanting to let her go. He took her tearstained face in both hands, his thumb grazing the darkening bruise where Cooper had backhanded her. "Are you all right? Did he hurt you?"

"I'm fine." Her lips trembled.

He tucked her head underneath his chin, savoring the warmth emanating from her, knowing both of them could be lying on the ground this very instant, bodies growing cold. He focused on the clear blue sky overhead. The sun was shining, and they were alive. He couldn't ask for more.

He wanted to tell her he loved her, but there would be time enough for that later, after he got her safely home. He'd take her on a picnic. They'd find a new spot, and they'd make new memories.

He'd tell her he loved her.

And he'd ask her to marry him.

Her eyes widened as she saw the blood coating his sleeve. "You're hurt."

"Nothing serious. Just a flesh wound." He glanced at Red. "I need to see about him."

"Soon. Let me see how bad you're hurt." She rolled up his sleeve and winced at the torn flesh where the bullet had plowed across his arm. At that moment, a dozen men rode into the clearing, led by Sheriff Dawson.

Chaos reigned as the sheriff and his men asked questions, loaded Cooper's lifeless body onto Giff's horse, bandaged Slade's arm, and saw to Red. Slade led Mariah away from the carnage, helped her mount, then swung into the saddle behind her. She'd been through enough, and he was taking her home.

"Donovan?" Sheriff Dawson strode across the clearing, hat in his hand. He cleared his throat. "Harper didn't make it."

Slade shook his head and glanced at Red's lifeless body. No matter what Red had done to Mariah and her family, he tried to make up for it in the end. "If it hadn't been for him, I'd be dead by now. We both would. May God have mercy on his soul."

"Ma'am?" The sheriff twisted his hat and squinted up at

Mariah. "Right before he passed, he asked me to tell you he was sorry."

Mariah's lip trembled. "Thank you, Sheriff."

✱　✱　✱

Night fell, and Mariah dozed only to start awake over and over, the events of the past two days seared into her brain. Slade's chest cushioned her head, his arms wrapped securely around her. She was safe. Safe in his arms. Frederick—

No, she wouldn't think about Frederick. Or Red.

"We're almost home."

She sighed and tightened her arms around his waist. "I don't think I ever want to ride a horse again," she murmured.

He chuckled.

She grew serious. "Do you think Buck and the others found the cattle?"

"I don't know. But if they didn't, we'll manage. Isn't that what your grandmother always says?"

"Yes. Grandma has a lot of faith."

"Then we'll have faith and take it one day at a time. Together." He brushed her temple with a featherlight kiss.

Together.

She liked the sound of that.

The ranch house came into view. It looked like every lamp, lantern, and candle in the place cast out a beacon of light to welcome them home. Slade stopped at the front door and dismounted. He reached for her, and she slid into his arms, her hand on his makeshift bandage. Her stomach flipped anew at how close she'd come to losing him.

She swayed on rubbery legs, exhaustion taking over. Slade slipped an arm around her waist and led her toward the door.

"They're back!" Jim yelled as he raced through the doorway, Buck right on his heels. Jim barreled into Mariah, nearly knocking her down, but she hugged him tight, thankful to be home.

Buck grabbed Slade in a bear hug, the two of them slapping each other's backs. No words were exchanged, but Mariah figured none were needed.

Jim looked up at her, his eyes bright. "Buck led the posse that caught the rustlers."

"They got the herd back?"

"Yep. Every single one."

"Praise the Lord!"

"Mariah?" Her grandmother stepped through the door.

Mariah let the older woman wrap her in her arms.

"Are you okay, child?"

"I'm fine, Grandma. Really." Mariah shook her head, dimly aware of others—a woman and two young girls—in the shadowed doorway. "Just so tired, I can hardly stay upright."

The other woman stepped forward. "Slade?"

"Ma?"

Mariah's weary gaze focused on the middle-aged woman standing in the doorway behind her grandmother. She blinked once, then twice.

Slade's mother had finally arrived.

Mariah woke not long after sunup. Lying still in her bed, she let the events of the last forty-eight hours wash over her. Nightmares of the ordeal plagued her, but she prayed they'd fade with time. Her thoughts turned to home. Last night, she'd been so tired she couldn't think straight, let alone take in the implications of the arrival of Slade's mother and sisters.

Worry inched its way into her heart. Would the fact that his mother had finally come make a difference? He'd said they would take it one day at a time. *Together.* Had he meant it? Had he meant they could share a future together?

There hadn't been time to discuss anything. Had she and Slade overcome their differences and battled Frederick only to face more obstacles?

What was his mother like? Did she hate Mariah's father the way Slade had? Did Mrs. Donovan blame Seth Malone for stealing the gold and leaving her husband to die? If she did, Mariah would feel the brunt of her anger and bitterness just as she'd faced Slade's.

Trying not to worry, Mariah dressed and made her way downstairs. Nervously she entered the kitchen and found herself gazing into a pair of eyes the exact shade of Slade's.

"Hello, dear." Slade's mother turned to the stove. "I made some coffee. I hope you don't mind."

Mariah shook her head, wondering at the smiling, friendly woman. "No, not at all."

Still feeling weak, Mariah sat at the table. Mrs. Donovan

placed a cup of coffee in front of her and patted her on the shoulder. Anxiously Mariah glanced toward her grandmother's bedroom.

"I peeked in on her a few minutes ago. She's still asleep." Mrs. Donovan took a seat across the table and caught her gaze. "It's a good thing I got here when I did last night. She was fit to be tied, and I don't blame her. What a terrifying ordeal."

"For you, too, what with Slade gone."

"True." Mrs. Donovan smiled, her clear, blue eyes kind. "The lot of us just buckled down and began to pray. That's all we could do." Mrs. Donovan traced the wood grain on the table with one finger, a frown creasing her forehead. "There is one thing, though."

"Ma'am?"

"Last night, your grandmother introduced herself as Sarah Malone. You wouldn't happen to be related to a man named Seth Malone, would you?"

Mariah took a deep breath. "Seth Malone was my father."

Mrs. Donovan's face paled. "Oh, my, what has Slade gone and done?"

★   ★   ★

Slade knew something was wrong the moment he stepped into the kitchen. He glanced at Mariah's stricken face and then at his mother's.

"What's wrong?"

His mother released a sigh. "I've just discovered that Seth Malone was Mariah's father."

"I didn't want to tell you in a letter. I thought it best to wait until you got here."

"I don't understand." His mother frowned. "Maybe you'd better start at the beginning. Or at least explain how you found the Malones."

Mariah spoke up. "Just before he died, my father confessed to stealing Mr. Donovan's share of the gold, and I wrote a letter asking his forgiveness."

"I see—"

"Your father stole all of the gold. None of it belonged to him."

"Half the gold belonged to him." Mariah threw him a defiant glance.

So they were back to square one?

"The deed—" Slade cut in.

"She's right," his mother interrupted.

Slade stared at his mother. "What did you say?"

She looked apologetically at him. "I'm sorry, Son, but if you had just told me you had gotten that letter . . ."

"What are you saying?" Dread clutched at his gut.

"Slade, your father was a violent man. You know that." Her gaze begged him to understand. "Buck and the girls were too small when he died to remember much of his rages, but I know you do."

Slade clenched his jaw, remembering all too well his father's temper. "Yes, ma'am, I do."

"Then you'll also understand why I never argued with him or contradicted what he said."

He waited, knowing there had to be more.

His mother took a deep breath. "When Jack and Seth Malone became partners, I thought it was the best thing that could have happened to Jack. Seth seemed like a decent sort. I hoped Jack would straighten up and quit drinking. But it didn't help. They started prospecting and before long, they found gold. They didn't want to leave the site unattended, so Seth agreed to stay while Jack went and filed a claim. But greed overtook your father, Slade, and he filed the claim in his name only."

Slade tried to make sense of it all. "Then how did Seth Malone end up with all the gold?"

"When he found out what Jack had done, they had a terrible fight."

"Did Papa shoot Mr. Donovan?" Mariah asked. "The wanted poster . . ."

"I'm sorry, Mariah, but yes, he did. They were both pretty riled up by that time." She twisted her hands in her lap. "Seth took the gold they'd found and left town. He said if Jack wanted the claim that badly, he could have it. But by then, the vein had just about petered out. There wasn't much more gold to be had."

"Why didn't you tell me?" Slade clenched both fists. "All these years, I thought Pa told the truth about the gold."

"After he died, I didn't see any point in bringing it up." She shook her head. "I never dreamed Seth's daughter would try to make amends. I'm sorry."

Slade glanced at Mariah, who gazed at him with wide,

accusing eyes. He felt as if his throat might close up and choke the life out of him. "Yeah," he croaked, "I'm sorry too."

Then he bolted for the door.

Blindly he strode past Mariah's garden, down the thorny path, toward the creek behind the barn. He stopped, breathing heavily.

Why? he railed silently. Why hadn't his mother told him the truth? If she had, none of this would have happened. He wouldn't have made a fool of himself and taken Mariah's home away from her.

Every unkind word he'd said, every time he'd declared the ranch—the *entire* ranch—belonged to him and his family came back to taunt him.

He'd thought he was doing the right thing. But all along he'd been in the wrong. His father had cheated Seth Malone first, but he'd never seen fit to share *that* fact in his drunken rages.

Slade slammed his fist against a tree, and pain shot through his injured arm. He growled, relishing the throbbing ache. Why hadn't he seen it? He should have known his father would twist everything to his own purposes. But he hadn't wanted to see. He'd wanted someone to blame for the poverty they lived in. For never having enough to eat. For living on the wrong side of the tracks. For being laughed at because of his threadbare clothes. And his own father had been the one to blame. Not Seth Malone.

Gradually his anger leached out of him, until he stood

broken and ashamed, weighed down by the guilt of what he'd done, the hurt he'd caused.

Forgive me, God. I've made a mess of things. My stubborn pride has cost me the woman I love. What do I do now?

The only answer was the light breeze that stirred the trees lining the creek bank. He closed his eyes and sighed.

He'd gotten the same answer today that he'd gotten from God two days before. Silence. And he couldn't blame God either. Slade had brought this trouble on himself. If he hadn't come to the Lazy M and demanded the deed to the ranch, things would be exactly the way they had always been.

Slade just wanted to provide for his family. He'd believed all the gold had belonged to his father. He thought back to the first day he'd shown up at the Lazy M. Even then, Mariah had insisted half of the gold belonged to her father, but he hadn't believed her. The deed proved otherwise. But even the deed had been wrong.

And now, so much bitterness stood between the two of them that she would never forgive him. He couldn't even forgive himself. He stared at his reflection in the sparkling stream. Only one thing would make this right. He slapped his hat on his head and headed for the barn.

CHAPTER TWENTY-NINE

"You're leaving."

Slade froze at the sound of Mariah's voice. Then he pulled the cinch tight. The slap of leather against leather resounded in the quiet barn. "That's right."

"You weren't even going to say good-bye."

His gut twisted at the accusation in her voice. He rested his forearms on the saddle. How could she say that? He'd almost ruined her life, had tried to steal her ranch, and she wanted him to say good-bye?

"Right again."

"What about your family?"

"They'll head for the train station tomorrow. Buck will see that they get back to Galveston."

343

"I can't believe you're just going to ride away." She moved in front of him, her brown eyes sparking with anger. "Like nothing's happened. You talk about caring for your family and how you want to make things better for them, but when the going gets tough, you run away."

He glared at her. "I'm not running away."

One eyebrow lifted. "Aren't you?"

He wanted to take her in his arms and hold her. He wanted to kiss her and tell her he'd never leave. He wanted to tell her he was sorry. Instead, he turned away. "No. I don't belong here. I never did. All my life, I thought my father was in the right, and then I find out he lied to me. He tried to cheat *your* father. Not the other way around."

She flung out both arms. "Half of that gold belonged to your father, Slade. They *both* tried to cheat each other. So we're even."

"We're not even. Not after what I did." He reached for the reins of his horse.

"All right! Leave, then." Mariah turned away, her whispered words barely audible. "You've got a chance to make something of this ranch, something of your *life*. But you're throwing it away because of your thickheaded pride."

Slade reached her in two strides. He grabbed her by the shoulders and spun her around to face him. Sparkling tears clung to her lashes and pooled in her brown eyes, nearly undoing him. "I can't stay here. Don't you understand? I almost destroyed your life. And your grandmother's and

Amanda's." He faltered, his chest tight with bottled-up guilt. "I asked God to forgive me today, and nothing happened."

The tears shimmering in her eyes spilled over as she reached up and touched his face. He trembled at her gentle touch.

"I forgive you, and God does too. I know He does," she whispered. Her gaze searched his. "You came here intending to take the ranch away from me, but you've given it back. If it hadn't been for you, Frederick and Red would have drained off the cattle until there wasn't anything left."

He shook his head and pulled away. Stalking to his horse, he gathered up the reins again. "People don't forgive and forget that easily."

"They do when they love someone."

The softly spoken words pierced his tightly held remorse. He turned and found her gazing at him, her eyes pleading with him to reconsider. He dropped the reins and closed the distance between them, stopping within inches of her. He stared into her heart-shaped face.

"Do you?"

Her lips parted. "Do I what?"

"Do you still love me?" His heart pounded as he waited for her answer. "After . . . after finding out the truth?"

"Yes," she whispered. "Yes, I love you."

His heart took wing at the small, feathery sound of her admission.

Unable to stop himself, he gathered Mariah to him and lowered his mouth to hers. "I love you too."

Her lips were sweet and gentle and everything he'd dreamed they would be. Finally he lifted his head and gazed down at her.

"I'll stay. On one condition."

"What?" She gave him a dreamy smile, twining her arms around his neck.

"Will you marry me?"

Epilogue

THE WAGON SEAT must have lengthened at least a foot since the first time they'd ridden into town together. Somehow there was plenty of room for both of them now.

Mariah released a contented sigh and snuggled close to Slade's side.

He smiled at her and, holding the reins in one hand, wrapped his other arm around her waist and kissed her soundly.

Trying to hold on to her good sense, she swatted him on the arm. "Slade, somebody might see."

He laughed and glanced around at the open countryside. "There's not anybody around for miles and miles."

"Wisdom is just over the next rise, and you know it."

"Well, I'd better be quick then." He grinned and pressed another kiss to her lips.

"Stop that." She laughed, leaning away.

As they rode through town, Mariah couldn't help but feel as if everyone they saw was staring at her. But she didn't care. Let them look. She'd found the man of her dreams and wanted everyone to know it. Soon she'd be Mrs. Slade Donovan.

The Lazy M ranch house would be overflowing with her grandmother and Slade's mother and sisters, especially when Amanda came home, but they'd make do.

"Whoa."

Mariah glanced at the bank. "Why are we stopping here? I thought you wanted to get some things at the mercantile."

Slade jumped down and held out his arms. "I do." His large hands spanned her waist as he lowered her to the ground. "But we've got a little business with Mr. Tisdale first."

The banker welcomed them into his office. "Mariah. Mr. Donovan. What can I do for you?"

"Morning, Mr. Tisdale." Slade reached into his shirt pocket. "About this deed . . ."

Turn the page to preview
another novel by
PAM HILLMAN

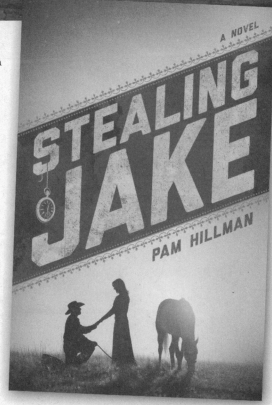

"[Hillman is] gifted with
a true talent for vivid
imagery, heart-tugging
romance, and a feel for
the Old West that will
jangle your spurs."

JULIE LESSMAN, *author of the*
Daughters of Boston series

TYNDALE
FICTION

www.tyndalefiction.com   Available now exclusively in e-book format.   CP0631

Prologue

Chicago
October 1874

"WHERE'S MY LITTLE BROTHER?" Luke glared at the man with the jagged scar on his right cheek.

"You do as I say, kid, and he'll be along shortly." Pale-blue eyes, harder than the cobblestone streets of Chicago, bored into his. "Otherwise, I'll kill him. Understand?"

Luke stood his ground, memorizing the face of the man who'd paid off the coppers.

"Get in." The man motioned to a wooden crate not much bigger than an overturned outhouse.

Luke crammed in, the three other boys squeezing together, making room. Nobody said a word. Nobody cried. They didn't dare. Scarface would kill them if they disobeyed.

Luke knew he'd been stupid. He'd tried to teach Mark the art of picking pockets, and they'd gotten caught. But instead of going to jail as expected, money had changed hands, and they'd been handed off to the man with the scar.

And now Luke would be shipped out of Chicago. Without Mark.

He pulled his thin coat tight around him and curled into a ball for warmth.

Bam! Bam! Bam!

Luke shuddered with every slam of the hammer against the nails. He drew his knees to his chest, shivering. This time not from the cold.

Bam! Bam!

He pinched his eyes closed, fighting the urge to throw up.

His heart raced faster than the first time he'd picked a pocket.

Where was Mark?

Chapter One

Chestnut, Illinois
November 1874

THE ILL-DRESSED, GRIMY CHILD jostled a broad-shouldered cowboy, palming the man's pocket watch. Gold flashed as the thief discreetly handed his prize to another youngster shuffling along the boardwalk toward Livy O'Brien.

Livy didn't miss a thing—not the slick movements, not the tag-team approach. None of it.

Neither boy paid her any attention. And why should they? To them she was no more than a farmer's wife on her way home from the mercantile or maybe one of the workers over at the new glove factory.

If they only knew.

Her gaze cut to the man's back. When he patted down his pockets and his stride faltered, she made a split-second decision. As the thin boy with the timepiece passed, she knocked him into a pile of snow shoveled to the side of the wooden walkway. She reached out, pulled the child to his feet, and dusted him off so fast he didn't have time to move, let alone squirm away. She straightened his threadbare coat, two sizes too big and much too thin for an icebound Illinois winter. "Oh, I'm so sorry. Did I hurt you?"

Fathomless dark eyes stared at her from a hollow face. Eyes that reminded her of her own in the not-so-distant past. She wanted to hug him, take him home with her.

"No, ma'am." The words came out high-pitched and breathless.

"Hey, you!" The man hurried toward them.

Fear shuddered across the boy's face, and he jerked free of her grasp and darted down a nearby alley.

Livy let him go and stepped into the man's path, bracing herself as he slammed into her. The impact sent both of them hurtling toward the snowbank. The stranger wrapped his arms around her and took the brunt of the fall, expelling a soft grunt as Livy landed on top of him. Her gaze tripped off the end of her gloved fingers and collided with a pair of intense jade-green eyes. She stared, mesmerized by long, dark lashes and tiny lines that fanned out from the corners of his eyes. A hint of a smile lifted one corner of his mouth.

A slamming door jerked Livy back to reality.

Heat rushed to her face, and she rolled sideways, scrambling to untangle herself. What would Mrs. Brooks think of such an unladylike display?

"Ma'am?" Large, gloved hands grabbed her shoulders and pulled her to her feet. "Are you all right?"

"I'm fine."

"Those kids stole my watch." A muscle jumped in his jaw.

"Are you sure?" Remorse smote her with the same force as that of the stranger's body knocking her into the snow. She'd reacted, making a split-second decision that could have resulted in catastrophe.

"Yes, ma'am." He patted his sheepskin coat again. Suddenly he stilled and removed the watch from his pocket. "Well, I'll be. I could've sworn . . ." He gave her a sheepish look. "Sorry for running into you like that, ma'am."

Livy breathed a sigh and pulled her cloak tight against the cold. Disaster averted. *Forgive me, Lord. I hope I did the right thing.* "That's all right. No harm done."

The stranger pushed his hat back, releasing a tuft of dark, wavy hair over his forehead. "I don't believe we've met. Jake Russell."

Her gaze flickered toward the alley that had swallowed up the boy. She didn't make a habit of introducing herself to strangers, but revealing her name might keep Mr. Russell's mind off the boys who'd waylaid him. "Livy O'Brien."

"It's a pleasure to meet you, Mrs. O'Brien."

"*Miss* O'Brien," she said. At least the gathering twilight masked the flush she could feel stealing across her cheeks.

Was it her imagination, or did the grin on Jake Russell's face grow wider?

"Pleased to meet you, Miss O'Brien. May I escort you to wherever you're going?" His eyes twinkled. "It'll be dark soon, and a lady shouldn't be out alone after dark."

Livy sobered. She'd never claimed to be a lady. The tiny

glow inside her faded with the setting sun. Mr. Russell would never be interested in Light-Fingered Livy O'Brien. "No thank you, Mr. Russell. I'm not going far. I'll be fine."

"I'd feel better, ma'am." He gestured toward the alley. "Especially after what happened."

He held out his arm, one eyebrow cocked in invitation. Her emotions warred with her head. She shouldn't allow such liberties, but what harm would it do to let him escort her home?

Just once.

She placed her hand in the crook of his arm. "Very well. Thank you, Mr. Russell."

"Call me Jake."

Livy's heart gave a nervous flutter. Did Mr. Russell mask his intentions behind a gentlemanly face and kindly words? A common enough practice where she came from. "I'm afraid using your given name would be a little too familiar. I don't know anything about you."

"Well, I can remedy that. What do you want to know?"

Livy shook her head, softening her refusal with a smile. It wouldn't do to ask the man questions about himself. If she did, then he'd feel at liberty to ask questions of his own. Questions she didn't want to answer.

He chuckled. "You sure are a shy little thing, Miss O'Brien."

Better to let him think her bashful than know the truth. A couple of years ago, she might have spun a yarn or two to keep him entertained, but no longer. If she couldn't speak the truth, she'd say nothing at all.

Her silence didn't stop him. "You must be new around here. I don't remember seeing you before."

"I arrived in Chestnut about two months ago."

"That explains it. I've only been back in town a few weeks myself."

Livy darted a glance from the corner of her eye to study him. Discreetly, of course—she'd at least learned *something* from Mrs. Brooks. The top of her head barely reached his chin, and broad shoulders filled out his coat. A late-afternoon shadow dusted his firm jawline.

He stepped off the boardwalk and helped her across a patch of ice. Her stomach flopped when his green eyes connected with hers, and she blurted out the first thing that popped into her mind. "Oh? Where've you been?"

She could've bitten her tongue. She shouldn't have asked, but curiosity had gotten the best of her. What made her want to know more about Jake Russell? Mercy, why should she even wonder about the man? He wasn't anyone she should worry with.

If only her foolish girl's heart would listen to reason.

"Taking care of some business in Missouri. It's good to be home, though."

They ambled in silence past the Misses Huff Millinery Shop and the recently opened Chinese laundry. The scent of green lumber tickled Livy's nose, bringing forth the image of the fresh sprig of mistletoe hung over the door of the orphanage.

The boardwalk ended just past the laundry. Livy gestured

into the gathering darkness. "It's a little farther down this way."

"I don't mind."

The snow-covered ground lay frozen, Livy's footprints from when she'd trekked into town the only evidence of anyone being out and about on this frigid day.

They rounded the bend, and Livy eased her hand from the warmth of Jake's arm when they came within sight of the rambling two-story house nestled under a grove of cottonwoods. "Thank you, Mr. Russell. This is where I live."

*　　*　　*

Jake studied the building before returning his attention to the petite lady at his side. He'd known the moment he laid eyes on her that they hadn't met. He would have remembered. "This is the new orphanage, isn't it?"

"Yes. That's right."

"I heard someone opened one up. 'Bout time. Lots of young'uns needing a place to stay these days."

"We already have five children in our care."

They stepped onto the porch, and she pushed the hood of her cape back. Light from inside the house shot fire through reddish-brown curls and revealed a smattering of freckles across a pert nose.

She'd knocked the wind out of him earlier, and the feeling came back full force now.

Whoa.

Jake stepped back, putting some distance between them.

He didn't have the time or the energy to be thinking about a girl, no matter how pretty she might be. His days and nights were chock-full as it was. He tipped his hat. "Good night, Miss O'Brien."

Her smile lit up the dreary winter landscape. "Thank you for escorting me home, Mr. Russell. Good night."

He headed back toward town, rehashing the brief conversation he'd had with Livy O'Brien. She'd sure seemed reluctant to talk about herself. Come to think of it, she hadn't told him much of anything.

Did he make her nervous? He should have told her who he was, but the thought hadn't crossed his mind. Knowing he was a sheriff's deputy would have put her at ease, but she hadn't seemed the least bit interested in who he was or what he did for a living.

He continued his rounds, confident he'd find out more about Miss Livy O'Brien soon enough. It was part of his job, plain and simple. He chuckled. He didn't remember anything in his job description that said he needed to investigate every beautiful lady he ran across. Still, it was his job to protect the town, and the more he knew about its inhabitants, the better.

Not that Chestnut needed protection from Livy O'Brien. A pretty little filly like her wouldn't hurt a fly.

His steps faltered when he stuffed his hands in his pockets and his fingers slid over the cool, polished surface of his father's gold watch. Not prone to jump to conclusions or get easily flustered, he'd been certain those kids had lifted his timepiece. How could he have been so mistaken?

Good thing he'd bumped into Miss O'Brien, or he would have had a hard time explaining why he'd chased an innocent kid down the street.

Still, he had reason to be suspicious. There'd been reports of scruffy young boys like the two tonight roaming the streets of Chestnut. Urchins from back East, Sheriff Carter said. Run out of Chicago, they rode the train to the nearest town large enough to provide easy pickings.

He settled his hat more firmly on his head. Those raga-muffins didn't know it yet, but they shouldn't have stopped in Chestnut. The town wasn't big enough for thieves and robbers to hide out for long.

Jake clomped along the boardwalk, part of his thoughts on the youngsters, part on the girl he'd left at the orphanage, and part registering the sights and sounds of merchants shut-ting down for the night.

He hesitated as he spied Paul Stillman locking up the bank. An urge to turn down the nearest alley assaulted him, but he doggedly stayed his course.

The banker lifted a hand. "Jake. Wait up a minute."

A knot twisted in Jake's gut. Would Stillman call in his loan today?

The portly man hurried toward him, his hand out-stretched, a wide smile on his florid face. "Jake. How're things going?"

"Fine." Jake shook the banker's hand, the knot intensify-ing. Mr. Stillman's continued grace made him feel worse than if the banker had demanded payment on the spot.

"And your mother?" His concern poured salt on Jake's unease.

"She's doing well."

"That's good. I should be going, then. I just wanted to check on the family."

Jake rubbed his jaw. "Look, Mr. Stillman, I appreciate all you've done for my family, but I'm going to pay off that loan. Every penny of it."

The banker sobered. "I know you will, Jake. I never doubted it for a minute. The last couple of years have been tough for you and Mrs. Russell."

"Pa wouldn't have borrowed money against the farm if he'd known. . . ." Jake's throat closed. "If the crops hadn't failed the last two summers, I could've made the payments."

The banker took off his glasses and rubbed them with a white handkerchief. His eyes pinned Jake, razor sharp in intensity. "That investor is still interested in buying your father's share of the Black Gold mine, you know."

"The answer is no. I'm not selling." Jake clenched his jaw. He wouldn't be party to more death and destruction.

"That's what I thought you'd say." Stillman sighed. "I admire your determination to protect miners by not selling, but as much as I'd like to, I can't carry that loan forever."

Jake shifted his weight, forcing his muscles to relax. It wasn't the banker's fault that life had dealt him a losing hand. "I know. This summer will be better."

"We'll see." Mr. Stillman stuffed the cloth in his pocket, settled his glasses on his nose, and tugged his coat close against the biting wind. "I'd better get on home. This weather is going to be the death of me. Say hello to your mother for me, will you?"

"I'll do that. Good night."

The banker waved a hand over his shoulder and hurried away. Jake stared after him. Would this summer be any different from last year? It would take a miracle to bring in enough from the farm to pay off the loan against the defunct mine.

A sharp blast rent the air, signaling the evening shift change at the mines. Jake turned northward. The low hills sat shrouded in a blanket of pure, white snow. Peaceful.

An illusion. The mines beneath the ground held anything but purity. Coal dust, death, and destruction existed there.

Along with enough coal to pay off the loan.

Jake turned his back on the mine and walked away.

Mrs. Brooks glanced up from the coal-burning stove when Livy entered the kitchen. "How'd it go?"

Livy took off her cloak and hung it on a nail along with several threadbare coats in varying sizes before moving to warm her hands over the stovetop. She closed her eyes and breathed deep. The aroma of vegetable soup simmering on the stove and baking bread welcomed her home. "Nobody's hiring. Not even the glove factory."

Mrs. Brooks sank into an old rocker. The runners creaked as she set the chair in motion. "What are we going to do?"

Worry lines knit the older woman's brow, and Livy turned

away. She rubbed the tips of her fingers together. How easy it would be to obtain the money needed to keep them afloat. Livy had visited half a dozen shops today, all of them easy pickings.

She slammed a lid on the shameful images. Those thoughts should be long gone, but they snuck up on her when she was most vulnerable. When Mrs. Brooks's faith wavered, Livy's hit rock bottom.

She balled her hands into fists and squeezed her eyes shut. *Lord, I don't want to go back to that life. Ever.*

Livy forced herself to relax and turned to face Mrs. Brooks. "Maybe the citizens of Chestnut will help."

"I've tried, Livy. A few have helped us out, mostly by donating clothes their own children have outgrown. And I'm more than thankful. But money to keep up with the payments on this old place? And food?" Her gaze strayed toward the bucket of coal. "Except for our guardian angel who keeps the coal bin full, most everybody is in about as bad a shape as we are. They don't have much of anything to give."

"Don't worry, ma'am." Livy patted the older woman's shoulder, desperate to hear the ironclad faith ring in her voice. "You keep telling me the Lord will provide."

Mrs. Brooks smiled. "You're right, dear. He will. I've told you time and again that we should pray for what we need, and here I am, doubting the goodness of God. Let's pray, child. The Lord hasn't let me down yet, and I'm confident He never will."

The rocker stopped, and Mrs. Brooks took Livy's hand in hers and closed her eyes. "Lord, You know the situation here. We've got a lot of mouths to feed and not much in the pantry. Livy is doing all she can, and I thank You for her every day. We're asking You to look down on us and see our need. These children are Yours, Lord, and we need help in providing food for them and keeping a roof over their heads. In Jesus' name we pray. Amen." She heaved herself out of the rocker and headed to the stove, a new resolve in her step. "Call the children, Livy. It's almost time for supper."

Livy trudged down the hall to the parlor. The short prayer had cheered Mrs. Brooks but hadn't done much to ease Livy's worry. She'd have to find some way to bring in a few extra dollars if they were to make it to spring. Otherwise, she and Mrs. Brooks and the small brood of children they'd taken in would be on the streets of Chestnut before winter's end. The elderly woman would never survive if that happened.

A wave of panic washed over her like fire sweeping through the slums of Chicago. Livy couldn't have another life on her conscience. She took a deep breath. They weren't on the streets yet. And as long as they had a roof over their heads and food on the table, there was hope.

She stepped into the parlor. Mary, the eldest child at twelve, kept the younger ones occupied on a quilt set up in the corner. The two boys, Seth and Georgie, stacked small wooden blocks, then howled with laughter when they knocked the tower down, only to start the process again.

"Libby! Libby!" a sweet voice trilled.

Livy held out her arms as Mary's little sister, Grace, toddled to her. "Hello, sweetheart."

The toddler patted her cheeks. "Libby's home! Libby's home!"

Livy nuzzled the child's neck, inhaling her sweet baby scent. Grace giggled.

"Yes, Libby's home." Livy glanced at Mary and the other children. "It's almost time for supper. Go wash up now."

Against her better judgment, Livy's mind conjured up flashing green eyes as she wiped Grace's face and hands. Would Jake Russell call on her? Why would such a thought even occur to her? What man who could have his pick of women would call on a girl who lived in an orphanage, a girl who came from a questionable background and didn't have a penny to her name?

And one who'd sprawled all over him like a strumpet.

Mercy! What if Miss Maisie or Miss Janie, the Huff sisters, had witnessed such an unladylike display? Her reputation would be in tatters. Not that she'd brought much of a reputation with her to Chestnut, but Mrs. Brooks had insisted she could start over here. There was no need to air her past like a stained quilt on a sunny day.

Maybe she wouldn't see Jake again. Or maybe she would. Chestnut wasn't that big.

More importantly, did she want to see him?

She didn't have any interest in courting, falling in love, and certainly no interest in marriage and childbirth. She knew firsthand where that could lead. Rescuing children from the streets fulfilled her desire for a family, and she'd do well to remember that.

Georgie shoved ahead of Seth. Livy snagged the child and tucked him back in line. "Don't push. You'll have your turn."

When all hands were clean, Livy led the way to the kitchen. A scramble ensued as the children jockeyed for position at the long trestle table.

Mrs. Brooks clapped her hands. "All right, everyone, it's time to say the blessing." Her firm but gentle voice calmed the chaos, and the children settled down. "Thank You, Lord, for the food we are about to partake. Bless each one at this table, and keep us safe from harm. Amen."

The children dug in with relish, and Livy took Grace from Mary's arms. "Here; I'll feed her. Enjoy your supper."

Livy mashed a small helping of vegetables in a saucer and let them cool.

"Grace do it," the child demanded.

"All right, but be careful." Livy concentrated on helping the child feed herself without making too much of a mess.

Thwack! Thwack! Thwack!

Livy jumped as loud knocking reverberated throughout the house.

"I wonder who that could be?" Mrs. Brooks folded her napkin.

"I'll get it." Livy stepped into the foyer. Resting her hand on the knob, she called out, "Who's there?"

"Sheriff Carter, ma'am."

Livy's hands grew damp, but she resisted the urge to bolt. The sheriff didn't have reason to question her or to haul her off to jail. Jesus had washed away her sins and made her a new creature. She wasn't the person she'd been two years ago. She prayed every day she wouldn't let Him down.

Some days were harder than others.

She took a deep breath and opened the door, a smile plastered on her face. "Good evening, Sheriff. May I help you?"

The aged sheriff touched his fingers to his hat. "Evening, ma'am. Sorry to bother you, but we've got a problem."

"Yes?"

The sheriff glanced toward the street, and for the first time, Livy noticed a wagon and the silhouettes of several people.

Mrs. Brooks appeared behind her. "What is it, Livy?"

Sheriff Carter spoke up. "There's been a wagon accident. A family passing through on the outskirts of town. Their horses bolted. I'm sad to say the driver—a man—was killed, leaving three children."

Livy peered into the darkness, her heart going out to the little ones. "Are the children out there? Are they hurt?"

"They're fine. Nary a scratch as far as we can tell. We thought the orphanage might take them."

"Of course." Mrs. Brooks took charge. "Bring them in out of the cold. Livy, go fetch some blankets. The poor dears are probably frozen with cold and fear."

Livy ran, her mind flying as fast as her feet. Less than an hour before, they'd prayed for help to feed the children already in their care. How could they manage three more? Of course they couldn't turn them away. They'd never do that. But would she be forced to do something drastic to feed them all?

Lord, don't make me choose. I'm not strong enough.

Heart heavy, she found three worn blankets and carried them downstairs.

Mrs. Brooks met her in the hallway. "They're in the kitchen. Mary's already taken the other children to the parlor."

Her arms laden with the blankets, Livy followed Mrs. Brooks. Two girls huddled together on the bench at the table, their eyes wide and frightened. Poor things. If only she could take them in her arms and tell them everything would be all right. It must be. She'd beg in the streets before she'd let them all starve.

She searched the room for the third child. Her gaze landed on a tall, broad-shouldered man with a tiny dark-haired child nestled snugly inside his sheepskin coat. The man lifted his head, and Livy came face-to-face with Jake Russell. She saw a fierce protectiveness in his haunted eyes.

"I don't believe you've met my deputy, Jake Russell." Sheriff Carter waved in Jake's direction.

Dread pooled in the pit of Livy's stomach, and for the space of a heartbeat, she stared.

"Pleased to meet you, Deputy Russell," Mrs. Brooks said, her attention already on the two little girls at the table. "I'm Mrs. Brooks, and this is Livy O'Brien."

Livy jerked her head in a stiff nod. For a few moments tonight she'd let her imagination run away with her, thinking maybe Jake Russell would call on her, that he might want to court her, that maybe he thought she was pretty.

And maybe he would. Maybe he did.

But it didn't matter. It *couldn't* matter.

Jake Russell was an officer of the law, and Livy had spent her entire life running from the law.

Acknowledgments

THIS IS MY SECOND OPPORTUNITY to work with the amazing team at Tyndale House. There are many working hard behind the scenes whose names I don't know, but as someone who's worked in the corporate world for years, I realize it takes a team to get any job done—and done well. My hat's off to each and every one of you. Special thanks to my editors, Jan Stob and Erin Smith. I'm learning from the best, and the stars in my eyes prove it. And be still, my heart: Jennifer Ghionzoli, I adore the cover of *Claiming Mariah*. Thank you!

Thanks to my agent, Steve Laube, the bottleneck in the middle of the hourglass that keeps my writing career flowing at a steady, even pace. He advises quietly but firmly, and from a wealth of knowledge I can't begin to comprehend.

I can't begin to list the authors, agents, editors, and contest judges who had a small (and sometimes very large) part in the development of this story. But special thanks to Charlene Glatkowski and Leigh Germann, who read the rough draft of *Claiming Mariah* long ago. Your insights helped take the story to a higher level.

To The Seekers for everything. It's so good to know you're all just the click of an e-mail away. Thank you for the laughs, the sisterhood, and the sounding board on everything from plot points to what to cook for dinner. Leave no woman behind!

Robin Caroll. Ah, dear friend. Without a shadow of a doubt, I know you're there, day or night. I'm sure you snicker at some of my lame questions and "duh" moments, and you probably roll your eyes when my "Help!" e-mails pop up in your in-box, but I'll return the favor by programming my magic formulas into your spreadsheets. Promise!

This acknowledgment wouldn't be complete without special thanks to Daniel Byram and Sean Hillman who, years and years ago, put away their PlayStation games long enough to name the main characters in *Claiming Mariah*. I'm very proud of the young men you've both become.

About the Author

AWARD-WINNING AUTHOR PAM HILLMAN writes inspirational fiction set in the turbulent times of the American West and the Gilded Age. Her debut novel, *Stealing Jake*, was a finalist in the International Digital Awards and the 2013 EPIC eBook Awards. *Claiming Mariah*, her second novel, won Romance Writers of America's prestigious Golden Heart. She lives in Mississippi with her husband and family. Visit her website at www.pamhillman.com.

have you visited
tyndalefiction.com
lately?

YOU'LL FIND:

- ways to connect with your favorite authors
- first chapters
- discussion guides
- author videos and book trailers
- and much more!

PLUS, SCAN THE QR CODE OR VISIT BOOKCLUBHUB.NET TO

- download free discussion guides
- get great book club recommendations
- sign up for our book club and other e-newsletters

Are you crazy for Tyndale fiction? Follow us on Twitter **@Crazy4Fiction** for daily updates on your favorite authors, free e-book promotions, contests, and much more. Let's get crazy!

CP0021